THE STRING KEEPER'S WISH

BY

BETH LAUREN PARRISH

Dedication

To all the equines in every dimension, you have my immense
gratitude. Thank you for teaching us so many lessons.

Acknowledgments

To my amazing husband, Charlie. Thank you
for all that you are and continue to be.

To my friends and family, thank you for your support and
especially for your willingness to read.

To all the dreamers in the world, remember to take inspired action!

Finally, special thanks to my editor and sister, Michelle Cohen.
Sister Code!

CHAPTER ONE

Briggs, The String Keeper

There is a space between worlds that is so discreet, few people can sense when they're visiting. You go there often when you stare at something for too long. It's a feeling of suspended animation or floating amongst the clouds. Some go there more often than others. This space is a comforting feeling; one of no obligations, rules, or errands to run. It allows you to feel connected, relaxed, and quiet, even for just a few seconds. Some feel like they are flying, doing flips, or spinning in place. Others just breathe and feel nothing at all. You even forget that you're in your human body, until you hear a voice or a noise and it brings you back.

Briggs lives in this space.

Just like a pleasant doorman who would greet you from a long day, she lights up when you arrive. Briggs guides you further into this space, or back to your world, depending on which you choose. She floats along, between the realms of reality to guide all who ask for assistance. She's like the reassuring whisper you hear in your mind when you're about to take a dive into the deep end, or the relaxing murmurs you hear when you're underwater in the bathtub. When you feel completely at ease to take these internal time-outs, those are the moments when Briggs shows up to join the party. Being with Briggs is a sort of rendezvous of your soul, linking up with her realm. She also loves to bump into your energy when you feel completely stressed out. She gives you a comforting sense of knowing you're always on the right journey, even in the direst of times. Briggs holds your soul in her arms, gives it a big hug, and then sends you back into your world when you're ready.

She is truly the mistress of "zoning out." When you feel yourself staying longer in this state, you can smile and know that Briggs is taking care of one of your most basic needs; the need to chill out and feel safe again.

Briggs lives within the strongest string of the Universal Web that has yet to be found by the evil entities, the Murmori, who suck up the life force of their victims to grow more powerful. They cause nightmares, finding the humans without control of their thoughts. Briggs resides in this hidden string, in a place where no dreams can be found. She can hear the thoughts of all Earthlings and other dimensional beings, while in this void-like string.

Centuries ago, Earth had direct access to other dimensions, when linked to the Universal Web at its peak vibration. Earth was known as one of the main gateway planets for inter-dimensional travel. However, the Murmori seized an opportunity for dominion over Earth, severely damaged the Web, and nearly all travel was brought to a halt. By fostering fear and chaos, the Earth's vibration lowered significantly, which dismantled all but one of the strings that attached the Web.

A very specific vibration, one that hasn't been felt in many lifetimes, is the only hope for initiating the strings to Re-Connect to the Universal Web. When the other strings were dismantled, Briggs' fellow String Keepers were called home to their respective planets. She was given the option to return and not be left all alone. She decided to stay. Briggs remained hopeful that her friends would return to Earth and join her once again. She had hope for the Earthlings. Despite the failed attempts for Re-Connection, Briggs believed it was still possible.

The hope is, once the Earth's vibration spirals back up, the former String Keepers, all benevolent and extremely powerful entities, may travel back to Earth in droves and assist those who cry out in the most anguish. Especially the ones being preyed upon by the Murmori.

Briggs had many failed attempts to restore the Universal Web. She would try to whisper to as many Earthlings as would listen. The

Murmori's hold was simply getting too strong. She was beginning to run out of ideas until she bumped into an energy named Naomi Drake, a horsewoman who was desperate to leave her planet behind. The only thing keeping her on Earth were her horses. This gave Briggs inspiration for a grand plan.

Since Briggs' string was the only one left to allow for short bursts of inter dimensional travel between Earth and her home planet, Gavrantura, she sent this transmission:

Earth's horses hold a pivotal role in the universe. They have evolved from carrying the weight of humans to creating powerful connections with them. Connections desperately needed to elevate Earth's vibration. I believe it is time to send our beings into horse form. I will take it from there.

The transmission was received. The council on Gavrantura quickly responded and asked for advice on which beings to send where. Briggs assured them that she would find the best Re-Connectors. *I need to contact Levidia now. She will most certainly know who is best suited for the mission. It is time to collaborate with the Earthlings' guides. They can no longer attempt this alone. This is our last chance.*

CHAPTER TWO

Levidia

Once Briggs sent her transmission, she then called upon Levidia, the Head Angel on Earth. Levidia is a gorgeous guardian angel. She can pop in and out of dimensions on Earth as often as she pleases, much like a ghost traveling through walls. A quick glimpse of her would make you gasp immediately. She has long, flowing white hair, with magnificent, yet very kind blue eyes. For those that can see her, she reminds one of a fashion model in a Vogue magazine, wearing the most brilliant and dramatic clothing for every occasion.

Levidia was napping on a cloud, when she heard Briggs. She quickly jumped into a keen state of wakefulness. There was an urgency in her voice. "Levidia, hear me, please. The council on Gavrantura has agreed to a new plan. This could be the answer to jump start the Re-Connection of the Web. We need to create a willing team of humans across the planet, bypassing the time-space continuum. They must be ready to make the most profound shifts, in order to elevate Earth's vibration." Briggs sounded desperate toward the end of her message. Levidia yawned and leaned over to see if Prometheus, her Pegasus was still floating around. He flapped his wings and flew toward her, as he felt her wishing him over. "Dear friend. Sounds like we have quite the job ahead of us." She stroked his neck. She then had tears in her eyes. "I do hope my observation skills are up for this task. Choosing the best candidates hasn't been my forte of late. Briggs might disappear forever if we don't succeed."

She had met Prometheus during her first encounter when she was upgraded from spirit guide to Head Angel. This Pegasus, twice the size of any Earthly horse, was honored to become Levidia's main steed in her travels. So many had forgotten what it was like to ride on his back, that he had doubts to whether anyone would believe in his existence again. When Levidia appeared on his ethereal plane, they had an instant connection.

A moment later, Briggs had materialized on the cloud beside the pair. She was engulfed in a sparkling tube, emitting rainbow light. This was the last string. Whenever she materialized on Earth, it surrounded and protected her, from any other energies or beings intending harm. It was the only connection point between Gavrantura and Earth. Briggs, equally as tall as Prometheus, looked him square in the eye and spoke boldly. "My idea actually involves sending Gavranturans into horse forms. I can usher them in through the string, as long as I know where to send them." Prometheus spun around and then pawed the air in a half rearing motion.

Briggs nodded triumphantly at his reaction and continued, "Once the humans are chosen and trained, they will be connected to the horses from Gavrantura."

Levidia let out a nervous laugh and hesitated to respond. "Well, why ever not? Briggs, darling, you are one of the brightest minds this galaxy has seen in years." Then doubts began to creep in. "But, do you honestly think the humans will be able to hear these beings through the horses?"

She posed this question to Briggs with great anticipation. She knew that Briggs could hear the innermost thoughts of humans who went to visit with her. Briggs nodded slowly. "Beloved Levidia, there are some here on Earth who long to speak with horses on a very deep level. I truly believe it will be possible. However, the next important question we should ask is this; will the other humans believe these horse communicators? Or will they just be written off as crazy, like so many of the past Re-Connectors here?"

"Do you really think it will work this time? This is truly our last chance. If we fail, your string, *your final* string will be dismantled." She paused for a moment and then her mind began to race, "Now, where on Earth will these beings be sent? What kind of horses and what time period? Have you considered all the options? The Murmori would never suspect an infiltration if we step back in time; especially considering how those evil ones are so linear. Pushing forward night by night."

Levidia stopped her thought process and took a deep breath; she had just remembered something. She closed her eyes and suddenly jumped out of focus, as if she was a malfunctioning television with lots of static around her whole body. A few minutes passed and she came back fully, this time even more vividly in front of Briggs. This quick investigation confirmed her suggestion.

"Please, tell the Gavranturans to send their being into a Roman war horse. I have just observed how they are valued immensely and have bestowed upon them, many a wonderful caretaker, called Strators. These Strators just might be open to our ways." Levidia hopped on Prometheus and they spun around Briggs, who was listening closely and taking notes inside the string.

Briggs watched the pair for a few more moments, as she relayed her message to Gavrantura. The string she inhabited began to vibrate fiercely and then hummed an intense note that would make a thunderstorm seem like a quiet lullaby. Levidia threw her head back and then locked eyes with Briggs. They both knew in that instant that a major decision was made. The excitement over choosing the first being to travel into a horse form had created that deafening sound.

Briggs explained, "The Gavranturans have chosen five other beings to jump into horse form, once the first is successful. Your task, Levidia, is to make contact with the human candidates and convince them of their daunting mission."

Levidia took a deep breath and tried to shrug off the looming sense of finality. She was about to fly off with Prometheus toward her first prospect. She looked back over her tense shoulder, "Briggs. What if this doesn't work? I will miss you so much and the humans...they will lose their ability to dream and imagine. Prometheus and I will be stuck..." She couldn't even say the rest out loud. *Nobody will ever know we exist. They won't see or hear us any longer, while we just float around aimlessly.*

Briggs whispered to Levidia confidently as she floated upward, "It has already begun. The Gavranturans just told me that the one in Roman times is ready to discuss the mission with his human. You see, this time-space continuum can be quite convenient for planning. Wouldn't you say?"

Levidia sighed. She thought, *Oh Briggs. How I wish I had your optimism.* She had to focus hard on the exact human she had in mind. She was about the same age as the one who just agreed. A test was needed first. She had to be sure to choose the right one this time.

CHAPTER THREE

The Murmori

They waited for her to drift off to sleep. Like so many of the youngsters on this planet, she was brimming with life force to continue feeding their never ending thirst for power. That power was in each and every human's imagination. They were so vulnerable, so open and giving of their energy. Devouring the power was getting easier, especially without anyone to stop them. They talked amongst themselves in the shadows, in between the nightmares they conjured up.

We are getting closer to owning this entire planet. The humans will never even know what they have lost. Their screams and trembling and tears are fuel to our fire. Let them sleep and feed us, sleep and feed us. Let them forget how to enjoy things. Keep them in the dark, in fear, and forever lose their sense of reality. Then we will have the power to fly around everywhere and keep all the light out. Then we will have won completely. Our kind will never need to find another planet to feed from. Earth is ripe and perfect to devour.

They felt her deep in slumber and began to hover over the one called Abigail. She was one of their favorites to prey upon. Her energy was mesmerizing to feast on. The Murmori pushed and pulled to get as close to her as possible. Suddenly, out of nowhere, a bright light blinded them and they all jumped back in astonishment. An angel was protecting Abigail. They were outraged and perplexed. They were reeling with anger, since they assumed all the angels had disappeared by now. There was no denying how powerful this angel was. They had to leave or be drowned out by the light. The Murmori quickly scurried off to find their next victim.

CHAPTER FOUR

Abigail Freedman

It began as the typical kind of disjointed dream that Abigail often had throughout her young life. Images of dark faces swirling around until just one became very clear. She fell deeper into sleep and could see the crystals forming on this face. It was making her nauseous with its penetrating eyes. It was ravenous and began drooling white frothy foam over her head. Then in a flash, it got sucked away. A new, more soothing face appeared over the scary one. It was the most loving being she had ever encountered. She was shining and smiling with such a glow that Abigail felt she might even need to squint to continue looking at this effervescent, angelic figure. There were blue lights twinkling all around her entire body and Abigail could now see that she was holding a huge white wand. As she swished the magical device in front of Abigail, a series of golden globes began to circle all around her. The angel then motioned toward Abigail to take a closer look. Within the center of these floating globes was a very long, vertical tunnel heading up toward the sky. Inside was a rope. Abigail then felt that she had been placed inside the tunnel and was holding this rope, trying desperately to climb. She detested this exercise in gym class and wondered why on earth she was being asked to do such a daunting task.

The angel told Abigail that she could get assistance and reach the top by simply choosing one of the floating orbs swirling around. As Abigail wearily looked around, she noticed that none of these globes were speaking to her. They all looked the same and were actually becoming a bit of an annoying distraction, rather than looking like any type of help to reach the top of this seemingly never ending tunnel.

Then, as if something clicked in, like finding the right key among a series on your key chain, Abigail could sense there was a golden orb inside of her body. She immediately focused on that and said aloud, "I choose the globe inside of me." It was as if a rush of super-heroine strength poured into every cell of her being and she suddenly began quadrupling her time up the rope, effortlessly floating up, climbing with ease, hardly losing her breath. And then she reached the top. She giggled in relief. The angel nodded and simply said, "I think you are indeed the one."

Abigail awoke with a start and stumbled into the bathroom. She wiped her face with a washcloth and attempted to focus in the mirror. Just like most of the nights of her young life, she had hardly slept. Her nightmares would poke and prod her until she awoke, breathless and staring at the dark ceiling for hours, as her mind raced with images of being squished by walls or led down steep embankments that made her stomach drop like an intense roller coaster. Her brown eyes blinked slowly several times and she thought about how the nightmare actually shifted. It was the first time she felt any inkling of hope in the night. She then narrowed her eyes as she focused on her thick, frizzy hair that seemed to go every which way. She groaned as she realized she was nearly out of the hair smoothing cream she had finally convinced her mother to buy. She pumped the last bits out of the bottle and smoothed out as many of the fly-away wisps as best she could.

Her mother, Evelyn, was an English teacher and thought spending too much money on frivolous things was absurd. She liked to remind Abigail of this fact, often. She could recite her mom's response verbatim: "We are on a tight budget. Your father and I are teachers, not entrepreneurs, and we need to make sure we can save for your college years." *Mom is going to be really upset. This bottle costs over $20 and it only lasted two weeks! I simply can't go to school with my hair this crazy. I know they will all laugh at me.*

She was fifteen years old and about halfway through her

sophomore year in high school. She had a handful of acquaintances, not bonded enough to call real friends. They didn't talk much. They were mostly people who didn't mind her sitting with them at lunch time. Her teachers acted like automatons, anticipating the bell to ring as much as she did. The majority of the students were caught up with staring at their phones. They would bump into each other as they were texting, viewing online 'viral' videos, and all other forms of technology her parents banned her from.

Besides the occasional sci-fi movie she watched with her father, Albert, when her Mom wasn't home, she felt so disconnected with this world. She secretly wished she could be whisked away somewhere else, somewhere foreign, like in all the books she loved to read. Abigail's imagination consoled her. She could escape and create anything she wanted, away from the ultra pretty, gossiping girls and brusque boys who never looked twice in her direction. She could fly around the mountains, pretending she was an eagle and watch all the glorious happenings in nature from far above; until her homework got in the way.

The most interesting part of Abigail's life was her walk to and from school. She only lived two miles away and insisted on walking, even after her parents begged her to take the bus.

"It's just not very safe, Abigail. I want to know you arrived at school without any mishaps."

"But you *know* how awful those kids are. They seem to love teasing the only anti-technologically advanced kid in the school." She shuddered at being enclosed in the yellow vessel, even for those few minutes, trapped with those instigators. "Besides, I love the exercise." Abigail rationalized. Her Dad shrugged. He knew he couldn't argue with that. He was, after all, a physics teacher and the soccer coach at an all boys private school. He wished his daughter would show some inclination toward being more athletic.

There were other reasons for walking. She adored being in nature. The birds' songs were always a little different each day. Her heart would skip a beat when she encountered something new that would flutter, slither, or crawl on her path. Abigail sensed these creatures held secrets to other worlds. At least that's what she hoped. Ever the dreamer, she would often get lost in the moment of leaves dropping off their trees, grateful for the reprieve of her terrifying images in the night.

Nearly every evening, she would dread going to sleep, anticipating being shackled by fear, hearing screaming and incomprehensible chatter that was determined to keep her doused in panic. Abigail didn't know that those nightmares represented a particular group of dark entities that preyed on the young, the weak, the stressed, and the sick.

She relished everything about her daydreams, getting lost in her nature abyss, until an acorn would fall on her shoulder, causing her to look at her watch. *Oh crap. I'm going to be late for geometry, again. Who thought doing math first thing in the morning was a good idea? I can hardly remember what day it is.*

On her way home from school one Friday, she decided to take a detour into the woods toward the waterfall. She loved coming here after a particularly stressful day at school. Today was one of the worst.

Thomas, the boy who sat behind her in English class, very quietly put gum in her hair. She knew it was him, since he couldn't wait to see the look on her face when he casually leaned over as the bell rang and whispered, "Are you trying a new look with your hair, Abigail?" She ran her fingers through her curls, secretly wishing he was giving her a strange compliment. Then she felt it and grimaced. He laughed so hard. Oh how that laughter cut deep. *No way,* she thought, *Now I'm definitely going to have to ask Mom to cut it. Ugh.*

As she ran to the bathroom with tears in her eyes, she vowed that when she got to college, she would keep her hair short and never have to sit in front of crude boys like Thomas again. She went through her backpack and found an elastic band. Rather than try and fight getting the gum out now and be late for yet another torturous class, she decided to just pull it back and hide it under some more of her unending thick curls in a ponytail. She never favored this look, since she felt it made her widow's peak too pronounced, but decided in this instance, it was much better than the alternative; attracting more attention by being late.

She tried to take some deep breaths, as she learned from her parents. *Breathing brings you back to yourself, to your essence.* Her father explained. *Once you can remember to breathe really well, all your cares can subside. You are one with the universe.* She thought, *But how can I feel at one with the universe when little prats like Thomas get away with torturing me?*

Abigail was clearly not paying attention as she walked toward her tranquil spot, deep in anguish and attempting to logically console herself. Nothing was working. She stepped on a twig and it snapped, quickly bringing her attention back to the path she was walking on. She could hear the waterfall getting closer, which gave her some comfort, and was utterly taken aback, at what she saw next.

CHAPTER FIVE

Sergius Strabo (Rome, 401 A.D.)

It was close to the fall of the Roman Empire. Those humans who were in charge of the cavalry horses care were called Strators. They were required to sleep with the horses in the stables, to prevent theft, as well as charged with keeping impeccable care of the horses' well being.

Sergius Strabo, a young man of seventeen, was one such caretaker to the horses. Although lower ranking, his role was undeniably essential. Sergius knew every inch of his horses' bodies. They were often coming in from conquests with various scrapes and rub marks from the abrasive warriors. He brushed, watered, fed, and exercised the horses meticulously.

Sergius' father taught him from an early age how to handle some of the most unruly of steeds. Sergius knew he had to be calm, focused, and fearless. Once he took over his own stable, he felt honored to carry on the family tradition. Although most of his time was around the animals, he felt there was a presence around him, watching him, guiding him. He never spoke of this to a single soul. He just knew it was there and it gave him comfort on the loneliest of evenings, after sweating more than any human should in one day.

Before bedding down on a patch of straw next to his favorite horse, he would sing to the beloved beasts. It wasn't a mighty war tune, simply a soothing melody. This singing made all the horses in his care feel at ease. Sensing that each outing could be their last, they treasured these peaceful moments with Sergius.

On a particularly windy morning, Sergius awoke, startled by a shrill whinny coming from his newest charge, Mercury. His nostrils flared and his huge chestnut neck arched above the stall door. Sergius then heard a large pounding on the wall. Mercury was attempting to jump out, slamming his front hooves against the stone walls. Once in front of him, Sergius raised his arms and began singing his evening lullaby. Mercury lowered his head, took a deep breath and softly nickered to Sergius.

What happened next was the most startling part of this interaction. Sergius could hear Mercury speak to him in his mind. Sergius stumbled backward and fell into a huge pile of manure. This did not even faze him. It was what this horse just conveyed that truly made him gasp.

"Good sir, I come from another world to make friends, learn of your species, and remind you of your purpose. I know that you were chosen to be the best caretaker of Horse. My true name is Dotune. Please hear me!"

Suddenly, there was a pounding on the stable door. The soldiers demanded all the horses to be readied for their next battle. Sergius scurried to his feet, stood at attention, and attempted to gather his wits about him. He took several glances back at Mercury while going through the check list in his mind for the preparations. He thought to himself. *I must have been dreaming. Did that horse really speak to me? What if he perishes in the next battle?* Before he could think of another question, Dotune answered, *You will see me again. We will have more time later to get acquainted. For now, know this in your heart. I will return.*

Sergius began to lose hope that he would see his new friend again. Flavius Stilicho, Sergius' general, was on a campaign against the Vandals. When Stilicho went into battle, he chose Mercury as his main steed. Mercury, or now called Dotune, as Sergius had learned, gained more insight into the Earthlings than he could have ever predicted.

Dotune quickly realized that many human beings were fierce and not heart-centered in the least. Most he encountered were blood thirsty, ego driven, and extremely insensitive. One would think that this would have discouraged this Gavranturan, yet quite the opposite transpired. Realizing that his strong and fast body was admired and utilized to its maximum potential during their conquests, Dotune had faith that humans could eventually learn how to connect with him. They could be encouraged to lead their lives in other ways, instead of the "survival and conquering" modes displayed predominately in this world.

Although grateful for his mission, he was eager to go back and relay his adventures to the council. He longed for the connection of love and joy that was so easily fostered on his home planet. Dotune knew he must be patient, for his instructions at the council were quite clear. "In one Earth year time, we will send for you in a most unique way. Please be open to all that you encounter. There are many journeys about to transpire. You will know soon enough."

Upon his return from a major battle, Dotune found comfort under the care of his Strator, Sergius. He noticed this human was curious about communicating, yet still unsure. This brought Dotune hope in transmitting his wealth of knowledge to humanity. This took some adjustments; especially when he first began to convince Sergius that he was indeed talking to him.

Good sir. I am ever so thankful to be back in your care. Would you be so kind and hear more of my story? I do believe we will be great friends on this journey.

Dotune sent these words to Sergius as he was just waking up one morning. He had just dreamed of an angel on a Pegasus. She was offering him a magical sword that would allow him to hear the thoughts of his horses. Still thinking he was in a dream state, Sergius shook his head and began doing some push-ups to pop his body back into wakefulness faster. After getting his blood pumping, he glanced over at Dotune's stall. He stared at Sergius and snorted.

You do hear me, correct? I need to know. Would you please nod your head if you can, good sir?

Sergius couldn't fight what he heard anymore. He had thought he had just imagined the original encounter and was now convinced he was going mad. He nodded slowly, then took off to grab a shovel and dove into his chores, hoping the horse would leave him alone for him to process what was happening.

Dotune sensed Sergius' resistance and felt content knowing that he was at least acknowledged. He began to observe his human more closely, in silence. He moved quickly, efficiently, and was an incredibly stoic young man. As the soldiers would burst in, disturbing his calm, he would jump into a posture of respect, carefully listen to instructions, and then immediately switched gears to the next task that had to be done. He never wavered in his duties, unless he was near Dotune. Sergius was suspicious of this talking horse, yet it was becoming clear that he was having trouble avoiding the impending conversation.

Sergius broke the silence one evening as he was drinking a strong drink called mead, that was passed around after a marriage ceremony he attended. His cousin had just taken himself a stunning bride, after settling into office at the Senate. Sergius was clearly intoxicated, stumbling around the stables in the dark. "Oh, what will you speak of next, my fierce friend? Dotune, was it? Please, relay your stories to my ears. For these ears are ever so tired of hearing the unending congratulatory wishes for my cousin and his new wife. They are the epitome of a gorgeous couple and I can only now dream of finding a future as bright. Please, dear foreign horse. Help me change my thoughts of longing into imaginings of the mysterious."

Dotune nickered, as he was overwhelmed with relief to begin communicating fully. *Dear Sergius, my faithful and hard working Strator. What I am going to tell you might sound too incredible for those ears you speak of. With that said, please listen with your heart. This, believe it or not, is exactly what you are doing right now. That is actually how you can hear me. We have a heart connection which allows this transmission to take place. However, I am getting ahead of myself. Well then. Let me begin with how I arrived here and what the plans are as I know them to be.*

Sergius sat down on a pile of neatly stacked horse blankets. He felt like he needed to get comfortable and his legs were a bit too wobbly anyhow. Dotune continued.

My soul is ever expanding and it originated on a planet called Gavrantura. Our String Keeper, Briggs, met an angelic being here on Earth named Levidia. She was summoned by my council to choose an appropriate time, place, and body for my soul to jump inside. She must have been watching you and known you would be open to hearing me, for here I am talking with you. This body's original soul, a kind one named Mercury, graciously agreed to leave and journey back to my planet, so that I might embark on this mission. Once you and I make a connection, a grand plan will be presented to us. The council told me that Levidia herself would be here soon to explain the next steps.

Sergius took another swig of his drink and threw his head back. He closed his eyes for a few moments. As he opened them again, his blurry vision was that of Dotune's eyes staring into his intensely.

Dear sir, can you hear me? Have I lost you?

Sergius steadied himself with his free hand and stood up slowly. He stood at attention and mumbled, "I am your humble servant." He then promptly passed out and slept all the way through the night. Dotune closed his eyes and imagined what Sergius might be dreaming about.

Levidia appeared just moments after Sergius fell asleep. She waved her wand in front of Sergius, and then Dotune. She smiled and bowed, thanking them silently. "I will be back again soon, Dotune darling. This young man is troubled with his sense of duty. He really thinks he has gone mad. Be patient with him. I know there is something very special about him. He could hear you, after all."

He went back to munching his hay. He realized that when she waved her wand in front of him, a story of a young lady named Abigail was implanted in his essence. He was instructed to visit her in dream time, tell her about Sergius and the larger plan to Re-Connect the Universal Web. Levidia smiled and then disappeared, just before Dotune could respond. She was clearly in a rush. She had to make sure the next horses would be ready.

CHAPTER SIX

The Small Herd

His body was relaxed and statuesque. He flicked his tail, pricked his ears forward, and turned his head to get a better look at something that floated past. It was just a pine needle. He sighed, allowed his head to lower, and closed his eyes. His legs carefully locked into position, securing his body to drift off for a nap. His journey could now unfold. In this world, he was called Horse.

Soaring over the dense treetops, the Lauren, sent by Briggs, circled down over the nearest bit of open land where she knew she would find Rafi. It was time to initiate the plan. This Lauren was an ancient messenger, one who had always assisted the String Keepers. She held in her wings the most precious, elegant chords, with instructions for this particular horse. She was known as a butterfly on Earth. Laurens took the form of anything that could fly. They especially liked the form of hawks, crows, dragonflies, and even swarms of bees. Her striking orange colored wings and green body floated down softly on a blade of grass, adjacent to a small glistening pond where this horse appeared to be waking up from a very relaxed state. Rafi began to quench his thirst in the hot sun with his eyes still half closed. She watched him carefully for a moment. Her antenna moved from side to side, sensing whether or not this was indeed *the* one to choose, the one Briggs had chosen. His eyes suddenly opened widely, sensing a presence. As he blinked slowly, the Lauren glimpsed into his large and dark eyes, filled with their own galaxy within. Her wings shuttered three times and she knew that was the answer. She could see glimmers of his home planet inside his enchanting eyes.

She dashed up to his sleek ear and whispered to him, "You are to move quickly to the West and stop at the first mountaintop. There you will find what you're looking for. It is time, my friend, and you must not waste any earthly minutes. I will find the others to join you. Good luck."

His head shot up dramatically, and with water still trickling from his muzzle, he let out a huge and powerful whinny. He knew his moment had finally come to make haste.

Rafi felt pride in his very first mission and galloped as fast as his hooves would negotiate the terrain. He knew he had to move quickly once a transmission had been received. It was of the utmost importance to stay within the time frame of the Laurens' messages. Each mission was orchestrated in such a way to allow for specific beings, at exacting times, to unite and push against the Murmori. As far as he knew, each attempt had failed. He secretly wished that he could be the one to help change that.

The world rushed by him and he slowed only when he thought he might step on a rock and bruise his hoof. The footing kept changing on this path from grassy plains, to sand, to rocks as he got closer to the mountaintop.

As he approached the snow-capped rock, known as the mountain of the West in this area, he collected his powerful body to a rhythmic trot. He arrived at the base and slid to a stop. Sweat was dripping from every part of him. His stomach and nostrils were moving in unison with his rapid breathing. Then he saw them. Two young mares appeared. They were clearly startled by his dramatic entrance. He decided to slowly walk toward them, lowered his head and nickered softly. They raised their heads high and snorted loudly.

The two mares examined the young stallion carefully. The horses used telepathy to communicate. *You must be him!* He replied, *Well, I guess I am. The Lauren sent me, you realize.*

They nodded and let out a big sigh. They then began to lick and chew as if they just digested the thought of all of this. The buckskin stallion spoke again, *My name is Rafi. The Lauren sent me here to find you and we are to commence on a grand mission. What are your names, my lovely new friends?*

They took turns getting to know each others' energy. Shantoo was a frisky chestnut mare and slightly suspicious of the new horse. She nipped at his flank and he spun around wide eyed, ready to kick. She backed off immediately from his response, conveying that she was indeed eager to get to know him, without a major tussle. Brouteen, a small dark bay with black mane and tail, was very pushy and immediately enjoyed being in Rafi's space, sidling up right next to his massive seventeen-hand tall body. Once the official introductions were made, the three of them began mutually grooming each other with intensity. After they found all of their itchy spots, they ran around the base of the mountain in a playful, wild sort of way. Each one took turns rearing up, spinning, and playfully pushing each other around, swishing their tails and tossing their heads up and down rapidly. Only a few moments went by and the crack of rock echoed loudly above them. They all spooked and ran together at full speed. None of them knew where they were going, only that they needed to be away from the dangerous rocks heading toward them. After about five minutes of racing, they finally slowed down once they found themselves in a forest.

The Lauren rested on a maple leaf, just above the three horses. She spun around in excitement once she realized that everything was being orchestrated perfectly. It only took a few dives down to get the attention of an old rattle snake, who was quietly sun bathing on a rock. She startled him enough to initiate the start of that avalanche. He looked up in the sky as she spiraled higher and higher in the air. As the old snake became focused on her, his tail rattled in the same rhythm as the Lauren's fluttering wings. His tail was just close enough to disturb a few pebbles, which then hit against a few more rocks, to create the whole galloping scene rolling. *That worked out even better than expected.*

She gazed down at the path of strategically placed crab apples. She had the help of another Lauren, a huge raven, shake those down for her several minutes prior to the snake's assistance. The horses were taking the bait. They followed each apple, crunchy loudly, and all fell at once, seemingly swallowed up by the earth itself. This exact portal, set up by none other than Levidia, was to lead them to their prescribed destination. She saw their manes fly upward suddenly and then vanish under the leaves. It was as if they never existed in this land. *Yes, it worked! They are on their way!*

CHAPTER SEVEN

Naomi Drake

Unbeknownst to her, Naomi had been monitored closely. Levidia seemed to think she would be an excellent candidate to join the two others prepped for the mission. After all, Naomi was searching for meaning and connection outside her daily life. She was heart driven with everything she did.

Even though Naomi had obtained a law degree, she gave it all up before even taking the Bar exam. Upon graduation, she took a part time job at her childhood stables. She had found her bliss that summer and couldn't imagine life without horses. It was then she decided to follow her passion to became a horseback riding instructor. While she loved her career, she never made a huge amount of money. Naomi secretly longed for the security of knowing a paycheck was always going to come each week. She was moderately happy in her life. The kind of happy that seemed to have an effervescent glow on the outside, advertising a sort of fake contentment, all lit up like a marquee at a movie theater. Yet for those who could sense deeply, she had a certain vacant, distracted sadness about her. She woke up each morning with soreness from being on her feet all day long. Her body felt years older than it really was from the arduous tasks of an outdoor woman.

She purchased Willow Tree Farms after her husband of four years passed away unexpectedly. She had finally grown accustomed to an amazing partner who loved the horses as much as she did. Her life flipped upside down when that phone call came in. He left her in a flash, just as he had shown up. She was ready to end it all and join him, when her husband actually came to her in a dream. He insisted she move away from their old apartment near the stables where she worked, begin again, and start with her own barn. The life insurance money was barely enough to get her business started up again, but she went for it. That dream shook her to her core. She could still see him so vividly and hear his words. *Naomi. Now is your chance. I will always be there to watch over you. I will leave you feathers to let you know you're on the right track. These horses need you. You have a gift. Please don't throw it away. I love you.* She never had any kind of spiritual experience until then. After that, she began to notice so much more.

Naomi attempted to sit every morning on her couch and listen to the sound of her breathing. She read an article about meditation as a form of therapy. She tried incessantly to get her negative thoughts out of the way. Each time, she would get frustrated, restless, and would go outside to clean stalls.

One day, while particularly annoyed at herself for not succeeding in the art of meditation, she felt a tickle on her nose while in the middle of a lesson. It felt like she was wearing a pair of glasses which were sliding down her nose. She rubbed her nose forcefully and said, "Go away! Leave me alone." This startled her student who was already nervous. Naomi quickly became embarrassed, "Oh, sorry, I think I just felt a bug on my face. Keep trotting on please. You're doing great."

She noticed that feeling on her nose, the next time she tried to meditate. Naomi realized it was an invitation to relax and believe in something other than what she could decipher with her five senses. She hadn't told anyone about it and let herself enjoy the secret sensation.

"Heels down, breathe, and look where you're going please." Naomi repeated these phrases more times than she had ridden a horse. She has logged close to 16,000 hours of riding in her life so far. Every student she encountered would need some variation of these words repeated to them. Naomi wondered if it was a parallel to life. *Steady yourself, breathe, and know where you're headed.* Naomi didn't have too many people to talk to about such philosophies. The horses were great listeners, yet didn't hold up their end of the conversation. Her students were just happy to ride and get a little bit better each time. Most weren't into deep conversations. They were often reminded to switch off their phones before mounting. That was one of Naomi's pet peeves. She once had a beginner rider answer her phone in the middle of a lesson and brag about how cool it was that she was on a horse. It made Naomi's stomach turn and she politely took the phone away and whispered a grateful 'thank you' to the steady lesson horse catering to the oblivious rider.

In between lessons and schooling her horses, Naomi would sit and write about her life. She felt it was the only way she could express herself completely. With the loss of her husband, she was lonely. Nights were the worst. She would type away at her computer until her eyes would become heavy and sleep was inevitable. Her dreams had become extremely vivid and were becoming more nerve-racking than she could recall as a child. In them, horses would get loose and run down the road, riders would fall off left and right, and her husband would show up. For some fleeting moments, she felt all was right with the world; until he would leave promptly again, reminding her of her heartache when she woke up each morning.

One such morning, as she wiped the tears away, she felt particularly spacey. She began putting on the multiple layers she needed to keep warm during the feeding process. Her boots were next to the door, still caked in mud from the previous night's trudging, and as she slipped her feet in, she felt something hard on her toes. She squealed, jumped back, tripped, and landed on her side. She assessed if anything was broken and realized she would just be bruised. Naomi crawled tentatively over to the suspect boot and turned it over. It was filled with cat food. It seemed the mice were beginning to store for the winter. She decided to clean up the mess later, carefully inspected the other boot and then limped her way outside to feed. She decided in that moment that it would probably be a fantastic idea to look for a working student soon. Twelve horses was quite a lot for one person to handle, even if she did consider herself an accomplished horsewoman. She couldn't bear the idea of getting hurt and having nobody lined up to help out.

After the chores were over and the happy sound of munching echoed in the barn, Naomi called the local paper to place a request in the help wanted section. Before she knew what to say, she felt a tingling on her nose and words that were not hers began streaming out over the phone. "Yes, that's right, applicants must be twelve years or older, with parental permission of course." She hung up the phone, trying to figure out where the words came from. *I should have written this out first. I can't believe I just blurted out what was in my head. Maybe I should call back and tell them to wait.*

She looked down and saw a beautiful brown and white feather. As soon as she picked it up, she heard a hawk right above the barn. Naomi took that as a sign to leave it be. The birds seemed to be the ultimate messengers. After all, she was told to follow the trail of feathers.

She prepared herself for the first lesson of the morning and heated a wet towel in the barn's microwave to wrap around Keeper's cold bit on his bridle. She was always thinking of little things to make her horses' lives happier.

CHAPTER EIGHT

Abigail's First Encounter

The three horses' hearts beat rapidly as they fell down the portal, then felt a jolt of air push them upward. Before they fully panicked, a soothing sound of a waterfall relaxed them. They landed in a large pool of water and began to swim, fighting to keep their heads up as they worked their hocks fiercely through this foreign stream. They finally reached land and shook off the excess water. Then it happened. They saw their first human and all three froze in fear.

This human was much smaller than the three of them anticipated, yet her movements were jerky and tense. They sensed a great sadness in her and decided that it was probably safe to approach her, slowly. She gasped at the sight of them. There was an unspoken curiosity among all four of them as they stared at each other. She immediately sat down on the ground and began to cry. The horses looked at one another and decided to start to sniff this human and nudge her on her shoulders. She sniffled and reached up, with her eyes closed, and began to caress each of their muzzles. They could feel her sadness surrendering to the most innocent joy. They nickered softly to her and she opened her eyes and smiled. She whispered, "I don't know where you came from, but I'm so happy you're here."

The Lauren was above the three of them and watched closely. She quietly flew down toward the stallion's ears again; whispering what was requested next, "Allow her to ride you. Then follow me." He thought this was very strange indeed, but who was he to question the Lauren?

Horses! Horses! Abigail looked around in amazement. Of all her years of reading countless books about horses, she fantasized of the day she could finally meet one of these creatures up close. Her parents were by no means able to pay for riding lessons, so she simply kept this wish to herself. But here they were, three beautiful horses just glistening. It looked like they had all been swimming together. *Am I dreaming? I'm going to close my eyes and open them again to make sure. Nope, this is no dream. They are really here.*

They surrounded her as Abigail giggled and pet each one of their soft muzzles. An overwhelming sense of joy took hold. She thought, *This just doesn't happen to any ordinary, frizzy-haired-with-gum-adornments-girl from upstate New York.* They all looked like they had never seen a person before, but seemed very brave to walk right up to her and investigate. She decided to stand up slowly and walk around them. They mouthed at her shoulders and then one of them knelt down next to her and motioned with his head to hop on. She couldn't believe this was happening. *Did this horse just invite me on his back?*

Abigail hesitated. She then had a flash of excitement wash over her. She took a deep breath, slid her small frame on him carefully, slowly, and was suddenly grasping at this stallion's mane for dear life as he stood up. The horse could sense this whole experience was unsettling for the both of them, so he walked very calmly and steadily. He seemed to be following with his eyes the flight of an orange colored butterfly. The two other horses got very excited and started prancing around the two of them. They motioned toward the butterfly and they all took off. Abigail held on tightly around his neck, closing her eyes, and praying that her butt would stop bouncing so badly on his back. She could feel him sense this and he began to slow from a gallop to a beautiful rocking canter. She was then able to sit up and allowed her hips to relax and follow the motion. *So this is what it's like. No wonder all of those books talk about being one with the horse. This is amazing!*

They hurried after the Lauren, taking care to keep the human with them. They realized too late that they were heading right back toward the waterfall. They could feel the sense to jump and jump they did.

29

They splashed right through the powerful waterfall into another portal. All they could hear was the terrified scream of the human child and they plummeted down into a misty setting. As if caught by a spider web, all three horses were suspended in the air, bouncing slowly up and down. Abigail leaned over and wretched a few times and then sat up with very wide eyes.

Am I dead? I can taste the bile from getting sick, so maybe not. What just happened? Where are we?

Abigail stroked the neck of her valiant steed and softly apologized for making a mess on his barrel. He simply lowered his head and waited. She looked around and realized there were fireflies coming toward them. Though this suspended feeling was a little uneasy, the glow exuding from their approach was mesmerizing. *Am I in Never land?* Before she could come up with another question, a voice boomed from above, "No, my dear, you are in another land, one of vast importance to humans, who have simply forgotten it exists." Abigail looked up to see a huge angel like woman floating down on top of a Pegasus. She introduced herself as Levidia, a guide for a very special journey, for a very particular young lady.

"What I am about to tell you will most likely make your brain fuzzy, Abigail Freedman. I've been watching you for quite some time. I know that you have nightmares often, yet remain hopeful that your life can get better with your frequent daydreams. Am I correct in this assessment, darling?"

Abigail was dumbfounded. *What the heck is going on? Oh crap. I think I am going to be sick again.* Levidia put a hand on Abigail's back and the nausea dissipated immediately. Abigail finally responded quietly. "Yes. You are correct. What I don't understand is why you've been watching me? And how? And from where? And where am I again?"

Levidia stifled a laugh and took in this fretful young lady. She decided to ask a simple question. "Abigail, all of your answers will arrive with clarity in a timely manner. I am here to ask if you are willing to commence on a mission of great importance. It would mean the end of your nightmares and the beginning of something even grander in your life. Are you willing to take a leap of faith, just as you did on the back of this stallion a few moments ago?"

Abigail was convinced they chose the wrong girl. *But I'm so sad and freaked out. Why would they want me?*

As if the horses could read her thoughts, they encircled her on this floating platform. Even though they didn't speak, she sensed a quiet reassurance from her new found friends. This journey wasn't something she could begin to fathom. She was hanging on very tight to the stallion's mane, trying to breathe, and still determining if she was dreaming or not. She took one hand off the stallion's dark wiry locks and pinched her cheeks a few times. She finally sighed and nodded, as if quietly accepting this challenge, yet still really unsure what to make of all this.

Levidia took her by the waist, hoisted her on the enormous Pegasus, and off they flew. She barely had time to wave goodbye to her new friends as they spiraled up a long corridor in the sky. Abigail almost passed out but kept on pinching her now very red cheeks to keep herself focused on what was unfolding.

CHAPTER NINE

Convincing Abigail

They flew up quickly, and then hovered in a rocking pause. The Pegasus, Prometheus, flapped his wings very softly and Abigail could feel a vibration all around them. Suddenly, the darkness of the tunnel began to open up with little bits of light. So small in fact, that Abigail thought at first she was just imagining, hoping beyond hope to actually see something. Then the small light bellowed out into a large circular door in front of them. They were sucked in rapidly and Abigail screamed a blood curling scream. She screamed louder than she ever had, yet no sound actually came out. It was if the light had buffered all the sound and the fear. Then a huge rush of peace filled Abigail's body. They had arrived in a garden that looked like a lavish waiting room. There were intricately designed chairs with leaves, flowers, and bits of moss sticking out. The ceiling had huge skylights, but there wasn't sky up above. It was a swirling light, much like Abigail had seen in some of the photos in the big picture books her Dad showed her as a child. They looked like cosmos, just swirling. Levidia motioned for Abigail to sit.

"I am sure you have a million questions right now. Before you speak, please let me explain a few things to you. It has to do with your nightmares you have nearly every night. Those nightmares are caused by the entities called the Murmori. They prey on you while you sleep and they're beginning to find ways to suck out humanity's imaginations without their knowledge. They're planning to keep humans in a cycle of fear and anxiety, without even knowing what is real anymore. Does this make sense to you at all? If you could, please place your hand over your heart, and let a question bubble up from that space." Levidia spoke in hushed tones.

Abigail wanted to burst out with all of the wild questions swimming in her mind, but was too afraid to say anything. She dutifully took one long, deep breath, placed her shaking hand over her heart and closed her eyes. Levidia was right. Abigail understood and felt a surprising wave of trust sweep over her. She opened her eyes, gazed at Levidia and asked, "What can I possibly do?" Levidia smiled.

"Now that is a wonderful question. Well done, Abigail." Levidia gained a spark of hope that her young traveler was much more eager than even she had predicted. She quickly gained her composure and looked into Abigail's curious and unwavering eyes. She continued in a more serious tone, "You are here in order to take on a mission of utmost importance in the universe. I have so much information to relay to you, yet realize that I can't unload it all at once. I don't want your mind to explode, after all."

Abigail leaned her head back on the huge armchair and closed her eyes. "The nightmares are getting worse. I feel like they are pulling me deeper into a world that I can't escape. I wake up shaking, not knowing what to do or who to reach out to. If what you're saying is true, then humans have a pretty dismal future. But seriously, why are you even considering me? This seems way over my head and much too big of a mission to do by myself, especially when I'm only making B's and C's in high school."

Levidia sat down next to Abigail and held her hand tightly. She placed her other hand on the top of Abigail's head. "Here you will find a variety of ideas, most of which will take you to dark places. Doubt will creep in and you will never believe in your own potential. This is what the Murmori are counting on. I am here to convince you otherwise. Abigail, you have an enormous amount of power. Even with these terrible nightmares, your imagination grows stronger during the day. You refuse to be brought down. That's why I have chosen you to help. Do you remember your dream with the golden globes and the rope?"

"That was you?"

"Yes. I was testing to see whether you could really understand your inner strength. You see, if you don't believe in yourself, all will be lost. Humans will be stuck in fear mode. I will no longer exist, nor will any other of the Earthly spirit guides. And worse, the Murmori will have succeeded in dismantling the entire Universal Web. They will cut off this planet from inter-dimensional travel. Humans will never again be able to accept assistance from benevolent beings."

"Wait. What? What's the Web thing? This is so crazy."

"The Universal Web was comprised of thousands of strings all around the planet. Each string represented a portal which allowed for inter-dimensional travel. Every string except for one has been dismantled by the Murmori. This is our final attempt at Re-Connecting the Web. If you are successful, the Earth's vibration will rise and the strings will come back online."

"But how am I going to take on such a mission? And you do realize that I'm only a teenager?"

"Believe me, you will not be alone. You will be part of a team. "

Abigail drew her hand back and turned briskly toward Levidia. "A team? You said you've been watching me. You should know that I don't have any friends. My parents hardly know what to do with me, and well, honestly, I just don't know how to relate to others. Who did you have in mind? What does this all mean, really?"

Levidia took a long deep breath and stared up at the swirling ceiling. She was gathering her thoughts and could hear Briggs whispering to her. *Only tell her what she needs to know right now. Don't overwhelm her, dear friend.*

"I really can't tell you who you'll be working with on this mission, since they haven't been confirmed yet. I can tell you, however, that the three horses you met today play a key role. Abigail, do you realize what's at stake here? I understand believing me in blind faith is incredibly daunting, but take a look around you. Did you ever imagine such a place existed before? Don't you think other humans deserve to find out more about the existence of a place like this and so

34

many others? We must take the power away from the Murmori before it's too late. Humans could become like robots, simply existing, without any creative thought to speak of."

Levidia continued. "Many have attempted this type of mission, yet were thwarted by others or their own insecurities. You must believe that you can make a difference. But most importantly, you must believe in yourself, no matter what. Are you ready to take on this challenge?"

Abigail retorted, "Do I have a choice?" Levidia lowered her head, "You always have a choice, my dear. I will leave you here for a few minutes and come back for your decision. Feel into your heart space again and really know that whatever you choose, it will be right."

She floated through a door that wasn't there a few minutes ago. Abigail watched her leave in amazement. She thought, *Well this was not what I thought an after-school program was supposed to be like.* She laughed at herself out loud. She could feel the tears streaming down her face, as she understood how much bigger she was about to become. She knew this was what she had always dreamed of and couldn't believe it was actually happening. Getting whisked away to another world, yet having to go back to hers wasn't what she had foreseen. Perhaps that was the point.

She looked around at the decor again and decided. As if reading her thoughts, Levidia slipped right back in and smiled at her with the most grateful looking smile Abigail had ever experienced. She gulped softly and thought, *If I am really here for a very specific reason, I better focus. This is not geometry. This is a very special secret mission from another dimension. What will I be capable of? This ought to be interesting.*

Levidia now demonstrated that she could indeed read Abigail's thoughts. "You will surprise yourself, darling. Let's start with where you are, since I'm sure that is foremost in your wonderment. This, you see, is a gateway in between dimensions. It was created with the last string of the Universal Web that remains intact. The Murmori managed to dismantle the strings, yet guides like myself and a few others managed to keep this one hidden. You see, the fallen strings, if reunited, will allow the Universal Web around Earth to initiate inter-dimensional travel yet again. When other beings can travel here, they can defeat the Murmori. You will be trained inside of this string. Come with me, Abigail Freedman."

Another big gulp, which was audible this time, came out of Abigail's body. Levidia just nodded and motioned to the hidden door. They walked through together and Abigail's body immediately started floating. She grasped at Levidia's arm, desperately trying to navigate the zero-gravity chamber. As Abigail's body flapped about she engaged her abs and was able to hover for a few moments, then began drifting again. Levidia quickly asked, "What made you steady for those moments?" As she tried to think about the strange sensations of all her body parts fluttering about, she took a deep breath and realized it. "Oh, I just focused on my inner stomach muscles and oh, right, there it is! That's the *key* to being centered." She let out a giggle of relief from realizing that she knew this all her short life and finally felt it work, immediately. She breathed deeper into her belly, found herself getting very steady, and discovered her independence from Levidia's arm.

"You're keeping up very well. Wonderful job, Abigail! You have already unlocked the first key in your training. *You* have the power to control all of your situations. Just remember to breathe into your center, your power, and it will all settle into place." As soon as she finished speaking those words, they moved into yet another room. This time it was filled with bright lights and flying dust particles, like miniature glowing spirals, in every color spectrum, whizzing around, making her feel extremely dizzy. While at first Abigail was mesmerized by this site, she struggled with puzzling out this next test and her tears began to stream yet again. She was being incredibly brave, but her exhaustion began to take over. Levidia knew this was happening and pointed to a corner of the room where two lounge chairs were beckoning them over. Abigail was most grateful to be able to just stay still for a moment. Levidia leaned over and whispered,

"You are ready for phase two, but you must rest first. This must be done in stages, since it's becoming apparent that your body really can't handle too much more. Close your eyes here and you will be taken back. I will find you for the next phase. Rest well."

Now Abigail was having her doubts again, wondering if it really was all just a dream. Her mind was swirling with thoughts and she just wanted them all to stop. She wanted quiet. She closed her eyes and her body was then gracefully placed on the bank of the waterfall again, with those gorgeous beasts grazing alongside her.

CHAPTER TEN

Joe

Abigail stretched, rubbed her eyes, and looked around. She grinned as she realized that the horses were still there. She looked out toward the horizon, past the dark mane of the stallion, and noted the sun was getting ready for slumber. She then realized how late it was and bolted upright. The horses raised their heads quickly and pointed their ears toward her. Those ears were like radar, sensing all of the things around them, ready for running, relaxing, or expressing their emotions. Abigail took a moment to realize that her movements really shifted the energy of these gorgeous creatures. She reminded herself to breathe deeply, find her center and slow down. As soon as she did, the two mares began to encircle her and softly nuzzled her back, arms, and hair. Abigail got chills from this interaction and found comfort stroking each horse. She softly told them that she would return in the morning and gave a huge hug to the stallion, which at first made him very tense. As soon as he felt her love pouring through, he relaxed and hugged her body closer to his chest with his immensely strong neck. Abigail sighed and waved goodbye to her new friends. *How am I going to explain all this to Mom and Dad?*

Abigail walked into the house casually with the clear intention that her parents would not even notice anything awry. She assessed it would be fairly easy to keep this experience quiet. Her mother was busy staring at a cookbook in the kitchen, while chatting on the phone with her friend. Her father was in the living room, catching up on the latest scientific magazine. She whispered hello to both of them and they nodded with sweet smiles, recognizing that their daughter was home, yet not quite realizing just how late it was. It still didn't stop her heart from racing. She tiptoed into her room and then grabbed a pillow and screamed into it. She screamed so much that she made herself dizzy. She sat down on her bed and tried desperately to calm her mind, hugging her pillow tightly. *What in the world is happening? Did I just dream all of that up? Should I tell my parents? They are probably just going to think I am nuts. I just need to talk to someone! I hate feeling so alone.*

Abigail suddenly stood up, tossed her abused pillow down and had an eerie sense that someone was watching her. This was a creepy feeling, yet she felt like it was almost to be expected at this point. She looked out the window and sure enough, a lean looking man with a huge black cowboy hat was leaning against the tree, staring in at her. He tipped his hat in a funny sort of hello and Abigail opened her window.

For most folks, Joe, the cowboy guide, doesn't show up all that often. He does, however, hang around people who are absolutely in a tizzy about what they are doing and can't seem to relax enough to see the other side of their whirlwind. He can be found chewing on a long piece of straw, leaning up against a tree, just ready for you to turn around and acknowledge him. Once you do, a huge sigh of relief comes over you, the dust settles, and you begin to remember what you were planning on doing in the first place, before you got your knickers in a twist. Joe loves to just chuckle at us modern folks and will remind us to slow down and enjoy the scenery.

"Evening, little Missy. I believe you were hoping for someone to lend an ear. My name is Joe. I don't come around these parts too often, but I was summoned here right quick when I heard the news. Seems like the folks around here are about to embark on a demanding mission. Heard you're the one to lead them. What do you know so far?"

Abigail studied this quaint man, speaking like he just walked out of one of those old western movies. He was completely relaxed in his body, yet had a grandeur about him that made her want to gather her thoughts in a most particular way. She didn't want him to think of her as a silly teenager. "Well, sir, I was told to prepare myself for assisting humanity against the Murmori. I am not exactly sure how this is going to play out, except that I did learn how we have very great powers from within. I guess I am supposed to spread these ideas somehow." Even with his attire and old time speech, implying that he could be a true cowboy, Abigail was careful not to mention the horses she encountered just yet. She felt like they were a precious secret, only to be shared when the timing felt right.

"Well, that sure does sum up why Briggs sent me here."

Abigail gave him a quizzical look, "Who is Briggs?"

"You mean to say you don't know the String Keeper? Thought for sure they would have sent you to her first. That's usually the way you folks are introduced to the other realms."

"No, sir. I really have no idea who you're talking about. I met an angel, err, of sorts, on a Pegasus."

Joe's eyes widened as he leaned closer toward the window. "You mean to say that you met Levidia. The Levidia? Well I'll be. This sure is a bigger mission than I anticipated. Maybe I ought to come back tomorrow so we can have a longer discussion. You have to be in school or something like that?"

Abigail suddenly realized that she had no idea what day it was. She looked down at her calendar on her desk, nodded and sighed with relief. It was indeed Friday. She looked up and quietly said, "Tomorrow is Saturday, Mr. Joe. My parents have a pep rally at their school, so I should be free all day. I am sure they won't mind if I stay home. They know how I shy away from the crowds at the private school functions."

"Well, all right then. I will be back when the coast is clear. Until then, get some rest. You're going to need it." Joe tipped his hat yet again and walked away into the woods, vanishing after just a few seconds.

Abigail continued to stare out the window, wondering what else was going to happen. She decided that she had to come up with some way to stay looking normal to her parents and grabbed a school book to put in front of her so she could continue staring blankly. Then the knock on the door came, "Dinner's on the table, honey. Come on out, please." Abigail knew that tone. Mom was on a mission of her own and Abigail was going to hear about it while munching on cantaloupe, a mixed green salad, and a new invention of the evening. It seemed to be some sort of pot pie, made with sweet potatoes, tofu, and Abigail was not sure what else. She really didn't care, since it had a hint of cinnamon that made her happy. She was imagining what was going to unfold tomorrow, as her mother rambled on and on about encouraging Abigail to take all the Advanced Placement classes she could next semester. This apparently would help get credit for college. Abigail nodded when appropriate and politely said that she would look into it. Her mother was well meaning, yet could be somewhat overwhelming.

Abigail looked over at her father who was clearly zoning out in a similar fashion. Once her mother started to wind down, he finally chimed in during their dessert of chocolate pudding, saying that any advanced classes Abigail wanted to take would be wonderful and he would happily assist her in the math and science areas. Abigail was grateful for the interesting dinner, mostly that it was finished, so she could quickly retreat to her room. She nearly forgot about the gum in her hair. Abigail thought, *That seems like ages ago now.* She sighed again and decided not to bother her Mom with it. *Guess I will have to be creative with the scissors tonight.* She started in on the delicate chopping away of her wild curls. *Just get this done, go to sleep, and it will all become clear in the morning.*

CHAPTER ELEVEN

Joe's Lesson

Abigail came back to consciousness slowly. Evelyn shook her on the shoulders softly, "Abigail, wake up. You were moaning so loudly, we could hear you from our bedroom. Are you okay, honey?" Abigail squinted and nodded slowly. "Of course," she responded, startling her very concerned mother. She quickly changed her words. "Of course I'm all right, Mom. I was just having a very intense dream. I think I am beginning to find a truly magical place." Her mother nodded and assumed she was still sort of dreaming. She stroked Abigail's hair, "Would you like cereal or eggs for breakfast?"

Abigail couldn't even think of eating. Her mind was spinning. She shrugged and said, "I will grab something in a little bit, Mom, thanks anyway." Evelyn smiled and shut the door behind her. Abigail threw herself back onto the bed as she recalled her dream of horses, an angel woman, a large Pegasus, swirling lights and a cowboy. She let out a little squeal. *Not even a dull moment in my sleep.* "Precisely," echoed a booming voice from her closet. Abigail bolted up with an adrenaline rush so strong she almost passed out. In that moment, she recognized that voice, and realized it wasn't a dream after all.

Joe slowly slid open the closet door, as he took in the frightened youngster, her eyes frozen up at him. He knew it was time to reveal more of the secrets.

"Mornin', Miss Abigail. Sure didn't mean to spook ya. I've been patiently waiting for you to wake back up into this realm. Your Momma sure is a sweet lady, being all concerned for you. Are you ready to hear some more about all of this here excitement?"

Abigail's heart started to slow down as the adrenaline rushed out of her body. She was still a little light headed, yet found some strength with some deep breaths. She began to sit up very squarely on the edge of her bed, hands folded neatly in her lap, shoulders back, and simply said. "Please share with me all you know."

Joe laughed a belly laugh so big it could have woken up the neighbors. Abigail was a little miffed that he was laughing at her and immediately shushed him. "Not to worry your pretty head there, miss. No one else can actually hear me but you in this moment. I am just tickled by your curiosity. Most youngsters want to cut right to the chase. I will tell you near as much as I can until we have to shuffle you off for the next phase. I am pretty darn sure that Briggs would like to be seeing you next to catch you up on all of these dimension hopping happenings. She is the String Keeper, after all."

"The String Keeper?" Abigail whispered in a fascinated way.

"Yes, I know her very well and she loves it when I offer up her description in this particular way." Joe handed Abigail a rolled up parchment. On the top it said:

Briggs is the last String Keeper between Earth and a planet called Gavrantura. She also likes to call herself the "zoning out" mistress.

As Abigail continued to read, the enchanted parchment literally lit up in a bright white light as her eyes met each word. It was a magical feeling just to skim the page.

*There is a space between worlds that is so discreet, not many people can really sense when they are visiting. You go there often when you stare at something for too long...*Abigail continued to read.

"Wow. I can totally feel this energy of Briggs. What a beautiful description and I love how the words light up on the page. Wish all of my papers in English could do that. Maybe I could get better grades?"

Joe laughed again, "Little miss, I think getting good grades is the least of your concerns at the moment. We need to catch you up on a lot of information, since you were apparently whisked right into an advanced class of energy work before you were properly briefed on addition and subtraction."

Abigail gulped, and then nodded. She smiled nervously when she realized that the flips in her stomach was coming back to get her all jumpy again, as she thought about all of these new sensations. Then she could feel herself zone out again.

She quietly said to Joe, "I guess I go to see her a lot; especially while in geometry." She giggled to herself. "Can I actually chat with Briggs? Do you have more to tell me, Mr. Joe or do I just go right to her now?"

"Ah, now you're sounding much like the youngsters I know. Just hold on to your hat and let me mention a few more details."

Abigail got a little more comfortable and placed a pillow behind her back. She took a deep breath, steadied her racing mind and looked up at Joe with her arms crossed. She wanted to believe all that was happening, but she kept getting a feeling like maybe she was still dreaming. She shrugged internally and turned her attention on the old cowboy in her bedroom.

Joe nodded and said, "Well then, let's begin."

"What if you could go anywhere you dreamed up? Would you want to learn how to travel so easily to any place at all, just as easily as you are breathing? What would that feel like, Miss Abigail?"

Abigail leaned her head back and closed her eyes. Then, being the clever girl that she already was and becoming even more so with every second, she exclaimed, "Well, I think I kind of already do that with my imagination!"

"Well, hold on there just a little minute. You can imagine you are there, yet are you really there? How do you know?"

This got Abigail's wheels turning for sure. She cocked her head to the side, played with her curls, and then scrunched up her face in a focused way.

Joe saw this internal struggle and decided to intervene. "Please relax. Really, the more you just allow for this idea to sink in, the more you will realize what I'm telling you. You can go wherever you like and actually interact with others just like you. You're a brilliant young lady who is willing to explore the unimaginable. Those who are more asleep around you would scoff at what I'm fixing to have you grasp. You can send your energy wherever you like and move the moon and stars if you take the notion."

"Whoa. Wait. Are you talking about stuff like in the movie, *The Matrix*? Are you saying that we are simply like computer programs and we can press restart and add a new game to be installed on our journey?"

"No, Miss Abigail. It isn't quite like that. It isn't nearly as morbid as that movie would like to impress on you youngsters. You're more of an infinite being. One that can actually be where you are *and* where you would like to project yourself to be, in any moment. Kind of like running two different movie screens at the same time. Even more than two, if you get really talented at this stuff. One might get slightly fuzzy and muted while the other becomes more clear, depending on where you focus. Are you catching my drift?"

Abigail realized she was starting to chew on her hair and quickly spit it out with this question. "I think so." Her thoughts immediately went to the three beautiful horses she had left yesterday and she yearned to be with them.

Joe could sense a longing in her and asked quickly, "I'm speculating there is a place you would like to be right now, am I on the money, you reckon?"

Abigail couldn't contain herself anymore. She burst with exuberance, jumped up and said, "Yes!" Hoping she didn't seem too silly. She still felt the need to be somewhat formal with this old time cowboy ghost or whatever he was.

Joe began giving her clear instructions. Abigail couldn't believe what she was hearing. It was like someone was handing over a map to the inner world that she only dreamed up in glimpses during her daydreams at school.

"You see, all you need to do is sit quietly, breathe in and out deeply and you will be getting into the space you need to be in, little darling.

We call this meditation. Once you are just noticing your breath and allowing any of your wild young thoughts to just drift, you get to find a still point. From there you can either ask questions about anything or simply enjoy the quietness of your mind. When you're fixin' to travel, you just bring your awareness to where you really want to be with all of your heart's desire. Then, just like a magic spell, poof, you are there."

Abigail stared blankly for a moment and replied, "Poof?" The amount of information was daunting. She wanted to think about something else and then suddenly became very self conscious that she was still in her pajamas.

"Before I attempt any of this, let me throw some more clothes on, okay Mr. Joe?" Joe chuckled and said he would step back into the closet for a few minutes until she was ready. Abigail scurried around her dressers for a few moments, threw on some jeans, a long sleeve flannel and her favorite pair of shoes, and leaned against the bed. Finally, she whispered, "all right, I am slightly more decent."

She reluctantly took some deep breaths, closed her eyes, did everything he had just instructed to the tee, and suddenly, she was sharply whisked out of her room and onto a tree branch, directly above the stallion she had so desperately wanted to be close to again.

Abigail grabbed hold of the branch as tightly as she could. She gasped. *I am having trouble believing all of this.* As soon as she thought this, she was brought right back into her bedroom.

Joe immediately responded. "That, Miss Abigail, is what I am here to do. Take away those doubts. Believe in what you once thought impossible. Otherwise, Levidia's decision about you will have been in vain. You just gotta believe." Joe patted her on the shoulder and left her alone to contemplate what she had just learned.

Abigail stumbled out of her bedroom. She found her way to the living room couch, next to the scientific magazines piling up due to her father's notion of keeping every bit of 'new knowledge' at hand. She took one look at them and felt her brain get squishy. *This is too much. Brain about to explode. Must go for a walk and get out of my*

46

head. She decided to head out and see if the horses were still there. She found them in the exact same spot.

The stallion was buckskin in color, a sort of champagne color, with a long, flowing black mane. The others were bay and chestnut. The three of them were stunning. She watched as they took turns grooming each other, chomping on their necks. They looked like swans, as they arched their heads around each other. Abigail attempted to stay quiet as long as possible, trying desperately not to disturb this intimate moment. Suddenly, the stallion's ears pricked forward and his head shot up, doing his best giraffe impression. When he spotted her behind a tree, he nickered softly.

My new friend is back. Rafi was most excited about the next step in his journey and was positive this creature would be able to guide him along for whatever his purpose was to be in this world. He made the typical beckoning sounds that a horse makes, in order to reassure her that he wanted her to visit with him. She slowly moved around the tree from where she was hiding and Rafi moved in close next to her.

The other two horses began trotting in a circle around the child and the stallion. They had grown tired of waiting overnight, as they each took turns standing guard.

While Abigail absorbed the energy of the horses, Joe, who had followed her, watched curiously at the three restless beings, thinking, *This is going to be some ride.* As soon as he thought this, he caught sight of a beautiful orange butterfly that was fluttering between the oak tree branches, just above the stallion's head.

Joe whispered to Abigail, "Hey, little miss, look above you. This is another messenger."

She had nearly forgotten all about Joe, with the thrill of seeing these beloved animals again. She looked up and smiled, "Hello. My name is Abigail. I am ready."

Abigail looked a little higher, above the orange fluttering wings, to see Joe tipping his hat to her from the tree top and then quickly evaporating.

The Lauren was most eager to share her latest message with the young girl. It was *the* message from Gavrantura's history. She fluttered and swooshed to get the frizzy haired thing's attention and created a thin film of translucent webbing that served as a miniature movie screen. The images created a story that was sent to Abigail's mind telepathically. Abigail leaned against the stallion's shoulder as she took in this fantastical show, watching intensely as she learned about why he was here with her.

She learned all about Dotune, Gavrantura, and the destruction of the Universal Web. The Lauren explained how she was chosen by Briggs and Levidia to help humanity bring their vibration to a higher level to Re-Connect the strings of the Web.

Abigail took a deep breath. Her mind was flashing and reeling in so many directions. She looked back at the horses around her and felt a deep sense of honor and then panic washed over her.

This is so much bigger than I realized. Why am I being asked to do this? She posed the question to the valiant steeds around her. They sent her their first heart centered message that she could finally hear for the first time.

Abigail could feel the message inside of her, as if all the horses were speaking in unison. *We would like you to know that you are obviously very special. You can now hear us and it is your job to begin hearing others on this level. We would like for you to be brave, join us on this journey, and invite as many others that you can inspire to be open to creating a new way of living.*

Abigail sat down and cried. She didn't know how to handle this. It was clearly overwhelming her. *I am not special. Nobody even realizes I exist in school. My parents are always hoping that I will be someone special. I always feel like I am disappointing everyone somehow. I try hard, but I just don't feel like someone worthy of all this. I have no idea how this is happening. I really think this is a huge mistake. If the entire planet is truly counting on little Abigail, then we are in some deep poop.*

Rafi looked toward the other horses and addressed them. *I'm at a loss. She clearly can't see what Briggs and Levidia see. What should we do?*

Brouteen suggested, *Let's have her just go home. There's really nothing more we can say to her.*

Rafi then turned to Abigail. *Sweet young lady. Never fear. You will find your courage soon enough. Find your way home, but please don't forget about us. We will be here waiting when you are ready.*

Abigail started to say something, but just sniffled and turned around quickly. She hurried back, tear stained and fretful. It would be just another hour before her parents got home. She decided to take a shower to clear her mind.

While shampooing her hair, Abigail was clearly overtired and getting loopy. She began creating some wild shapes out of her hair with the shampoo, allowing it to stand straight up like a Mohawk would on one of those older punk rockers. She nodded her head up and down, letting the soap fly everywhere. Then she froze. She felt a presence with her. This time, her adrenaline did not peak. It was a soothing presence. Under her breath, she whispered, "Briggs?"

She then could hear a whisper back. "Yes, it is me. I am so glad to finally make your acquaintance. I see you haven't lost your sense of humor in all of these adventures of late. I am so pleased that you're beginning to tap into your power and taking this all in stride. And speaking of strides, I am here to advise you to begin taking riding lessons immediately. That is all. Good luck, Abigail."

Riding lessons? What the? I've always dreamed of doing that, but there's no way my parents would be able to afford it. I did feel an amazing connection while riding that stallion. But seriously?

Abigail decided to focus on the task at hand. She rinsed the shampoo and quickly found the best conditioner in the variety of used bottles scattered around her. She did enjoy the process of smoothing out her hair, whenever possible. It always felt best immediately following a good shower. She wrapped her head in a towel-like turban and slipped on her pajamas. She fell into her bed, with the intention of taking a nap before her parents came home from the pep rally. She hoped all of her thoughts would disappear. She couldn't take any more surprises. She was asleep within moments.

CHAPTER TWELVE

The Parental Units

Dotune was waiting in Abigail's dream. He had been sent to her by Levidia. Abigail arrived in her dream time with such a curious nature, it reminded him of his first decision to travel to Earth. He walked up beside her and nudged her shoulder. She smiled and turned to him, with an inquisitive look, as if to say, who are you?

His first instinct was to make a quiet nickering sound, so it wouldn't startle her if he spoke. Then he realized, she had already showed up on this plane of reality, so he might as well begin his explanation.

"My name is Dotune. I am bonded with the caretaker, Sergius, who I would love for you to speak with sometime soon. Right now, all I can tell you is that you and he are connected in the most glorious way. I have experienced his generous spirit firsthand and I can already sense that yours is very similar. We will meet again during this dream time of yours. Until then, follow the path that you are set on."

Abigail woke up to the sound of birds chirping. She was surprised she had slept through the night. She looked out the window and observed a cardinal couple tilting their heads, clearly watching her through the window. Abigail could sense that they were thanking her for keeping the bird seed filled up on the side of the house. As she contemplated her latest dream, or encounter; combined with these cute birds, she felt relieved, *I didn't have a nightmare. This is interesting. And I am beginning to feel like Snow White combined with She-Ra.* She-Ra, "Princess of Power," was one of her all time favorite cartoon characters as a small child. It was one of the few shows her parents allowed her to watch. It was only shown on re-runs on Saturday mornings on an obscure channel that her father discovered in between the basic seven channels broadcast via the "bunny ears" antenna. These thoughts began to bring her to a slightly better mood than when she had her meltdown by the waterfall.

She thought some more about her long lost beloved character, She-Ra. *She rode a Pegasus which she communicated telepathically with.* This gave her goosebumps. *Oh my goodness. Talk about dreams coming true!*

Abigail shook her head and tore off the towel that was already halfway off of her slightly damp hair. She looked in the mirror and decided to simply pull her hair back in a pony tail. Her reflection didn't seem to bother her nearly as much as just a couple of days ago. She was beginning to realize that her heart was opening and her face was softening. She didn't feel as tense as she did that dreaded day she discovered the gum.

She heard a gentle knocking on the door. Rat ta tat tat tat. She perked up, as she realized that was her Dad's secret knock. She opened the door quietly. Albert grinned and handed her a page from the Sunday's "help wanted" ads. He had circled something and silently pointed to it. Her eyes widened as she read how the mystery was unfolding:

Working Student Wanted: Must be willing to muck stalls, clean aisle ways, groom horses, and take instructions cheerfully. All hours of work will be credited toward lessons with a successful local riding instructor. Applicants must be 12 years or older (with parental permission), have reliable transportation, and have a great desire to learn. No experience necessary. Will train. Apply in person at Willow Tree Farms.

Her Dad smiled and said, "Honey, I know things have been rough at school for you lately. Would you like to do this? I can drive you over this afternoon."

"Would I? Oh my. *Dad!* This is what I have been waiting for all of my life! Thank you *so* much for finding this!" She nearly knocked him down when she gave him a fierce bear hug.

He chuckled and said, "Well, then, let's plan to head out after lunch."

Abigail was so excited she started running around like a horse, all over the house. Her father kept laughing out loud. Abigail was glad that her Mom was still at the gym this morning, so she wouldn't wonder what got her all wound up. Her mother tended to shift her away from anything other than schoolwork. She figured that her Mom wasn't privy to this bit of news yet. Dad used the "secret" knock on the door after all. She simply couldn't wait until lunch time. She ran back into her room, bursting with energy, and managed to settle down in front of her notebook. She always wrote when her emotions got too overwhelming. She began writing about all of her latest adventures and realized that as her pen was moving feverishly, words that were not her own began developing on the page.

Have faith, my darling Abigail. This is your next task. Phase two has begun. Learn how to ride well. Listen to the horses. Share what you learn. Don't be afraid. It is time to make this great leap of faith with horses, humans, and the universe. Good luck!
Much Love, Levidia

Abigail stared at the page. *What the? How did she write this through me? I must be going mental. Phase two? This beginning has already been crazy enough.* She looked around the room and closed her eyes, trying to keep her thoughts from swirling around rapidly. *Well, maybe I will just focus on riding horses and this so called mission might not be so bad after all.*

Lunch time was a bit of a blur to Abigail. Her mother prepared a huge salad and watched Abigail closely as she inhaled every last bite. Evelyn looked quizzically at her husband. He mouthed the word 'teenager'. She shrugged and stood up to clear the plates. "I need to finish working on grading papers. Would you two like to do something this afternoon? I think it would be great for you both to spend some quality time together."

Albert looked at Abigail sharply, as if to imply that she shouldn't breathe a word about their plans. "That sounds like a great idea, Mom. Dad, what should we do?"

Albert squeezed his daughter's shoulder and took a moment to reply. "How about we take a drive around the countryside and discuss how things collide?"

Abigail stifled a laugh and said loud enough for mother to hear as she walked toward her study, "That sounds like a grand way to spend the day." Evelyn smiled to herself. She knew how her husband and daughter loved to do rhymes. She called out to them, "Have fun. Love you!" and closed the door.

Abigail whispered to her Dad, "Why all the secrecy?"

Albert said, "I'll explain in the car. Grab your coat."

Albert made sure they were clear of the driveway before he began his explanation. "Abigail, did you know that your mother was an avid equestrian?"

Abigail looked at her Dad like he grew another head. "Um, no way. Why wouldn't she have told me? That's kind of a big deal. You guys know how much I love to read about horses."

He proceeded to explain how she rode as a child and had a huge accident where the horse flipped over. She had broken her pelvis and she never wanted to ride again. The fear took over her love. "I think that's one of the reasons why you are such a huge blessing. The doctors told her that she couldn't have a child. Guess they were wrong!"

Abigail stared at her Dad in shock. This was the first she had ever heard of any of this. "So I take it Mom wouldn't want me riding then, right?"

Albert nodded slowly and then whispered, "Abigail, I think you should do what makes you happy. Let's see if you get this job and like riding before we say anything. Right now, she's been under a lot of stress at work, so it's probably best that we keep this to ourselves."

She couldn't imagine her mother riding horses. *And to think, I wasn't even supposed to be born. My oh my. This week is proving to be full of surprises.*

The drive to the stables was only fifteen minutes. Abigail could feel her stomach doing flip flops. Her Dad looked over at her in the passenger side and sensing her nerves, quietly said, "Just breathe deeply and imagine you have the job." *He can read my mind too, I think.* Abigail smiled and proceeded to breathe deeper. She then thought about Levidia's magical realm where she used her center to steady herself from not floating away. Her flip flopping stomach immediately settled and at that moment, she looked up to see the most glorious gate. Above her as they drove through, were two large metal horse heads, intertwined like swans, above a sign that said, "Willow Tree Farms." Her heart skipped a beat as they pulled right up to the first large building, surrounded by cherry blossoms.

CHAPTER THIRTEEN

Naomi's Working Student

Before she really grasped what was going on, Abigail was already sweating from mucking out three stalls of the twelve in the barn. About twenty minutes ago, her father had given her a congratulatory slap on the back, when the riding instructor, Naomi, asked if she could start today. He told Abigail he would be back in a few hours to pick her up.

Naomi was a short woman, with childlike energy. The only sign that she was perhaps aging slightly were the tiny gray hairs showing up in her carefully tucked-away bun. She had a bubbly personality as she asked Abigail all sorts of questions about horses and why she liked being around them. Although Abigail took note that as soon as Naomi approached a horse, her demeanor shifted into a very Zen-like state. It was almost like Naomi lost her own personality and became one with the horse in front of her. Abigail wanted to inquire further about this apparent shift in Naomi, yet she realized that a job was required of her and she did not want to pry too quickly and seem weird. Naomi could tell that Abigail was obviously very eager to please, when she pointed to the muck rake and wheelbarrow. "Could you please show me how to clean a stall properly?" Naomi tried not to laugh and covered up her amusement by nodding in a business like way. "Of course, follow me please."

CHAPTER FOURTEEN

Travel Time Approaching

Briggs and Levidia were relieved that Naomi and Abigail linked up as planned.

"My dear Briggs, you might be on to something. I will alert Sergius that his time to travel is arriving quickly. Will you reassure the horses from Gavrantura that the humans need time to process? I believe we can make this all work out perfectly if we send them all back in time to elevate Earth's vibration. This present time is becoming more desperate and I really don't think these new Re-Connectors will have any profound effect on the modern humans."

Briggs began to create more light around the string. It started to crackle as she spoke, "Levidia, you're a clever one. Gavrantura's high council has already advised the locations and time periods we should aim for. I will let the horses at the waterfall know. You know who we also need?"

"Daniel? Are you sure? He's not worn out from the previous missions? Do you think he is up for the task?"

Briggs spun around the string. "He's really our best bet. He knows how to teach, that's for sure. He might seem a bit prim and proper, but I believe the trio will see past that."

Levidia smiled halfway and nodded dutifully. "I will begin my traveling to and from, dear Briggs. Remember, keep these ladies in your sight. They will still need reminders that they are being prepped for something far greater than they can imagine."

Briggs allowed the string to get so bright that Levidia had to look away. "Levidia, I am trusting you to set these paths in motion. Good luck and ride swiftly."

CHAPTER FIFTEEN

Time for Riding

Several months had already passed since Abigail's first encounter with the three horses by the waterfall. Abigail would get up early to see them before school, as well as linger with them before returning home. It was only an extra ten minute walk out of her way. They were content to stay hidden. They told her that she would eventually be able to tell others about them, but only when the timing was just right. Abigail chatted with them about what she was learning at the riding school, including an in depth description of each school horse that so graciously assisted her. The stallion allowed her to ride him often, to get some extra practice. He reminded her to find her center, while allowing him to move freely. She learned how to ride with Naomi in an English saddle, although practiced bareback and bridle-less on the stallion. This proved to boost her confidence and stability ten-fold. Naomi remarked in her lessons, "Abigail, you are such a natural. It is a pleasure to teach you. Pretty soon, you will be ready to start jumping in your lessons, if you like."

Abigail was thrilled at the progress with all of these amazing horses to ride. At Willow Tree, one of her favorite rides included a spunky paint pony named Al, a paint pony, would buck if she lost her balance for just a moment. Talk about a learning curve! She also rode a lovely mare named Blueberry, who showed her where all of her itchy spots were during grooming sessions. If she wanted Blueberry to go a little faster, she would scratch her in those special areas while riding and Blueberry happily complied. Naomi also marveled at how well Abigail seemed to communicate with the horses. Little did she know that Abigail *actually* talked to them, every Sunday during work, and always while in the saddle during her now weekly Saturday lessons.

During one of Abigail's lessons, Naomi decided to school another horse and rode right alongside her. It was then that Abigail's mount, Keeper, told her to watch Naomi carefully. *Abigail, Naomi also has your gifts of communicating. She just doesn't know how to tap into her potential.*

Naomi's mount, Darby, got very fresh and crow hopped around the arena. Naomi stayed very calm and stroked his neck as she rode, to help settle him. Keeper then got very quick with Abigail and as she half- halted him back to find their balance again, he said, *Abigail, tell Naomi that Darby wants to be lunged for a few minutes and then he will be fine to ride.* Abigail gulped, since she wasn't sure it was her place to give instructions to her own teacher. She trotted around another lap and then finally developed the nerve.

Quietly, she halted in the middle of the arena, and then looked up at Naomi, who seemed surprised she had stopped riding. "Um, Naomi, this might sound kind of weird, but I am getting the impression that if you lunged Darby for a few minutes, he would be much better to ride." Abigail was a little shaky, yet certainly didn't anticipate Naomi's reaction.

"Huh. Abigail, funny you should say that. I was actually getting the same idea, yet wasn't sure if I should leave you in the middle of your lesson."

"Oh, it's completely fine, Naomi. I don't mind waiting."

Off Naomi went to get her gloves and lunge line. Sure enough, Darby was super excited. He proceeded to canter and buck about five times in a row, while staying in a perfect circle around Naomi. When he was done, he sighed, licked his lips and lowered his head, pointing his ears directly at Naomi. She smiled and said, "Abigail! I guess that's was just what he needed! Doesn't it look like he just thanked me?"

"I'm so glad it worked. Thanks for being willing to listen." Abigail was thrilled it all worked out.

Naomi hopped back on and Darby. It was the best ride she had all day. This got her thinking a lot more about Abigail, her beginner savant, as well as her own work with horses.

Naomi went home that evening with a wonderful sense of hope. Out of all of her students, the one she was most proud of, was her working student, Abigail. She felt today was a turning point in her education. She finally had the confidence to suggest something that most trainers would shrug off. It was clear that the horses were speaking to Abigail and Naomi was most impressed that she was able to hear them and verbalize it. As she drifted off to sleep that night, Naomi could sense something big was going to happen with her new protégé. She was eager to find out what that entailed.

Naomi's dreams were quite colorful and tonight wasn't any different. She found herself at the entrance of a huge castle, waiting for the gate to open. As the drawbridge lowered, Naomi felt chills up and down her spine. Four Knights on huge horses came galloping toward her, full speed ahead and then formed a circle around her. The first Knight asked what she was doing there. The second immediately drew his sword and aimed it toward her neck. The third jumped off his stallion and tied her hands behind her back. The fourth smiled, hoisted her on his stallion, and said, "Welcome to our world. It is time you learned the ancient ways before you continue further on your quest." They continued galloping off into a dense forest. Naomi was exhilarated. The nightmare turned into a thrilling dream.

Naomi awoke to a loud radio blaring, "Every Little Thing She Does is Magic," by The Police. *What in the world?* She sighed and pulled the covers up over her shoulders and took some deep breaths. She took a few moments to process her dream. She was so surprised it didn't end badly like usual. She felt empowered, rather than drained. She then got a strange feeling to pick up one of her training books by the bedside table. *Ancient ways? I wonder if this is what they meant.* She began reading the quotes that were highlighted from the last time she picked up this particular classic, *The Art of Horsemanship*.

Anything forced and misunderstood can never be beautiful. And to quote the words of Simon: If a dancer was forced to dance by whip

60

and spikes, he would be no more beautiful than a horse trained under similar conditions. -Xenophon, 400 B.C.

I think that if I become a horseman, I shall be a man on wings. -Xenophon, 400 B.C.

Naomi let the words sink in. She always trusted her horses to show her how to dance the way they enjoyed. She assisted in guiding them through movements that would increase their athletic ability. Sometimes it did feel like they had wings, especially when it all clicked together. Her nose began to tingle again and she noticed a large crow feather leaning against the window. She smiled.

CHAPTER SIXTEEN

The Fall

Briggs had discussed all the details with her home planet. She wasn't thrilled with the next step, but understood it was necessary to get the humans on board with the entire mission. She told Levidia something unexpected was about to happen and to send Dotune back to Abigail's dreams for assistance. Levidia had her doubts. "What if she gets seriously hurt? She's learning to ride so that she can learn a deeper connection with herself and believe in her own power. You told me that she needs this to continue the mission. What if this event throws all her confidence out the window?"

Briggs shook her head slowly. "It must happen. Believe me. This is her next test. We can only hope it will work out the way it needs to."

Levidia began speaking in a high pitched voice, "Briggs, darling, really. You are quite the gambler. This is getting silly. Why can't we just throw them into their missions already? She can learn as she goes."

"You're forgetting why the others didn't work out. Your impatience has cost us many strings, my friend. I really sense that the foundation *must* be set in. They need to find their inner power first. Every time I think about it, the string vibrates higher. It's got to be the answer."

Levidia sighed. There really wasn't any arguing with Briggs. She was right after all.

The last young one Levidia had asked to begin this quest, before Abigail, was so close to achieving success, but finally succumbed to her own doubts. She was far too entrenched in her world and refused to believe that any of Levidia's visits were real. That poor girl ended up on heavy medication for quite some time. Her family thought she had gone crazy. Levidia sent her as many good surprises, secretly of course, to make up for the mishaps.

Levidia was much more careful in finding Abigail. She observed her and her parents for quite some time before making the decision. She could sense a loving, supportive family unit that would inevitably assist in this wild journey. After all, Albert had dreamed of Levidia many times. His constant questioning about the physical universe called her into his dreams. They had long discussions about quantum physics. Things he only had a fuzzy recollection about when he woke up. She was pleased to find his daughter could be just as open minded as he was, once she convinced her to be more confident.

Abigail was flying high. She already had three lessons in a row where she learned what it felt like to jump with a horse. It was much different than the upward motion of that gorgeous Pegasus, months ago. That was a terrifyingly ecstatic feeling of floating above the world. Jumping actual riding horses was a powerful, intricate dance that required so much focus, body control, and sheer will.

Although she started out slowly for weeks of getting her positioning down over the ground poles, Abigail was slightly impatient to get to the real jumps. Naomi could sense this and put her on the steadiest mounts that would certainly take care of her over the cross rail courses she set up. Abigail was getting her timing down beautifully; staying in her two-point well after the jumps and being ever so careful to stay out of her mount's mouth. By her fourth lesson, she was moving up to some smaller vertical jumps and was promised to try some logs outside of the arena, to give her a sense of what cross country jumping felt like. She was approaching her last line before heading out of the arena and lost focus for a split second at the thought of riding out in the field. As she and her horse landed, she held her breath and wobbled. Her horse, Jasper, could sense her unusual moment of unsteadiness and was startled by this. The second stride after the jump, he stumbled and Abigail went flying over his head onto the ground.

Naomi immediately ran over to her very still body and knew it didn't look good. Abigail tried to sit up, yet felt the wind knocked out of her. Jasper stood over her body with his head down, in a very pitiful way. He knew he had made a mistake and was very sorry for his little friend.

"Take a moment to just lay there and breathe, Abigail. When you are ready to talk, just let me know if you can feel your fingers and toes and wiggle them around a bit." Naomi said with a very grounded, yet concerned voice.

Abigail simply blinked and tried to force a small smile to let Naomi know she wasn't majorly injured. Then she started to lose consciousness, feeling darkness all around. The next thing she knew, she was in the back of an ambulance, with Naomi. Abigail moaned a little that her head hurt and her next recollection was in the hospital room with a gown and her parents standing over her.

"What happened?" Abigail asked, as she then motioned for the bucket next to her. She promptly vomited a couple of times, looked around, and began processing what was going on.

Abigail's father put his hand on her shoulder, "Abigail, you had a good fall and knocked your head. The doctor said that the helmet saved your life, but you suffered a minor concussion and will need to stay here overnight. They are going to need to wake you every hour. I will stay here with you the whole time, okay?"

It was that moment that Abigail began to replay the jumping scenario in her mind and how she was getting slightly nervous about her next jump outside the ring. She lost focus and so did Jasper. *Oh my goodness. I am so lucky I was wearing a helmet.* She looked at her mother who had clearly been crying. She didn't know what to say to her at this point. *What a way for Mom to find out about my riding. We should have told her sooner.* Then she thought about the horses by the waterfall. She wondered if they were going to miss her tomorrow morning. All of these sad thoughts and the pain in her body took over. She started to cry, as she realized how she simply wasn't prepared to have any kind of accidents since she started this journey. *How can I continue on this path when I messed up so badly? Levidia is going to be so disappointed.*

Evelyn turned to Abigail with tears in her eyes. She began rambling, "Honey, I know you've been riding. Your father made me promise not to mention that I knew. After all, who does your laundry? I could smell that horse scent from a mile away. Anyhow, I agreed that it would be best for me to stay out of your riding experiences, for fear that I might cause you anxiety from my own nervousness. I just don't want you to repeat what happened to me. Keep riding if it truly makes you happy. I love you."

Abigail whispered she loved her back and was then transferred into her room for the night. As described, alternating nurses began waking Abigail up every hour to check on her in the hospital room. Each time, Abigail would mumble something to them about flying horses, angels, and Roman cavalrymen. They must have heard all of this a time or two before, as they hushed Abigail back to bed.

She cried for a few minutes, wallowing in self pity, and eventually just drifted off to sleep. Dotune was waiting for her.

"Greetings, Abigail Freeman. Levidia has revealed your life to me and how you are beginning to communicate with your horse friends. If you can remember from your last dream, my name is Dotune. I was one of the first to arrive in the form of these magnificent beasts. I was very skeptical at first, but over the past few months, I have learned much about the message these valiant steeds are here to bring humanity. Please do not feel sorrow about your incident. My planet has foreseen this accident and relayed how it was absolutely necessary to invite you to our realm and understand your next steps."

Abigail was stunned. *I was supposed to fall? Did they make that happen?*

Dotune gently nudged her in reassurance. Abigail quickly moved away, too annoyed to be consoled.

He looked over toward a floating chair heading her way. He motioned for her to sit.

She sat down and grasped at the sides tightly. She looked intensely at this muscular horse. She then asked, "What is it, exactly, that I am supposed to be doing here with you?"

Dotune walked toward her and she found a scroll tied in his mane. It consisted of symbols that were very intricate, yet made absolutely no sense to Abigail. Then, as she blinked a few times, it transformed into English.

Those who can read these words are destined to create peace and harmony in their world. You are certainly among the most cherished creatures on your planet. If you agree with what we are offering, many adventures will unfold before you. A simple exclamation of 'yes' will allow us to continue our explanation.

Abigail read it twice. *Well, I've come this far. What else is there for me to do? Stay in the dark and never know what I could have done to help?* She yelled at the top of her lungs, "YES," as if the scroll was far away and needed to hear her from all parts of the universe.

Suddenly, Abigail was being shaken on both shoulders. She opened her eyes to see a concerned look on her father's face. "Abigail, you're talking in your sleep. Do you remember what you were dreaming about? Do you know where you are?" He started asking her many more questions that he memorized from the last nurse's script from half an hour ago. It was now 1:30 AM and Abigail had four similar chats with nurses to check on her already.

Abigail stared out into space for a couple of minutes and then rambled on in a mumbled sort of way, "Oh my. Dad, I am so sorry. Yes, I am in the hospital. Got thrown off Jasper. But it wasn't his fault! And I was dreaming about, well, err, a mission. Supposed to help others in some way. They just asked if I was really ready. Sorry to startle."

Her father studied his daughter's face and realized she was really becoming quite a beauty, inside and out. He wasn't really sure what she was talking about and encouraged Abigail to go back to sleep. She nodded and rolled over, falling into a deep slumber right away. She was ready to get to the bottom of this mystery already.

She was surprised to find herself in that same comfy armchair, just floating around, with Dotune waiting. "All right, Miss Abigail, I am here to explain your purpose. First, let me tell you why you fell. It was a test to see if you could suffer a setback and still be willing to continue on with the mission. Let me ask you, what was the first thing you remember about riding horses?"

Abigail was beginning to get very impatient, desperate to know what was next. She stopped her feeling of wanting to float away by breathing into her center. She then felt a calming sensation, which grounded her little bum in the squishy chair. She realized that she *was* advised to take riding lessons. It was all part of the plan, so there really must be something to this inquiry. *Think Abigail. Think. All of this feels like such a blur now.* Then it hit her like a strong wave on the beach and she found herself saying the following words with the utmost confidence, "Pure love and connection." She immediately got very teary-eyed and embarrassed. She looked away.

"Precisely why you are here. It has nothing to do with domination, ego, or riding toward specific medals or glories. You love the interaction, or the journey, as many like to say."

Abigail took a cleansing breath and smiled. "Yes. I love the interaction, the feeling of moving with horses, sensing what it is like to move as powerfully as they do. I think they enjoy showing me what it's like to be in sync with them, so I might feel their freedom of movement."

Dotune stood up and motioned to a door that materialized in front of Abigail's armchair. Abigail put her hand on his neck and together they walked through it.

CHAPTER SEVENTEEN

A Strange Request

Naomi walked into her house, recalling the events of the day. Once Abigail's parents met her at the hospital and she explained what happened, they thanked her for taking such good care of their daughter. *It never gets easier, when students take a fall. I know this is part of life, yet I somehow feel terrible. How do I shake these feelings?*

She put some water on the stove for tea and sat down in her sparsely furnished living room. Her home was simply a resting point before and after her most sacred place, the barn. She lived and breathed horses, riding, and teaching. She couldn't remember a time when she went out into town without finding bits of hay or horse hair on her clothing. It was a passionate lifestyle where getting up early to feed, breaking ice on water troughs, and mucking stalls were just mundane chores that were well worth the reward.

Naomi glanced at the stack of horse magazines next to her and felt a flip in her stomach as one of the headlines jumped out at her. She picked it up and started skimming the article. Immediate tears ran down her cheeks. It was a story about a young woman who was on the Olympic track. She had been riding all her life and had secured sponsorship with a rescue thoroughbred that she saved from slaughter. They suffered a severe accident, causing her to be paralyzed and her horse to pass away. This athlete was clearly devastated until she met with an animal communicator, one who can hear animals' thoughts, to help her with continuing pangs of guilt. Her experience soothed her and it pushed her toward the decision to delve into animal communication and teach others how to connect with their horses on a deeper level. *This is what Abigail has been doing. I just know it. This is what I need. My soul is craving these kinds of conversations with horses.*

Her cell phone rang and startled her out of these longing thoughts. She looked down to see it was a private number, so she allowed it to go to voice mail. The teapot was screaming at her, so she jumped up and prepared her cup of Earl Grey. Once steeping, she listened to the message.

Naomi, please don't be alarmed. This is Abigail. I am actually leaving this message in a very unique way. I am all right, yet I am going to need your help. When you get this message, please go take a nap. I know this is a strange request, yet it will be quite the adventure. See you soon!

Naomi almost dropped her spoon filled with honey. She decided to listen to the message a second time. *What in the world?* She thought she was going crazy. Then she began putting all of these moments together. *Well, I have certainly been summoning a lot of requests. Perhaps this might be an answer to them. What do I have to lose?* Without thinking too much more, Naomi sipped her tea, drank about half of it and lay down on her couch, giving herself a mental note to turn the ringer off on her phone. She had a feeling that she didn't want to be disturbed during this nap. She drifted off quickly. Briggs was waiting to escort her.

"Naomi Drake. Allow me to introduce myself. My name is Briggs. I am the last String Keeper. It is my deepest wish to unite you, Abigail, and one other human to commence on a mission of most importance."

Naomi knew she was dreaming, yet felt the tingling sensation on her nose. *This is really odd. This only happens when I'm awake.*

Briggs smiled brightly from her rainbow lit encasement. "Indeed. You are in a half wake, half sleep state, Naomi. Remember how you decided that feeling on your nose was no longer scary? Let's multiply that trust by a thousand and pray that you believe all that I have to say next."

Naomi blinked several times. She really wasn't afraid. Very curious. But not fearful. "All right. Try me."

Briggs knew exactly what Naomi needed to begin to trust her. She sent out three huge bluebird feathers from the string that floated up and landed on Naomi's head. They both laughed and gazed into each others' eyes.

Naomi exclaimed, "Good one."

"Why thank you. You see, I do know a lot about you. Levidia, an angel guide, has been watching you. As we speak, she is making contact with another human to link up with you and Abigail. He will be from the past and must adjust to your present time. It will be your duty to get him acquainted with your time period, put him at ease, and then trust he will assist you two ladies on this grand mission."

"Mission? What in the world?"

"You should change world to universe." Briggs grinned and then pushed out a scroll to explain the details of the mission so that Naomi would be up to speed about the importance of the Re-Connection of the Universal Web.

Naomi read and reread the scroll several times. She finally looked up and whispered, "Briggs, did you know that I've felt so alone lately? Nobody here really understood me, until Abigail came along. If what you're relaying is true, then why would you choose me? It's only been a few months since I have felt a spark of hope. Until then, I felt like I just didn't even want to exist anymore."

Briggs closed her eyes and sent an image to Naomi's mind. It was one of complete freedom, riding horses in the sky, with her husband by her side again.

Naomi started crying and then quickly said, "Please don't tease me. What are you implying here? Will I get to fly free once this is all over?"

"You may do whatever you like, dear Naomi. That is what I'm trying to explain. If you can find it in your heart to believe you have a purpose, then you can imagine your way to that reality once the mission is complete. I'm afraid if you don't succeed, nobody will be able to imagine anything, any longer. The Murmori will see to that, I am sure."

Naomi shuddered as she thought about the part explaining the dark entities in the scroll. "Well then, I guess I have to just go for it." She sighed and waited for instructions.

Briggs nodded and invited her to step into the string with her. She then pushed her into Abigail's dream.

CHAPTER EIGHTEEN

The Meeting

Dotune and Abigail pushed through the large door at the same time, to find themselves in a room without walls, just swirling stars all around. Abigail began to feel slightly dizzy.

"Remember your first test with Levidia, Abigail? Breathe into your center." Dotune confidently walked toward a swirling spiral about ten feet in front of them. He then felt the urge to stand right in the middle of the spiral. Abigail watched him carefully, thinking to herself, *Gosh, how much does he know about me?* Sure enough, she found her power, strength and steadiness by breathing into her core. She slowly approached the spiral, watching the sparkling lights spin around in a clockwise direction. Dotune motioned for her to stand with him in the middle. He whispered, "Abigail, let me present to you what we are here to learn. Please, if you will, close your corporeal eyes for a moment and breathe into your heart. When you feel you are ready and completely connected to your heart center, open your eyes and begin to look at the spiral."

Abigail did as instructed, finding an enormous amount of energy run through her entire body, once she shifted her breathing from her core to her heart. It was as if she could hear her entire heartbeat outside of herself, coupled with a rush of love pouring in from the top of her head and up from the bottom of her sit bones.

She slowly opened her eyes and the spiral began to light up with the biggest words.

IT IS TIME TO LEARN THAT THERE IS NO TIME. YOU MAY GO WHERE YOU LIKE, WHEN YOU LIKE. CHOOSE

YOUR BEST TWIRL. ARE YOU READY TO GIVE IT A WHIRL?

Abigail chuckled at the curious sense of humor of this spiral. She rolled her eyes and then shook her head. "What in the world is this thing talking about?" On a whim, Abigail stood up and spun around several times and got herself dizzy, nearly falling on top of Dotune. Abigail said, "None of this is really making sense. But I will just go with the flow for now. I am so far gone, why the heck not? Where shall we go?"

Dotune chimed in, "Ah and when shall we go?" Abigail closed her eyes again and said quietly, "Okay, can we go where you came from? I gather that is the idea of this?"

"Yes! Although, we do need one more companion." A small device materialized and landed in Abigail's hand. "It would be of great satisfaction for you to leave a special message for your riding instructor to take a respite. She will meet us there."

"What? She's going to think I'm nuts. I am not sure this is a good idea." He already knew what action she was going to take. Abigail stared at the device, realizing that Naomi's number was already lit up and all she had to do was push the big send button. She was extremely relieved that it went to voice mail, yet was sure her message would raise an eyebrow or two out of her beloved trainer.

The device suddenly disappeared. He turned to Abigail and asked her to hold onto his neck, take a deep breath and remind herself what Joe had taught her to do. "This form of travel will take an enormous amount of faith." Abigail was again taken by surprise. *He really does know all about me.* She slowly put her hands on his crest and immediately started blushing. She gulped and wasn't sure if that sound was louder than her now rapidly beating heart. Even though she was in a dream, she was getting very freaked out about traveling through time. It took her a moment to regain her composure and as she took a deep breath, thought back to the specific protocol Joe taught her months ago. She was now having serious doubts about trying it again. "Err, Dotune, I'm not sure how to imagine where you

73

live."

"Just breathe deeper, all the way down into your toes and you will be able to see the images in my mind. As long as you have a hand on my body, I will be able to guide you back in time." Suddenly, Abigail saw flashes of an ornate building, with whinnying coming from inside. Soldiers were galloping toward a huge wooden door. Then, before she could take another breath, she was in a stall with Dotune.

"Wow. That happened *fast!*" Abigail was breathless. She realized that this was indeed a completely different time in history from where she was born. The armor for horses was organized in the most beautiful way around this barn. Each horse was groomed perfectly and the horses possessed a sense of strength that actually intimidated Abigail. Just as she was about to ask her guide a plethora of questions, she saw Naomi walk up to the stall door.

"Hey there, Abigail. Um, I got your message." They both burst into a nervous laughter which was quickly hushed by Dotune. He lowered his powerful chestnut neck so they might give him a scratch. He began slowly telling them both about his adventures. *It is a pleasure to meet more like-minded or shall I say like-hearted humans.*

Abigail simply grinned at Naomi, studying her face to get a sense of her reaction about all of this. To her surprise, Naomi seemed radiant and not in the least bit afraid of this interaction. Abigail continued to stroke Dotune's neck and confirmed with him that he was indeed the first horse to come from Gavrantura. Naomi couldn't hear Dotune and quickly asked if Abigail would interpret.

Abigail relayed what he had just told her, "My dear ones, please know that you are here with me, so we might learn from each other. I know you are certainly the heart centered humans I was put here to interact with. My last month on this planet was full of adventure and much sadness, as I saw many battles that humans were involved with. Although they do serve an unusual purpose of playing out different roles, I would much prefer to create, rather than destroy. Would you agree?"

They both silently nodded. He continued to speak as Abigail

listened closely and began interpreting again. "My planet is filled with joyous souls who desire to assist your planet. The soul of my planet decided to usher us to your planet to interact with humans in this horse form so that you might be more open to our help. It took some getting used to, yet I am enjoying the strength, power, and movement this body provides. You two, as well as Sergius, my caretaker, are the chosen Re-Connectors, destined to bring hope to your former gateway planet. My hope is for you to succeed, so that my planet and many others may flush out the Murmori, raise the Earth's vibration and allow inter-dimensional travel to commence. Levidia is attempting to convince Sergius to join you both on this mission. I hope you will meet him soon."

The two ladies exchanged quizzical glances at the thought of a Roman man just showing up.

Naomi studied this horse as he spoke telepathically to them. He was the most powerful horse she had ever seen, so it seemed quite fitting for him to be the 'first' as he mentioned, from this other planet. She hoped she was up to the tasks he had mentioned. Abigail was drifting in and out of sleep, realizing her little tired body was still in the hospital bed, with her sweet father sitting next to her. As she came back to this dream, she then observed how amazing it was that Naomi was there with them. She began to get really confused as to whether she was really there or whether she was dreaming all of this. Naomi then turned to Abigail, as if sensing this and said, "Abigail, I know this all might seem incredibly weird, yet I know I am in a more lucid dream. After I figured out how to meditate, I've been practicing traveling while I sleep. I've never told anyone about this until now. I really am here with you, so don't you worry about feeling like you're just making this up. We can talk more about this when I see you at home. I heard you only have to stay one night in the hospital. Get some rest now. I think we're going to have many more adventures like this very soon."

As they stroked Dotune's neck one last time, they slipped quietly out of the stall. Abigail suddenly had a burst of clarity. "Wait, Naomi, if this really is happening, I have a huge favor to ask of you. I have been keeping this secret for many months now. Even from before I met you. There are three horses who I think are very much linked to this grand adventure. I see them every day on my way to and from school. They are near that waterfall off of Cuba Hill Road. You know the one?"

Naomi's eyes widened. Abigail continued, "I think it might be best for you to pick them up and bring them to your big pasture behind the barn. You can tell them you're my friend. I have a feeling they need to be closer to other horses and of course, in your care."

Naomi took a deep breath and said confidently. "Well then, this will be quite an amazing test to see if all of this is real. If there actually is such a thing as real anymore." She laughed as she took a mental note to hitch up her stock trailer in the morning.

Both Naomi and Abigail found themselves waking up with sun rays on their faces. Naomi was still scrunched up on her couch in her home. Abigail could hear voices in the hospital room and realized it was a nurse telling her father that she would be discharged later that morning.

CHAPTER NINETEEN

Naomi's Surprise

There was a rustling in the woods. Six ears pricked forward, quickly toward the noise. A soft male voice whispered to them, "It's all right. I'm here on behalf of your little friend, Miss Abigail."

The three horses immediately lowered their heads in a relaxed state, recognizing how this human was somewhat ethereal and meant them no harm. Joe went on to explain about Abigail's accident and how Levidia had sent him to relay this message. He cleared his throat, as he pulled out the scroll and read with determination:

Dear Ones,
The time has come for your journey to begin. Another human, the one who has been teaching Abigail, will come find you. She will bring all of you to her home and keep you safe. Remember to be brave and know that you will remain together.

In case they needed confirmation, The Lauren, the beautiful butterfly that started them on this road together, showed up and fluttered all around Joe's hat in a most wild sort of way. He was about to start swatting her, since she was being so relentless on being seen, yet finally succumbed to her playful movement and chuckled to himself. *Ah, these little guides are so insistent. Can't say I blame them. Every bit of energy loves to show their light.*

The horses thanked Joe for his message and continued grazing in a very content manner. Joe tipped his hat to them and dissolved into the nearby waterfall.

Naomi got her wits about her, finished the now cold Earl Grey and decided to go hook up her trailer. She fed her horses breakfast and then wrote a note for the afternoon students that she might be a little tardy to their lesson. She left detailed instructions for who they would be riding.

She negotiated her big rig down Cuba Hill Road. She parked, let out a big sigh, and slowly lowered herself out of her dually truck. After she lowered the ramp on the trailer, Naomi began hiking. She heard the waterfall getting louder. To her amazement, she noticed the sound of horses' snorting. She stopped in her tracks once she spotted them. *Holy moly. There they are!* She got chills up and down her spine, goose bumps on her arms and legs and had to steady herself as she watched the gorgeous horses raise their heads up high, frozen in fear. The buckskin stallion whinnied loudly at her. What she knew as reality had quickly shifted.

Of course, none of these horses had ever worn halters or were accustomed to being put in a large moving box. She spoke quietly to them, while each nuzzled her outstretched hand. It was as if they had loaded into trailers all their lives. One by one, they loaded and happily waited for their journey 'home'. Naomi shook her head in amazement. *Well, I can't wait until Abigail hears about this. She will be so proud!* She carefully drove them home and was quite amused at how easily these 'wild horses' settled into their new surroundings.

Rafi was nervous, yet thrilled to finally be taking his next step on his mission. Once they arrived at this new home, he saw so many other horses across the fence. This comforted him tremendously. He began taking a poll among the others to see where they were all from. Only one actually responded that he was indeed from his original home, which puzzled Rafi at first. Then he remembered that only certain horses were sent from Gavrantura. The others were Earthlings, just like the humans. The one who responded was called, Keeper.

He had been with Naomi for ten years. Before that, he was simply found wandering the countryside. A nice older couple, who were out walking their dog, found him and called Naomi to pick him up.

Apparently, she was known to deal with unwanted horses and give them loving homes with a purpose. Keeper, the nickname that she loved to call him, was taught how to carry humans around. He did so well that he was able to teach youngsters how to balance themselves at any gait. He even fancied going over jumps and competing with the most adept students. Naomi was so fond of him that she would often take him out on private rides, choosing him over the 11 other horses at the stable. He loved her and wished she could speak with him, although there always seemed to be a strange wall, like static, whenever he attempted to communicate.

Now that Keeper had met Rafi, something told him that this was all going to change. He was hopeful that he could begin sharing more secrets with Naomi soon.

Keeper had a nice chat with Rafi and fancied talking with the youngsters as well. *So what do you think of Earth so far?*

Brouteen answered first, stomping her front black leg for dramatic effect. *It is quite remarkable. There is less to fear than I expected, yet I am still wary of what will happen next. Well, we know we've been quite safe for some time. Just hope it stays that way.*

Shantoo had more confidence. *Of course it will. We are creatures of love and light. Have faith, my friends. We have already been so blessed to meet two humans with wonderful hearts and now this dear elder has been waiting for us.* Shantoo lowered her chestnut head with flaxen forelock as a sign of respect to Keeper.

Well, what an honor it is to meet you. I am so eager to see how the humans will interact with all of us soon.

Once home, she hugged her mother and told her she was so happy to still be with them. Her Mom burst into tears and said, "Oh Abigail. I am so grateful you are all right. I am sorry I had to leave. I was just so emotional. I had a lot of time to think last night. I was up all night. I understand why you both kept this a secret. But no more holding back, okay? Is there anything you need?"

Abigail took a moment to respond. Keeping secrets was becoming the norm for her these days. She wanted to tell her everything but worried she would be sent back to the hospital, this time in another section. She decided to just change the subject altogether. "Thanks Mom. Actually, I think I would like some drawing pads. I know it's a strange request. I've never actually been into art, yet something tells me that I need to begin sketching some new ideas out." Her mother also shrugged just like her father did earlier and grabbed her keys to head to the art supply store. "I'll be back in an hour. Get some rest in your own bed now, sweetie."

Abigail had been drifting in and out of a nap on the way home from the hospital. She got a very clear image to begin sketching pictures. She didn't quite understand what that was about, yet at this point, she didn't think to question all that much anymore. After her Mom got home, she began making designs on a pad. She stopped thinking for those moments and allowed the pencil to just float along, doing what it wanted. She ended up making four beautiful spirals on each corner of the page. Then she drew a large spiral in the middle. Finally, she drew a figure eight around the entire pattern. She stepped away for a few moments and then began to stare at her creation. Her eyes relaxed and the spirals began to move. She smiled and then closed her eyes. Again, she was inside the spiral. Words around her lit up again. "Hello Miss Abigail, WHERE TO NOW?" She giggled and said, "How about back to my three horse friends?" Away she was swept and to her surprise, she was in the back paddock of Naomi's barn.

Abigail appeared in the middle of the pasture, giving the three horses a jump. It only took a split second to realize it was their sweet little friend and quickly began grooming her and tickling her. She laughed and laughed and then noticed how Keeper was staring at all of them from across the fence. "Hey there, sweet boy. What do you think of my friends?"

He whinnied and then spoke to her, *Well, you do realize we are from the same place. I was sent here to be a watcher and way shower for Naomi. Obviously your three friends were sent to you. This is going to be quite the ride!*

Abigail just laughed some more at the little pun he threw in there. *Keeper, I didn't even think to ask if you were from Gavrantura. Apologies for not asking earlier. I just thought it was cool that we could chat.*

Keeper puffed up a bit as if to remind her he was most important. *That is quite all right, young one. I realize that all of these interactions are so new to you. It is a most extravagant experiment. Please go find Naomi and have her come out. I want you to teach her how to communicate with us the way you do.*

Abigail froze. She hadn't seen Naomi in waking time since her accident. She wasn't really sure how she was going to react to all this. At least now, seeing the horses in the pasture, she must realize how all of this wild adventuring was indeed true and not some silly fantasy in and out of consciousness from the hospital.

She shook her head quickly, as if she was ripping a band-aid off her self-doubt. She climbed the pasture fence carefully, as her body was still aching, headed up to Naomi's house and knocked on the door.

Naomi expressed the utmost glee when she opened the door. She immediately hugged Abigail and wouldn't let go for some time. She finally let out a whisper, "How did you get here? I think it might be time for you to teach *me* a little more, right?"

Abigail let out a huge sigh of relief. "I learned how to change my attention to where I want to be, through a series of spirals. The spirals gave me a flash of insight, that I may do this type of travel, as long as I stay in present time. The spirals help me to focus and then it's like 'poof', there I go. It's really amazing."

Naomi sat down on the porch to take in what she had just said. She looked around for a vehicle that might have dropped her off, just in case Abigail was still out of it from her hospital stay. There wasn't a car in sight and Naomi realized it was time. She had to open up her perspective of reality in a much bigger way. The words she could muster came out slowly, "Oh. That's fascinating."

Abigail was so excited that Naomi wasn't freaking out, so she immediately began chattering away about Levidia, Joe and the mission they had encouraged her to pursue. "I'm really not sure how this is all going to unfold, Naomi, yet I do remember one of the assignments they gave me was to learn how to ride. I guess the main reason was so that I could meet you and we could team up!"

Naomi sat down on her steps and nodded. She smiled and then exclaimed, "Abigail, this mission was explained to me before we met up with Dotune. You are certainly confirming all of this. Whatever shall we do now?"

Abigail took her by the hand and led her to the horses. "Basically, I'm figuring out that if we just take our instructions day by day, there is no need to worry. Believe that all of this will unfold the way it needs to. The most important thing I have learned so far is," she hesitated as if she didn't want to sound corny, "You have all of the power inside."

"I was just told to teach you how to speak to the horses for real. Not just in dream time. I'm pretty sure it will come easily for you." She reached for Naomi's hand. Her trainer took a deep breath and let her head tilt back.

Abigail continued. "Close your eyes, listen to your breath, get really quiet and allow your thoughts to drift. Start breathing into your heart and feel that area begin to expand. Then imagine that same area in Keeper's body. Imagine your two hearts are breathing as one, expanding and touching. Then simply ask him a question. Let it be an easy one, like, hey would you speak with me? Then just wait."

Abigail and Naomi sat on the old wooden bench, overlooking the main pastures. Naomi took some deep breaths, got very still, and waited. She then whispered, "Where did you learn this? It's amazing how much this is like the meditation I've tried before."

"The horses you picked up at the waterfall taught me. We've been chatting for a long time now. I've even had long conversations with all of your horses. I know where Blueberry loves to be scratched and how Jasper was really sorry for the accident yesterday. Go on, give it a try. I really think it's the most miraculous thing, compared to all the other wildness we've already encountered."

Abigail stopped talking and thought Naomi might need some space, so she quietly stood up and started taking a stroll toward Rafi. He made a soft nicker at her approach and she scratched him on the withers. Naomi opened her eyes and realized that Abigail had left. She glanced over toward her new charges and saw her scratching the stallion as if they had known each other all their lives. The bond was indescribable. There was such softness and understanding, along with playfulness that horses only reserve for their kindred spirits. She closed her eyes again, asked Keeper once more if he would like to speak with her. This time she felt a conversation begin.

My sweet Naomi, I think you can finally hear me. I have been waiting so long to finally commune with you on this level. Bless this youngster for teaching you. First, I want to express my utmost gratitude for all that you have done for me and the horses in this world. Now, please let me know what kind of questions you have, as I am sure there are many.

Naomi jumped up from her bench, with her heart racing. "Abigail, it worked, I could hear him!" Abigail simply smiled and gave her a 'thumbs up' sign.

Keeper. Oh my darling boy. I love you so much. Thank YOU for all that you do. I am trying to think of a question, yet my heart and mind are racing too much. Let me just enjoy this moment for a bit and we can continue later. Seriously, I am still in such shock that we can talk now. Wow.

Keeper came trotting over and nuzzled Naomi. She wrapped her arms around his neck and began crying uncontrollably.

It is okay, Naomi. I knew this day would happen. Just relax. We have so much more to talk about. Allow Abigail to show you even more. Our journey has just scratched the surface. Oh and speaking of scratching, can you please scratch my belly right now. I get so itchy there.

Naomi bolted out of her emotional breakdown by these words, giggled and of course, began to scratch his belly. He immediately lengthened out his upper lip and moved it side to side to the rhythm of her scratching. She laughed aloud again.

CHAPTER TWENTY

The Choice

Sergius and Dotune discussed the two modern women. Sergius struggled to concentrate on Dotune, who was attempting to give him an accurate description of his encounter. "The young one is charming. I think she will be very suitable for this quest. The older one seemed nervous, yet she still made it here. She might take some more convincing to understand how her passion will inspire others. Her energy is sad, yet pure. It will need to become more joyful to help raise the necessary vibrations around the locations that are selected. Levidia has revealed more of the plan. There are certain parts of the Earth, in different time periods which cry out in anguish. She told me all of this last night, before you were sent out to exercise the other horses. We are to assist with raising the vibrations of these locations. Once they find joy again, the strings for the Universal Web will be restored. The Web is the main portal for inter-dimensional travel. Benevolent beings could then arrive here on Earth and cut off the Murmori's main source of power. Do you know what that source is, Sergius?"

Sergius just shook his head. He was having so much trouble following Dotune's rapidly firing words. "Murmori? What in the world do you speak of, Dotune?"

"They haven't arrived yet, Sergius. That is one of the reasons Levidia has chosen you. They arrive in another thousand years. Your dreams haven't been intruded on, thus your essence is incredibly strong. You are able to assist in this type of energetic work in a more powerful way. You can be one of the key Re-Connectors for the Web."

Before Sergius could respond, a soldier came bursting into the stable. "Sergius, you have been summoned by the general to meet him in Rome. You must take your best horse and ride swiftly to the gates of the Coliseum."

Sergius obediently saluted and began saddling Dotune. They took off at a full gallop once outside the stable door. Dotune began sending images and thoughts to Sergius as they rode. Fear, anxiety, and battles were lying ahead for their future with every huge stride taken. *We must get away, now. Otherwise all will be lost. Turn toward the forest, Sergius. Leave your world behind. I promise we will be safe.* Sergius took a deep breath and slowed Dotune down to a walk. "What if they catch us? Then all will really be lost. I might be sent away to become a Gladiator" Sergius retorted. *Trust me, head to the forest,* Dotune pleaded. Sergius stroked his neck, straightened up in the saddle, and spun him around a few times. When they settled, Dotune became increasingly antsy and started to paw the ground forcefully. Sergius thought about the mission Dotune explained. It all sounded so crazy. Then again, he was talking to a horse. He then turned away from the city that was beckoning him.

The next sight was practically blinding. A huge horse with wings descended upon them almost immediately after his turn on the haunches. Levidia had arrived in his conscious world for the first time.

Sergius did a flying dismount off of Dotune, dropped to his knees and lowered his eyes to the ground. "Take me if you wish, but please spare my horse."

"Sergius Strabo, I am not here to punish you. It is my honor to meet you in person. My name is Levidia and this is Prometheus. Don't you remember me from your dreams?"

He looked up slowly and whimpered to himself. Now he realized there was so much more than the reality he had grown up knowing. Talking horses seemed like such a mundane thing at this point. A flash of his dream from last month showed up in his mind's eye. Levidia had shown herself to him and attempted to convince him to listen to Dotune.

"Yes, I do now. How may I be of service?"

"Sergius, thank you for your acceptance. You are desperately needed for a secret mission. We have no time to waste. If you are serious about continuing on this important journey, please, follow me." Dotune lowered his head, raised his back, and just before he took off, Sergius found his stirrup, swung himself back on, and steadied himself in the saddle. Dotune was clearly determined to follow Levidia.

The flapping of wings was all Sergius could make out. He grasped the mane tighter and allowed his hips to relax with Dotune's amazingly huge stride, as they followed Levidia into the woods. The forest was brimming with wildlife and as they approached, all seemed to go silent. Levidia gracefully slipped off her enormous Pegasus. She waved them over to a grand maple tree that seemed to be shivering as they approached. Its leaves shook and the bark began to twinkle. As Levidia got closer her hands lifted up toward the first branch in her reach. She tapped it three times and a wide hole opened up on the main trunk of the tree. Levidia and Prometheus then flew away. Sergius glanced inside and saw the tallest woman he had ever encountered. He suddenly felt pulled inside the tree. He and Dotune were standing right next to this giant lady in an open hallway, filled with the perfume of cool moss and peppermint.

She welcomed him and said she had been waiting for this moment with much anticipation. This woman wore a gorgeous, woven top with browns and blues swirling together. Her dark hair was loosely moving with gray streaks. Large rings in turquoise adorned her fingers. Her body was covered with a delicate film of rainbow light. Sergius assessed that this woman was probably seven feet tall. Although her size was daunting, there was something about this woman that seemed very familiar. She felt Sergius searching his memory banks and finally whispered, "My name is Briggs. I am the last String Keeper. I am here to assist you on your journey. You probably remember me from a dream or a time when you 'let your thoughts drift' as you like to say."

Sergius nodded and realized he had done this often, especially when waiting for Dotune to return from his first battle. He knew what to ask next. His eyes became brighter and he took a deep breath, speaking in a hopeful manner, "Have you made acquaintances with the women, Abigail and Naomi? Dotune has mentioned that I am to meet with them."

Briggs put her large hand on his shoulder and said, "Briefly yes. Abigail has learned about me and we have chatted once. I did escort Naomi to your world yesterday in her dream. I am here to bring you all together. I will coordinate more official visits from now on. Are you ready to begin this journey? You will not be able to return to your time for quite awhile, if at all."

Sergius closed his eyes briefly, reaching out for Dotune's neck to stroke it quietly. He was a strong and stoic young man. He really didn't have much to leave behind besides honor and duty. This new adventure seemed to be a larger quest that had fallen upon him for reasons he had yet to comprehend.

"It is unclear why I have been chosen for such a mission. You do realize I am a glorified servant here? I tend to the horses. I am merely a lowly Stator."

"Sergius, I have been watching you for some time. You might feel your position in life is on a lower level, yet I can assure you, from my perspective it is much higher."

Sergius paced up and down the hallway. Dotune watched him carefully. He longed for his caretaker to know his own greatness. *Sergius, remember. You can hear me. This must make you realize how special you are. Please trust Briggs. And yourself.*

Sergius took a moment, sighed, looked at Dotune, then back at Briggs. "Yes. I believe I am ready for whatever might come about. I desire to assist. Horses and I are bonded, that I know. For if this journey has anything to do with that, which I suspect it does, please enlist my services."

Briggs smiled widely and clapped her hands above her head. A door appeared in front of the spacious hallway. The door was about nine feet tall, so Briggs could certainly enter without ducking. Sergius placed his hand on the doorknob and felt a cool rush from the steel door. It seemed to be pulsing and as he examined it closer, he noticed hundreds of tiny spiral shapes etched into every crevice.

He took a deep breath, opened the door with an authority that caused Briggs to do a partial curtsey to him in awe. He looked over his shoulder at her and actually stepped back, "After you, dear lady. For I believe you will need to assist in this next phase. Am I correct?"

Briggs let out a belly laugh which echoed all around them. "That is very astute of you, Sergius. Yes. I am honored to join you, as I would love to share a soul to soul meeting with Miss Abigail and her Naomi."

All three of them walked through the door and found themselves inside a small bathroom together. They were quite cramped and slightly shocked, considering the huge amount of space they were just sharing a moment ago. Dotune was especially nervous considering he was taking up most of the space with his large body. Briggs whispered, "Just push open this next door and we will see where we are exactly."

"You mean you don't really know where we are? I thought you created this door for us?"

"Well, I have an idea, but these portals do seem to have a mind of their own."

Sergius was alarmed, mostly from the tight spot they were in. He was in the dark and his chest was pushed against a small sink. "What is this sort of room?"

Briggs whispered, "It's where the modern humans go to do their private business."

"You mean they have a room for it? They don't just go outside?"

"Yes, there are many things you will learn here. This is quite the convenience. Although right now it might not seem like it."

Briggs pressed against Dotune's legs and tried not to trip over Sergius' feet as she grabbed for the smaller doorknob and pushed it open. She crawled through the seemingly miniscule doorway. She enjoyed a large stretch with her arms over her head once in the main room. She gasped when she realized exactly where they were and grabbed Sergius by the arm. Dotune froze as he realized they were in someone's home. It was not the most comfortable for a four legged beast such as himself.

Briggs regained her composure and calmly stated in a whisper, "Sergius, we have arrived in Abigail's home. I thought we were aiming for Naomi's place. It is much more discreet. I believe her parents are just in the next room. We will have to be very quiet for a few moments until I can reassess the best door to go through to get to Naomi's home."

Sergius scrunched up his face as if someone just punched him in the stomach. Somehow running into battles seemed much more feasible to him than bumping into a young girl's parent in the middle of their own home. He looked around in shock. He had never seen such strange furniture. There were small boxes with wires hanging out and the loud noise of the lit up box in the window, blowing cold air, made him hold his hands over his ears.

He then regained his composure and started scanning the room for hiding places. There wasn't much available. He tiptoed over to a window and looked out. There he saw a hammock suspended by two enormous oak trees. It looked so peaceful. The next thing he knew, he was on the hammock. Surprised by how he seemingly jumped from one space to another, he almost flipped over. Briggs did a twirl right beside him and before he could say anything, she chimed in with, "Well, are you really *that* surprised? By now, so many dimensions are showing up for you. You can simply imagine where you want to be and, just like that, there you are!" She collapsed on the lush grass beside him and looked up. "This is one of her favorite places for solitude. I remember her energy visiting with me often when she relaxes here."

Dotune began grazing happily next to Sergius, as he was getting the hang of the hammock, gently rocking side to side, feeling very grateful that Abigail's parents hadn't spotted them.

Briggs began creating a new portal around the hammock and the trees. The three of them made their way to Willow Tree Farms in a flash.

CHAPTER TWENTY ONE

Mission Revealed

"Evening ma'am. Evening sir." Joe was leaning against a cherry blossom tree, chewing on a piece of hay. He tipped his hat toward Briggs and Sergius. He then stared for a long time in amazement at Dotune. "I suppose you three are here to see Miss Abigail. She's sure been busy around here, lately, hasn't she?"

Briggs smiled and embraced Joe with a huge bear hug. "Dearest of Joes, thank you for joining us. Tonight we will celebrate and reveal the rest of the plan. I'm sure she will be pleased to see you again. It has been quite a few months, right? Time seems to get away from me, as you know."

Joe tipped his head back and then simply grinned. "You would know, sweet String Keeper. Time is a funny thing, ain't it? Sure is handy when we're fixin' to get together though."

Abigail was cleaning the stalls in the barn. It gave her a sense of peace. Even though she was still sore and bruised, she loved to help Naomi whenever she could.

She was pushing the wheelbarrow out of a stall when she stopped in her tracks. A tall, muscular man was standing in the barn aisle staring at her. "Excuse me, but." Sergius gasped as he realized he was speaking a foreign language and could understand himself completely.

Abigail stared at him curiously. She then started sniffing the air. It was at that moment, she realized how badly this stranger smelled. Without being able to help herself, she covered her hand over her nose.

"Is there something wrong with your face?"

"What?"

"Why are you holding your hand over your nose?"

"Well, you just have a different sort of smell than I'm used to."

"Smell? Really? What kind of greeting is that? I just traveled from a different time and place and that's what you have to offer as a welcome?"

"Excuse me? Who are you?"

"I am Sergius Strabo, the Strator from Rome."

"Oh my goodness. Dotune was right. Wow. I thought you would be older for some reason."

"Which one are you? Are you Naomi?"

"No, my name is Abigail." She grabbed the handles of the wheelbarrow and stood up straighter to address this formal young man. Abigail wasn't sure what to say next. She was nervous, just like she was around all young men her age. He circled around her a few times, inspecting her carefully. She became extremely self conscious, yet was struck by his dark eyes.

"Do you always spend your time caring for these horses in such a way? Where is the hired help?"

"You're looking at her," huffed Abigail.

"Why is a fair maiden such as yourself performing such a menial task? This is a man's job."

"Uh, I happen to like it. And news flash. Women can do what they want these days."

"Really?"

She stared at him blankly. She then sighed and put the pitchfork in the empty stall. "Follow me. I will take you over to Naomi. Oh wait, just a minute."

Abigail ran over to the marigold fly spray bottle and started spritzing him all over.

"What in the world are doing? Are you crazy?" Sergius quickly grabbed the bottle from her and held it over her head. She jumped up and tried to grab it again. He finally flung it into a stall and raised his hands up. "Stay back. I don't want you to cast any spells."

"What are you thinking? Dude, I am not a witch. I just like a barn to smell like horses and nothing else. Come on. Let's go."

As Sergius started to walk, he caught a whiff of himself. He thought this new scent wasn't so bad after all. It reminded him of the garden outside of his stables.

Naomi stepped out from the house and took in the menagerie of beings in front of her. She played with her bun nervously as she took in the likes of Sergius, Briggs, and Joe. Sergius did a strange sort of bow in front of Naomi. She nodded quietly and then looked toward the lean cowboy suspiciously. Abigail ran toward Naomi, "That's Joe. I just told you about him!" She was getting a little dizzy with the prospects of all the pieces coming into play. "And this is Sir-gee-us." Abigail displayed a hint of disbelief. "He's here to help. I think."

Naomi embraced him in a bear hug, "Well of course he is. Welcome dear man. How are you coping? Do you need something to eat or drink?"

Abigail scrunched up her face as she watched Naomi get so close to the stink.

Sergius had a glazed look in his eyes. "Do all women wear pants in this time?"

Naomi laughed. "Why yes, that's one of the many things we love to wear."

He nodded respectfully, then turned his attention back to Dotune.

Briggs tried not to show too much emotion as she watched them meet. Her heart was beating quickly with the prospect that these three before her, could be *the* Re-Connectors. She noted how Abigail was very stand-offish. Although Naomi's greeting made her feel more at ease. She hoped Sergius wouldn't fritz out from his new environment. She thought, *What in the universe was Levidia thinking when she put these three together?*

She motioned for them to all sit down in a circle. "Come, let's all gather around and get to the heart of the matter. You will get to know each other in due time."

Dotune stopped grazing and positioned himself in between Sergius and Abigail. They both instinctively reached up to scratch him on the neck. Their hands accidentally touched. Abigail was surprised that instead of recoiling from the dirty hand, she felt comforted. Sergius was surprised by the sensation, which was distinctly different from Naomi's embrace. Abigail grinned as she realized in that moment they had something in common. *Maybe there is a good reason he is here. He seems better with horses, than humans, just like me.*

Briggs started her explanation. "We are here to employ all of you with an elaborate undertaking. First, so that you understand this pressing matter, I must show you what the Murmori have been planning. I have overheard them on their way to and from different victims."

Briggs opened her large hands. Two spirals emerged and dashed in front of everyone. As they passed by, the following words from the Murmori were imprinted in all of their minds. *We are nearly finished with taking over the Earth. The humans will be our robotic slaves. The more we prey on them at night, the less they are able to use their imaginations during the day. Their fearful and anxiety-ridden energy allow us to grow stronger every night. There is nothing to stop us now. In just a few more months, we will have penetrated every human's mind and have conquered this planet.*

As they sat in the circle, they all shuddered. Sergius began to speak fiercely, "They haven't conquered me! When do we begin to fight them?"

Abigail was stunned at his reaction, but had to chime in. "I've dealt with the Murmori all of my life. Fighting won't help."

"Abigail, my people thrive in battles. Perhaps you just don't realize how strong we are. I would bet we could defeat these Murmori creatures with the right weapons."

"What kind of weapon would destroy a dark spirit? They aren't in physical form."

Sergius' mouth opened widely. "Um, wait, what?"

Naomi realized that Sergius was dumfounded. "I know exactly what Abigail is trying to explain, Sergius. If you would, imagine you are trapped in a dream and could never wake up. How would you fight something like that?"

Sergius stood up and paced around all of them. "This is absurd. Are you telling me, we are on a mission, without proper arms? How will we win?"

Abigail looked up at him. "All I know is that any type of aggression will make them grow stronger."

Sergius' eyes narrowed. "There is no other way."

They all turned to Briggs for guidance. She looked at the three faces for a few moments before she spoke. "The Murmori are defeated by love, joy, and light. We need your light, dear ones. Light can push away the dark."

Sergius shook his head. He asked, "What do you mean by light?"

Briggs put up her hands, spread her fingers and ten more spirals popped out of her fingernails. They spun around in a playful way and then all landed on Sergius' head. He wanted to fight them off, since they were tickling him like crazy. He swatted at them, only causing them to reposition themselves on different parts of his body. All of them burst out into laughter. This was the first moment that the tension lifted. He finally put up his hands in surrender. "Enough of this foolishness! What is our mission?"

Briggs smiled and said, "To find your lightness, like just now."

She continued, "This is undoubtedly a challenge for most humans, yet you have already come so far with your willingness to learn about jumping around in time and space. Basically, we want you to join other humans with horses around the world, through time and space. Specific places that need the most help. These places have the most vital strings of the Universal Web and must be Re-Connected. Incidentally, these places are the most depressed, fear-ridden areas, and are completely trapped in the Murmori hold. The areas on Earth that call out in the most anguish were the places that held the most joy at one time. Now they are losing their grip with reality. The humans there have forgotten that they can create their own realities. Their joy is evaporating by the minute."

"You three are to learn how to go to these places and find anyone who might have a glimmer of hope left inside of them. Once you do, you are to teach them what you have learned, so that they can spread the message and initiate the Re-Connection of the strings in their area. Once that is done, inter-dimensional travel will be available once more and the Murmori better watch out. Their rule will be vanquished."

"How is that done?" Naomi's head began to hurt. This sounded way more complicated than she could have even dreamed up.

Briggs continued, "The strings can be Re-Connected by specific energetic vibrations. The Earth needs to be vibrating at a higher level for the Web to be completely reconnected again. Singing the songs of the ancient ones was one of the best ways to go about this. There are other ways, that have to do with horses, and you will learn them all in time."

"Once you begin this mission, you will teach other humans how to find their power within and never look back. Too many people struggle with looking outside themselves for answers. Your job will be to become models of power, leadership, and above all 'joy spreaders'. For once you discover that you have all the answers, power, and joy within yourselves, anything is possible."

Naomi and Abigail looked at each other intensely. Naomi was the first to respond. "Joy spreaders? Seriously? I honestly don't think I have felt real joy in a very long time."

Abigail felt a wave of sadness. She hadn't realized how her dear trainer was so raw. She wanted to find a way to help this amazing woman, who had brought her so much joy. Then she realized she had the answer.

Abigail instinctively took her by the hands. "Here. Start with this. Naomi, you've brought me such joy with teaching me all about riding. Can you feel it pouring in from me?"

Naomi's eyes watered. She whispered, "Yes, I do, sweet girl."

Sergius looked at both of them longingly. He felt the pang of jealously he experienced at his cousin's wedding. He was always left out. Dotune sensed this and started breathing on the back of his neck. Sergius slowly allowed a grin to appear. *Yes, dear Sergius. You know the horses bring you a sense of joy as well. Feel into that, dear sir. You are more like these ladies than you realize.*

Sergius got very quiet and put one arm over his head, as if attempting to keep his thoughts from drifting out.

Uneasy and awash with emotion, Naomi pulled her hands away from Abigail suddenly and looked up at Briggs. "On a purely practical side, would this mission interfere with my business and taking care of my farm? Surely you must understand that it is just me running the whole place."

Joe chimed in immediately, "Why, Naomi, I'm sure glad you asked. This is precisely why I was asked to join y'all here. I am volunteering my farm sitting skills for you to feel at peace while you do your inter-dimensional gallivanting."

Naomi eyed him warily. Briggs put her hand on Naomi's shoulder and whispered, "He is by far the most exquisite horseman in this dimension you could ask for. Having him here is quite an honor." Naomi stood up, walked around the circle of beings and blurted out instructions, "So each of my horses get different vitamins and supplements. It is a complex procedure. Some have to be separated, depending on the horse, because the herd leader will always push the betas away from their buckets. And you have to really spread all the hay around. Do do know how much hay to feed a horse? Oh and the pony gets very little since she is starting to get a hay belly. Then you must check the stalls for manure twice per day. The water buckets get filled every evening. The fly spray is located in the middle of the barn, hanging outside the stall doors..."

Joe stopped her with a one large hand pressed over her mouth. When she tried to scream, he simply shook his head slowly. "Naomi! Please relax. I can hear the horses. Just tell me who is in charge and I will ask them."

"Oh." Naomi sat back down, clearly embarrassed from her compulsiveness. "Keeper. He's the one. He will tell you." She smiled shyly in Joe's direction. His eyes twinkled and he tipped his hat to her.

Briggs pressed on to reassure Naomi, "Remember, all of these travels will seem like you have been gone a long time, yet you will continue to come home quite regularly. In fact, after this first task, you will get to go home and sleep in your own bed."

Naomi nodded, though still skeptical, and reminded herself that she really wanted this.

Abigail was keen on starting right away. She turned to Briggs with a longing look. "Well, when shall we begin? I feel like I've been waiting for some time. What do we need to do?"

Briggs laughed and looked her in the eyes. "I knew you were pretty adventurous, Miss Abigail. I love your willingness to move forward quickly. I have a special message for you. Please give me a moment to prepare." Briggs stood up and began to spin in place. She spun three times, clockwise, then three times counterclockwise. She stopped and grinned. In front of all of them was a beautiful spiral getting bigger and bigger.

Joe stood up as well and tipped his hat in the form of a goodbye. "Wait" Briggs exclaimed, surprised, "You need to join us for this first part. Please, sit down again."

Joe's expression was both one of utter shock and confusion. "Ma'am, if it's all the same, I would rather just do the watching part. I 'spect Miss Naomi's horses will need some tending to."

Briggs raised her eyebrows. "Joe, really, Levidia insisted you know about the plan too. Now please, you can go over to the barn right after."

Joe shrugged and leaned back on the tree, with his eyes wide and let out a sigh.

The four of them watched as the spiral grew and then began to show small horses galloping up along the sides. They all cooed in amazement, to which Dotune lifted his massive neck and pricked his ears at the sight of his brethren so close. He whinnied loudly.

I miss them so, dear one. I would love to see all of them soon. It has been a year since I have been home to relay my stories.

Abigail stroked his mane and nodded. She couldn't imagine what it would be like to be trapped on a different planet in such a different sort of body.

Briggs took a very deep breath and closed her eyes. She placed both hands on her lap for a few moments and then a large scroll appeared in her hands. She carefully opened it and stood up to show the others. It was a message from Gavrantura. This is what it revealed:

The truth about this planet is just a whisper away. You find it most often in dream time. You are not alone and there are so many others who wish to help you. The closest ones that you know of take the form of horses.

Humans have, for the most part, been kept in a slumber state, unaware of this truth; some very deliberately, some self induced.

The amazing fact is: all humans, while in dream time, are fully aware of traveling to different dimensions. They sometimes travel so far, especially most recently, that they often forget who they are for a short period of time when they wake up in their bodies. People are searching for truth. You are all here to help them remember. You will travel consciously, deliberately, and with your most splendid hearts. You will be the ones to show humans that they have never been alone and they are truly remarkable beings in the universe.

Your first task will involve a dream-like adventure, although you will be fully aware of what is going on. You are going to make contact with all the other horse lovers who have this kind of awareness. Together, you will be shown how to make this truth palatable to the world.

Step into the spiral and you will be brought to home base. Are you ready?

Abigail felt overwhelmed, but decided to stare at Sergius. She thought about how he had already arrived here safely. This gave her courage. Naomi tried to hide that her legs were shaking. Sergius looked back and forth at the two of them and felt moved to grab their hands. They looked at him and gulped.

United for the first time, they nodded at each other. They bravely stepped forward into the spiral until they vanished.

Dotune whinnied to them and Briggs quickly turned toward him. "Oh my dear one, would you like to stay with me for a bit? You and Sergius will meet again soon. I feel you both have much to accomplish. Here is where you get to rest. Come with me to my home. You can rest and regroup with Gavrantura tonight. I am sure they have missed you and are eager for a full report!"

Dotune sighed and licked his lips. That was music to his ears. He missed the sound vibrations he was accustomed to on his home planet. Briggs had just brought him such hope.

Joe and Briggs looked deeply into each others' eyes. She placed her hands on his shoulders. "Dear sir, you are to tend Naomi's farm now. Thank you for all that you are and will be doing. They will arrive again soon. The horses will tell you what they need, especially the one called Keeper. He will be the one to chat with first."

Joe nodded and turned away, looked back again and whispered, "Well, I reckon those adventurers will be hankering for some dinner when they get back. I best get some fixings together after feeding the herd. You suppose they're truly up for this here task?"

Briggs smiled brightly. "Oh, Joe, what other choice do we have but to hope?"

They hugged and then Joe gave Dotune one last scratch on the neck. He headed toward the barn. Briggs and Dotune walked casually together into an opening of a cherry blossom tree.

CHAPTER TWENTY TWO

Daniel

Still holding hands tightly, Naomi, Sergius, and Abigail tumbled through space after walking into the spiral. They floated up and down and every which way, until they hovered over a starry figure eight just below their feet. Naomi kept spinning and Sergius flipped around several times. Abigail was the steadiest. "Hey you guys, breathe into your bellies. You will find your balance." This she knew from her first task. As soon as they relaxed into this, they were promptly placed on the figure. It moved them along the path, just like an automated walkway in an airport, hurrying them along to their boarding gate. They got very quiet. None of them had any frame of reference for where they were and decided to stay quiet, to not give cause for worry.

Levidia suddenly appeared in the middle of the figure eight and touched her wand to it in order to stop the movement. All three of them nearly toppled over. They found their bearings again as they watched Levidia spiral up a few more times above them. She turned toward them and then pointed to a flurry of snowflakes appearing in the distance.

"My darlings, it brings me great pleasure to introduce to you the home base of your training school."

They all stared at her in amazement. She continued.

"For what you humans are about to learn will take some practice. You didn't think you were just going to wing it, did you?"

They sighed in unison. Levidia waved her wand again and a huge tunnel appeared with spirals all around it. "Go now and take some time to get acquainted. It will take a fortnight for this training to sink in. Then you will be ready to go on your quests to teach the others out there."

The three of them walked into the tunnel, one by one and were suddenly sucked in, like a vacuum, toward a huge building in the clouds. It was marble like, suspended in the air, and a large door opened as they wandered closer.

A slender man was in the doorway, beckoning them over. He had blond hair and wore a dark suit, which looked like it had been neatly pressed that morning. He introduced himself simply as Daniel.

Daniel was also known as the 'precision' angel. A perfect gentleman, Daniel is the ultimate leader for all the type "A" personalities, hoping to make sure everything gets done well and correctly. He is the one whispering in the back of your mind, reminding you to double check your recipe for dinner, call your Mom on her birthday, and rinse your plate before you put it in the dishwasher. Daniel will always be there to remind you to be impeccable with your word and to feel good about what you're doing, always. He's the best supervisor and friend when you get a little lost or sloppy.

"I will be your guide during these training days. Please let me know if you have any questions. I will give you a short tour of the facility and then we will commence in the main hall to begin your basic level class."

Abigail became a bit rigid, as she never enjoyed the school environment. Naomi was having trouble wiping the smile off of her face. She always dreamed of going back to school, yet not quite in a dream state such as this. Although she was excited, she was still pretty nervous about all of this reality bending stuff. Sergius took in all of his surroundings, attempting to make sure in his logical mind that they were indeed safe. The inside of this floating building had every kind of spiral around the walls, floors, and stairways. It was enough to make one feel like they were being hypnotized. Sergius put his hands on the ladies' shoulders. He thought it would make them feel more supported. They all followed Daniel into each room that seemed stranger than the next.

The rooms were all pretty bare, except for a few pillows on the floors and large couches in some. The spiral theme continued and some would light up as they went by.

Finally, Abigail couldn't take it anymore. They were walking in silence for so long, she needed some answers. "Excuse me, Mr. Daniel?" He whirled around and gave her a stern yet inquisitive look.

"What are all these spirals for? They're actually making me dizzy." Abigail sat down on one of the pillows to catch her bearings.

"Oh, well, this is what you have come to learn. No need to fret. Come, let's go ahead and begin the class now." Daniel handed her a glass of water from the corner of the room that seemed to just pop out of one of the spirals in the wall. She drank slowly and Sergius helped her to her feet.

As they sat at a round table, Daniel instructed them to all take some deep breaths, relax and imagine their happiest moments with the horses in their lives.

Abigail immediately felt herself riding Rafi along the waterfall, the first time she felt the connection of floating along, being one with him.

Naomi giggled as she imagined doing a perfect jump course with Keeper.

Sergius was galloping along the countryside with Dotune, in complete awe of his amazing power and endurance.

"Very nice, my new friends. I can see you understand this connection beautifully. As your guide, I want to remind you that I can sense and see what you experience. I am one of the oldest horsemen in this realm and this is truly an honor to show you youngsters what I have learned."

They all opened their eyes and looked at Daniel in a new light. For some reason, none of them suspected he was into horses. He seemed much too clean, proper, and frankly uptight. Sensing their confusion, Daniel quickly cleared his throat and clarified, "You see, I am the first spirit who ever rode a horse on Earth. It has been quite some time since I have been able to interact on this level. My appearance might seem a bit prim, yet I assure you, I am full of surprises. I chose this look, since I want to appear honorable. I am certainly one who is proud of all that horses and humans have accomplished together so far. I have so much to share with you."

They nodded and waited for him to continue.

"What I want you to do now, is close your eyes and come back to that place with your horses. Once there, find a physical cue to attach to that feeling. Whatever will work to bring you back into your body. It might be touching your fingertips together, curling your toes, putting your hand over your heart, or shaking your behinds!"

This last comment created an inward smile for all of them. Once they decided on their cues, they opened their eyes. Sergius inquired, "So what kind of traveling are we aiming for?"

Daniel stood up and became much more animated. He walked around the table once, sat back down and proceeded to explain, "You will do as little or as much as you like. I just traveled around the world in that moment. Did you see it?"

They gave each other looks like their new teacher was completely mental.

"It really doesn't matter where your physical body is. This is the point. You can travel anywhere and to anytime with your minds. This is what you are going to practice, perfect, and perform. With these tools, my friends, you will connect with others like you and teach them how to do the same."

"Just so you feel more at ease, we do have a few specific locations and people in mind for you to visit."

"Let's get back to it. I am going to allow the screen behind me to explain the next steps. I will be here in case you would like me to press pause and we can dive further into any subject." He stood up and pulled out a remote control from the bottom of the table. He pressed a large red button and an enormous movie screen came into view.

Sergius leaned his head back. He was astounded. "What in the world is that? What kind of magic is this? Do you ladies know about such things or is this just as peculiar to you?"

Naomi grinned and went into teacher mode. "Sergius, this is all modern technology that Abigail and I are very accustomed to. Of course, this entire building and traveling is all new to us. The movie screen is something that was developed recently in our time, and we really love these forms of entertainment."

"Entertainment? You mean these enormous moving pictures are enjoyable to watch? I am just getting dizzy."

Abigail understood more than she realized. She preferred reading books, rather than staring at screens. "It will be fine, Sergius. I am quite sure you will relax about it sooner or later."

He nodded quietly and tried to focus on the screen again. He was grateful that Abigail had some reassuring words.

The moving pictures were like watching a physics class for Abigail, although with clever animation that had horses, humans, and more of the spirals.

Then a booming voice began to play:

Welcome friends. Thank you for being here. I trust you have learned phase one of this activity. Once you have a physical cue to bring you back to your bodies, the next step involves clearing your minds completely. If you can imagine you are stepping back from your bodies, onto a blank projection screen, you may then look at your bodies from the outside. It will serve you well to stay very neutral about how you feel. Simply observe your bodies and then begin to decide where you would like to go. Once you imagine where that is very clearly, see your body popping into this new place. It's a lot like picking up a doll and placing it in a specific room in a dollhouse.

Daniel pressed pause instinctively, as he saw all of their eyes glaze over. "All right, this may have been a little too much. Abigail, remember what Joe taught you? Does this sound familiar?"

Abigail blushed and looked around at everyone. She nodded and then said, "This explanation is a bit more, err, dry, I guess. Although I can see how it would work. Joe taught me to actually use my emotions to help me jump to where I wanted to be. With my intense desire to go somewhere, I just showed up. It felt effortless and surprised me big time."

"Good. Good. I can understand how that would work well for you." Daniel sighed and sat down for a moment. "This class was created for a variety of travelers. I guess it truly depends on how focused you can get your mind to be. Some need their emotions, while others thrive by staying neutral."

Sergius chimed in, "Yes, my emotions run deep, yet I can see where quieting them would help me focus. You are doing an exemplary service, Daniel. I can most definitely sense this must be challenging for you."

Daniel had tears in his eyes and spontaneously hugged Sergius. "Thank you. I really don't want to disappoint any of you, nor the horses. This is our last chance to make things right and I fear that these connections might be lost if you don't understand what we are asking of you."

Naomi took a deep breath and said, "Daniel, you must know that we are obviously very willing to learn. We are here, aren't we? I know that I can help others since I've been doing that in the physical world for quite some time. My skill set will most certainly come in handy for this other worldly mission. You can count on me."

Daniel smiled with gratitude and then looked toward Abigail. She blinked a few times, as if coming back from a visit with Briggs. She thought about how sensitive Sergius was with Daniel. She really hadn't given much thought to the feelings of her teachers before. She took a moment to respond. "Yes, of course. I've dreamed about this for quite some time. Seriously, my day dreams are always about flying around and visiting horses." She smiled and then got a little nervous, ready for the class to continue without all the attention on her.

Daniel turned around to cover up his emotional state and blew his nose. Sergius was intrigued and spontaneously grabbed the remote and started pushing the buttons. The screen began to play again. He jumped back and Naomi took the remote from him. "Let me save you from yourself."

He grinned sheepishly. They all looked up at the screen again.

Once you have locked into your new location and feel yourself materializing there, please remember that you are safe and can always come back to your original location by initializing your physical cue you established moments ago. That's really all there is to it when Daniel is guiding you, for he has the specific travel equations memorized. When you come back to your bodies, it will be as if you never left. Only seconds will have drifted away, even if you have been in your new location for hours, days or weeks. That is the only major disorientation that you must get accustomed to. The next phase will be discussed tomorrow. Thank you for your participation.

The three of them all looked at each other, then they focused on Daniel who was passing over three scrolls. "For the last part of this class, we will all practice going to the same place together. The instructions are here. Read it well and we will begin when I count down."

The scroll read:

You will assist with a young Comanche girl and the training of her horse. Imagine you are along a ravine and her horse is a Tobiano Paint. She is wearing deerskin, has dark hair with hazel eyes and she seems a bit frustrated. They call her Topsana and the year is 1859.

Can you see her? Remember what you have just learned. When you arrive, teach her how to communicate with her horse. She will be receptive to this information as long as you are gentle with your approach. We won't linger too long here, as this is just your first journey. There is much to continue doing.

Naomi asked a practical question, "Daniel, how will we communicate? I don't speak Comanche."

"Ah yes, I forgot to mention the beauty of this type of travel. Once you intend on the time and space to be in, you will actually take on the essence of the humans in that area. You will be able to speak and look just like them. Fear not. Great question. This is how Sergius can speak fluent English by the way."

Naomi nodded in approval. Sergius was impressed that he could continue becoming a master of languages.

Sergius felt empowered and changed the subject, "Daniel, what did they mean that you have the travel equations? What happens if we get separated from you?"

"Sergius, I promise we will all stay very close for this first task. The equation will be explained in more detail tomorrow. For now, just believe me when I say that you can simply imagine where you need to be and as long as you are holding onto some part of my body, I will get you safely to your destination."

Sergius looked deeply into Daniel's eyes for a few moments. He then softly said, "I trust you."

Suddenly, Abigail began to get really fidgety. She looked up at the others. "I'm not sure I am really ready. Maybe we can practice a little more with people we know?"

"Abigail Freedman, you are most certainly ready. You are more ready than any other fifteen year old that we know of on this planet. Remember what you have learned. You have the power." He began to count down before she could reply.

Naomi reassured Abigail, "Just take deep breaths. Pretend you are riding Rafi right now. That will remind you of your power, right?"

Abigail smiled. "Naomi, you always know what to say."

They found their still points within and a large spiral began swirling above all of them. Abigail and Naomi grabbed Daniel's arms, while Sergius placed his hands on Daniel's shoulders.

They could hear the rushing water of the ravine before they even opened their eyes. They smelled a sweaty horse nearby and heard a young woman grunting. They whirled around and saw the pair making circles around one another. The horse pinned his ears back and raised his neck up high, as Topsana attempted to jump on his back. Hooves stomped and spun around her.

"I need you to stay still horse. Please stop spinning around." Topsana suddenly froze, as she felt eyes upon her from the trees thirty feet away. She quickly dropped the rope of her horse and began reaching for her knife. Abigail appeared first and put up her hands in a quiet way.

"Please, we are not here to harm you. We have come to help you with your horse. I know this is going to sound crazy, but please listen." Abigail instinctively bowed in front of the young girl and then reached out to pet her horse.

Topsana got very defensive and yanked her horse away from Abigail. Abigail simply backed away and the other three quietly walked up to support her. Topsana's eyes grew very large and she began shouting at the visitors.

"Who are you? What do you want?"

Naomi thought it would be safer and less threatening to just sit down beside the troubled young woman. The others followed suit and began staring at the ravine. Naomi lifted her hand softly toward the horse. She practiced what Abigail had just taught her with Keeper. She sent him images of how they interacted with their horses. He lowered his head and started to nuzzle the four of them.

Still not convinced, Topsana stomped her foot and demanded answers. "I have no idea who you are. You are intruding on my land and space with my horse."

She glared at them and reached for her knife again. They didn't budge.

"If you don't leave, I will have to get my family to make you wish you did."

Sergius took in this defensive, scared young woman. He grasped at what to say next. Then the answer came in suddenly. "How would you do that if your horse won't let you ride him?"

Topsana burst into tears and fell onto the ground, a few feet away from the group. Abigail quietly put her arms on her shoulders and said, "It's really all right. We are here to help. We want you to hear what your horse has to say. I promise it will work."

Abigail's touch reminded her of a feeling as a toddler. It was akin to her great grandmother's embrace. Topsana's sobs quieted as she lifted her head and made a point to make eye contact with each of them. Then something clicked in. "You are my ancestors, here to assist?"

Naomi sighed and decided to play along, "Something like that. Listen, we want to teach you how to communicate with your horse. It is much easier than you think."

Daniel remained quiet and motioned for Sergius to do his thing.

Sergius stood up and after communing with her horse for a few minutes, grabbed the rope and a handful of black and white mane, then swung his right leg over. He was mounted and the horse took a couple of crow hops around, and then jumped into the ravine. Sergius proceeded to move with him effortlessly in the water. The horse seemed to really enjoy the interaction. He understood which way Sergius wanted to move with his leg cues. The weight of his rider was lessened in the water, which was only up to his belly. They moved like swans for a good few minutes. Then the Paint went toward the bank, jumped out and shook. Sergius laughed loudly and slid off the now relaxed steed and scratched him all over.

Topsana stared in amazement. "Please teach me."

Abigail initiated the conversation by explaining how to connect to your heart, then your horse's heart. The birds around them began to chirp louder. Topsana listened intensely with tears rolling down her eyes. As she began to practice what these strangers were telling her, the Paint circled around them and stopped right behind Topsana. He started to blow in her ear. His blue eyes got heavy. She got goose bumps up and down her arms and legs.

She leaned back on the ground and he started to nuzzle her hair. She grabbed a hold of his mane and he helped her stand up. It was clear they made the connection. She then rode him around the visitors and promptly trotted off. They watched her for a few moments. She turned around and charged toward them. She smiled and whispered,

"I will be forever grateful for this knowledge. I will pass it on to my people."

They all waved goodbye and stared in awe at this transformation. Abigail broke the silence. "Um, What just happened? Did we just create a rift in the universe from this experiment?" Naomi began to laugh nervously. Sergius focused on Daniel.

"Exactly! You see how this works, my friends?" Daniel said with a chuckle. "It is now time you understand the impact you have on Earth's vibration. The more lives you connect with, the better chance we have to Re-Connect the strings of the Web."

He quickly changed the subject. "Now, you need to rest and commune with your own horses again. Abigail, please find your way to your home. Naomi and Sergius can go back to Willow Tree Farms. Sergius, Dotune will be waiting there for you with much news to share. I believe he had his own journey back home this evening as well."

The three of them put their hands on Daniel's back and initiated their physical cues for travel. Abigail, Naomi and Daniel disappeared. Sergius was left on the ravine. He looked around and wondered why he hadn't left. He screamed at the top of his lungs, "I'm still here!" He paused to listen. There was no response.

"I need assistance!" His eyes dashed around and hoped he would see something.

"Help!" He started pacing and sweating. "Can anyone hear me?"

He suddenly wondered if Abigail made it back safely. This wave of emotion surprised him. He shrugged it off. *I need to have a plan. I can't believe this just happened. What if they never come back for me?* He closed his eyes and took a deep breath. He felt defeated. He sat down and leaned against a large tree. He closed his eyes and began to shake in fear. He had never felt this alone and confused.

Daniel arrived back in the castle to find a very concerned Levidia. "Daniel! We have a major problem."

His eyes were wide and he exclaimed, "What do you mean,

Levidia? Everyone did splendidly!"

"Yes, however, Sergius is still in Topsana's land."

"What?" He gasped.

"You forgot to tweak your equation to bring him back."

"Oh what is wrong with me?"

"Remember, his energy is so different from the ladies, that I am sure it was just an oversight."

"To think, we were so close to getting this first part of the mission flawless." Daniel then jumped up. "My deepest apologies. I will go back immediately. I hope he hasn't lost his mind. Oh dear. Levidia, I will make this right. You can count on me."

Levidia put her hand on his back, "I know, Daniel, I am quite sure you will never make this mistake again. It is very unlike you to slip up like this. Now go get him!"

Before she could finish her last sentence, he arrived at the ravine again. Daniel appeared right next to the tree where Sergius was frozen in fear. Sergius, still shaking, looked up and took in that his guide had returned. A wave of relief and anger swept over him all at one. He was about to take a swing at Daniel, who didn't move a muscle. He then saw how remorseful he looked and thought the better of it. Daniel didn't blame Sergius in the least.

"I am deeply sorry. This was entirely my fault. I forgot something about this traveling experience. There was a certain type of equation that you specifically needed to jump forward again. I forgot how different you are from Abigail and Naomi."

Sergius sighed in resignation. He didn't have any energy left to be angry. Daniel put his hands on his shoulders. Sergius then found himself on Naomi's couch.

Daniel returned to the castle, sat down at the round table, and tried desperately not to beat himself up about his mistake. *I am going to have to be extra diligent. This mission is so incredibly intricate.* He sighed, waved his hand in the middle of the table and grasped at his wine glass that wasn't there a moment ago. He took a long sip and sat back in his chair, allowing himself a much needed visit with Briggs.

Even angels needed time to rest.

CHAPTER TWENTY THREE

Home Again

Dotune was overwhelmed as he sat in front of the Gavranturan council. The celebration for his return was remarkable. Music played, while every kind of food whizzed around the room. Once someone chose a meal in their mind, a specific plate would hover in front of the hungry being, long enough to get their fill. Dotune relayed the many battles he participated in, the humans he encountered, and the feelings he had toward his experiences. Then he got very quiet and explained his amazing connection with Sergius. He told them of how he had a beautiful song for each horse and how he could hear him speak. He began to cry with how relieved he felt knowing there was an Earthling with so much love and devotion in his presence.

The council members looked around at each other and congratulated Dotune for his fine achievements. Then a choice was presented.

Gerseve, head of the High Council, walked toward Dotune and boomed so the entire council could hear, "Dotune, you have proven that we are certainly on the right track with our decision to send you to Earth. There is still much to be done if the Universal Web is to be Re-Connected. We realize that you must be weary. So we ask you, hoping for a completely honest and true answer. Would you like to continue in this form, take another, or rest here for awhile?"

Dotune closed his eyes and felt his body sway to the music playing in the background. While he felt at ease on his home planet, he truly enjoyed spending time with Sergius. He felt they were on the brink of shifting more Earthlings' perspectives and felt a calling he had never thought was possible in his essence.

"I would love to continue on in the same form, as long as I might visit back here more often. Would you agree to that?"

Gerseve nodded immediately, "We thought that was your answer. Of course, you may continue. As you will see with the other more recent horse forms on Earth, they are all able to reconvene here every time they go to sleep. You may now do this anytime you wish."

Dotune bowed to the council with gratitude and ordered up his most favorite dish, Grunips. It tasted like a combination of marshmallows and apricots if one were to eat this on Earth. He had a bit of a sweet tooth and had craved this meal for quite some time.

After overindulging, he pulled up a very comfortable chair that hugged him as he sat down. He fell asleep and was sent back to his magnificent chestnut body.

Abigail found herself swinging on the hammock and relaxed there for a few moments. She needed to catch her breath. She could see through the kitchen window that her mother was preparing dinner. Her stomach rumbled, she jumped up, and floating inside the house.

"Hi Mom, how's it going?" Her mother took a double take as Abigail walked in from the back door. "Wow, Abigail, I thought you were in your room."

Abigail gathered her thoughts and calmly said, "I was for a bit, then popped out to the hammock to have a nice meditation with nature."

Her mother gave her a sideways glance, checking to see if her daughter was really all right. "Well, dinner is almost ready. Please go get your father."

Abigail smiled and hugged her Mom, then headed over to the study. Her father was working on grading papers, with his spectacles nearly falling off of his nose. She poked her head in the doorway and said, "Dad, the feast is nearly ready. Shall we dine?"

He chuckled and looked up in a daze. "Why yes, my dear girl. That sounds divine."

"I just hope the fixings are incredibly fine."

"Your mother cooks so well, that's why she's mine."

"Ha! Good one Dad. Listen, I need to talk with you after dinner. Do you have time?"

"I will make some, if I feel inclined." Albert laughed and then winked at his daughter. "I do love these rhymes."

They were both giggling as they sat down to the table. Evelyn shrugged, as she knew by now how often those two had their inside jokes down pat. She presented them with sweet and sour meatballs over jasmine rice with steamed broccoli and melted butter. Abigail dug in like she hadn't eaten in a week. Evelyn and Albert exchanged surprised looks as they watched their girl inhale the 'divine feast'.

After dinner, Abigail was in a bit of a food coma, yet was still eager to have a chat. Evelyn decided to take a bath and leave the two alone. They sat down in front of the fireplace, with the sound of jazz music playing on the stereo. Abigail felt sleepy, yet wanted to share so much and ask questions of her physics teacher father.

Albert looked very content, "So what did you want to talk about?"

Abigail sat up a little straighter and proceeded to create a scenario for him to explore with his mind. "Well, Dad. If someone were to travel back in time, alter a bit of history, nothing major, yet it did change. What do you think would happen to the time traveler when they arrived back in their own time? Do you think a lot would change for them?"

Albert studied his daughter as she made this inquiry. It seemed like a fun topic to dive into, yet wondered where it came from. She typically enjoyed rattling on about horses, books, and sometimes the latest annoyance at school. There seemed to be a major shift in her. He decided not to think too much about this, since she was a teenager after all. He knew her interests would be rapidly changing in the next few years, or weeks even. He tipped his head back, took a sip of his gin and tonic and said, "Abigail, this is quite the interesting topic. Many theories are at play here. My take is that there are multiple universes. So no matter what the time traveler did to alter history, their own time period would remain the same. The history that they altered simply exists in a parallel universe. Kind of like train tracks that shift.

One train goes one way and then it switches and gets sent in the other direction. Every time something is altered, or a decision has been made, the train can switch to a different track. Are you on track with me?"

Abigail laughed, "Oh Dad. You and your puns. Yes, I get it. Thanks. I may have to disagree though. I have a feeling we can really make changes to the present if we travel back in time. So, would you believe me, if I told you that I might have found a way to switch tracks for the better?"

"Well, I believe anything is possible, Ms. Einstein."

Albert took a deep breath and a longer sip of his drink. He swished around the remaining alcohol and looked up at Abigail. "Keep me posted on your big bang theories, kiddo. Okay?"

She shrugged, realizing he was just humoring her and was slightly disappointed. "Thanks Dad."

He was left by his wild eyed girl and sat there with his eyes closed, humming along to Chuck Mangione's, "The Land of Make Believe."

Joe had just finished making supper when Naomi reappeared. He turned around from the stove and said, "Perfectly timed, weary travelers. I fixed us a meal fit for a prince."

Naomi grabbed a tight hold of the sides of the kitchen table, making sure she was really in her home again. Sergius arrived a few minutes later, looked around and felt completely out of place, sitting on the couch. He was more comfortable outdoors and this modern looking home was a bit daunting. He was still shaken from being left behind. His first instinct was to shout out and display his disdain for this whole ordeal. He then regained his composure as he noticed the delicious smells that were wafting from this kitchen. His hunger was overwhelming and he didn't want to seem ungrateful.

Joe didn't disappoint. As he told Naomi about all the horses' antics during feeding time, he dished out pot roast, corn bread, and mashed potatoes. Naomi was overwhelmed with joy to know that all of her animals were attended to and obviously understood, especially when

Joe joked about Keeper delegating who gets what from the side of the feed room.

They ate quickly, grateful to be sitting still, with settled stomachs. Sergius tried to explain what had happened with his later arrival. Naomi was shocked that something like that could happen. "Maybe we are all taking this a bit too lightly. It seems like we can get in some big trouble, being left behind. Oh my goodness, that's really freaky." She shuddered and then thought of Abigail's reaction.

"Listen, Sergius. I think we better keep this mishap a secret from Abigail. I'm really not sure how she is going to take this. She is still recovering from her own accident and it might put her off for the entire mission. Would you please keep it to yourself?"

"Yes. Of course. She is much younger than you and probably fragile. I truly felt helpless. I've never had that emotion before. Naomi, what do you do when you feel that way?"

Naomi was startled. She wasn't prepared for such a deep question from this stranger. She admired how he got right to the point. She was extremely adept at bottling her feelings since she had become a widow. She quietly responded. "Well, Sergius. I usually just go and hug one of my horses. They know how to comfort me, more than any other human. Oh and about Abigail. She is strong, but may not always show it. I wouldn't necessarily call her fragile."

"That is something I will need to learn more about. Most young women I know are quiet and submissive. But horses comforting us? That I understand completely. More so than any of these strange surroundings. I am grateful to be here, near your horses, Naomi. Thank you, gentle woman."

Naomi thought he was taking all of these changes in stride and then wondered about what he left behind. "You're welcome. Hey, what exactly is happening with the horses in your charge?"

"Oh, I was called away to Rome just before I came here. I am quite sure another Strator has taken my post. I don't think they expected me to return to my herd."

"Wow. Well, I am glad you made it here then."

Sergius took a long drink from his water glass. "Indeed."

Naomi then realized she had one more task that evening. She had to make her guest more comfortable. She jumped up from the table and went into the living room to put together a nice cot for Sergius. *She is a gracious host*, Sergius thought, *As I would be content to sleep in the barn.* She then showed him the section of the closet where she still kept some of her late husband's clothes. "You can wear anything you find." Sergius felt uncomfortable, as he didn't recognize anything hanging. He pulled out a shirt, put it on, and then walked back out to the kitchen. "Tunics are generally longer where I come from."

Naomi turned around quickly, trying not to laugh in his face. "Joe, can you please help Sergius find some pants." Joe smirked and brought him back to the closet for a tutorial.

Joe said his goodbyes and asked, "Oh, do you have any special dinner requests for tomorrow evening? I hear that tomorrow's class will require quite a few exercises that might make your mind melt. Brain food, perhaps? Power smoothies and the like?" He lifted a health food magazine that was on the coffee table, seeming proud of himself that he was learning about the latest human cravings.

Naomi laughed and put her arm around Joe's shoulders and whispered, "You know, dear sir, I might get way too spoiled around here. You just create whatever inspires you, all right? Thank you so very much and good night. I feel like I'm sleeping already!"

"That will happen as you get more involved. It will be challenging to tell just which reality you're in. It might do you some good to consult with a schedule book, especially if you want to keep your lesson appointments during the day."

Naomi nodded and picked up her datebook. She noted that she had three students coming tomorrow. Luckily, they started at eleven o'clock.

Sergius saluted as his form of goodbye to Joe.

CHAPTER TWENTY FOUR

Adjustments

Dotune opened his eyes and realized he was in a pasture with Rafi, Brouteen, and Shantoo. They ran like the wind in their five acre pasture, whinnying, galloping, rearing, and bucking. This woke up Sergius as he could hear them just outside the window. He quickly got dressed and stumbled outside.

It was quite the sight. The four horses were so powerful, playful, and joyous. He whistled to Dotune who threw his tail and head up in the air and snorted loudly three times at his human companion. Sergius laughed and ran out toward the gate. He unlatched it, found his way in the pasture and hopped on Dotune's back. They trotted around the others as they shared their adventures from the night before. Dotune wanted Sergius to know something very special, "My dear friend. I was given the choice to stay on my home planet. I decided to come back for you. I love you so much and feel we have much to do together. I hope you realize how grateful I am for your friendship."

Sergius leaned over and hugged Dotune's massive neck and whispered, "I am grateful as well, my friend. My deepest apologies for the prolonged waiting period it required. I was unsure in the beginning if I could put my faith in you. Thank you for your belief in me."

At that moment, Naomi walked out of the house and saw the joyful moment. She waved to Sergius and asked if he wanted some breakfast.

"Thank you, Naomi. I will be with you in but a few moments." He slid off Dotune and scratched his neck until his fingernails were black.

"I will see you later. Until then, run boldly my friend." He bowed respectively toward Dotune who sighed and pushed his head forcefully into the stomach of his human, which caused Sergius to laugh loudly.

Sergius and Naomi sat at the table drinking coffee and munching on English muffins. "What are these?" He stared at the first muffin and after smelling it, realized he liked the smell, and finished it in two bites. He then helped himself to another three after checking Naomi's face for approval. Naomi wondered if Sergius would relax at all. He was sitting up so straight and proper, it made her feel like a slouch. "Sergius, it's okay. You can be at ease here. You don't have any duties. But, if it would make you feel more comfortable, you're welcome to help out with the horses while we wait for our next class."

Sergius seemed relieved to hear this from his host. "Thank you so much, Naomi. It does feel very peculiar being here, without tending to my specific duties. Waiting to learn more is probably going to be the most challenging part of all of this. I realize we need to process, yet I am wondering if I will ever get accustomed to this era."

Naomi stood up and dumped the last bit of her now cold coffee down the sink. "Oh, Sergius. It really isn't that bad. We are free to do what we like around here. Less battles to be won, unless you count the ongoing struggle to make money and pay bills."

Naomi had a grin on her face, walked over to her living room, grabbed the remote control and placed it on the table in front of Sergius. "Here, press some more of those buttons and the magic box over there should give you more insight into my world."

He looked up at her and immediately started playing with the remote, as if he was a small child given the most precious gift.

She grabbed her hat, schedule book, and water bottle. "I'll be out teaching. Feel free to watch television here, hang out, or muck stalls. You know, whatever you like." She laughed to herself as she realized he probably didn't even know what 'hang out' meant.

CHAPTER TWENTY FIVE

Learning Curves

Briggs collected the three travelers, who were instructed to meet at 4 pm to continue with Daniel's teachings. She ushered each of them through special doorways to find the main castle door again.

Daniel was bubbling with enthusiasm. "Welcome back! Let's get right into it. This evening, I am going to show you how to create a travel equation to help simplify your journeys without a guide. When you learn the equations, all you do is imprint them on an object, much like a charge. Whenever you touch that object, you will be transported to your destination. Do you have any questions?"

Naomi's mouth was wide open in amazement. She chimed in, "Well, this is getting more intense by the minute. No wonder Joe said this would be a mind melter."

Abigail was nervous. This seemed way harder than geometry. She looked up at Daniel and said, "I'm not really sure what you mean by charging an object. Does this mean we will have to use electricity every time?"

Daniel smiled and jumped up and down, then said "Brilliant question, Ms. Freedman! The use of electricity wouldn't be very practical, especially if you are going back into a time where it hasn't been invented yet. The charge would entail using your energy and your inner power. You do realize there are spirals, or helices within your own bodies? They are the DNA structures which reside within you. When you are aware of your own helices, you may talk to them, get them spinning just a bit faster than they are now and the charge will be ignited. Pretty cool, right?"

"What is electricity?" Sergius felt like he was in over his head.

Naomi and Abigail suddenly felt very sorry for Sergius. They were struggling enough to keep up with Daniel. Sergius was so far behind in his comprehension.

Daniel was kind, yet needed to move things along. "Like I said, it hasn't been invented in your time yet, Sergius. It is a power source. Remember when you saw how lit up the modern homes were, without torches? I hope you are willing to go along with all of this and learn as you go."

Sergius put his arm over his head. As Naomi noticed his odd position, she took the opportunity to lighten the mood. She decided to stand right behind him and do the same. She elbowed Abigail to join in on the mocking. Abigail hesitated, then grinned and followed suit. Sergius turned around slowly. He exclaimed defensively, "What? I do this to help me think. I don't want the thoughts to get out."

Abigail laughed and Naomi winked at her. Sergius put his arm back down and stared blankly at Daniel. He didn't want to make eye contact with the two ladies. He felt embarrassed, yet was secretly glad they tried to create some lightness in the air.

Sergius wanted to change the subject. He looked around the room and saw the spirals all spinning faster around them. "Are the spirals here to help remind us of our power within?"

"Ah, now you're getting somewhere, Sergius. Well done!" Daniel sat back down and tapped on the table three times. A holograph appeared. The equation was presented for them to memorize. "You see, the equation represents where you are in the space-time continuum. When you begin shifting the equation, you can then pop yourself into any time and space you desire. Here, let's practice with something small. Let's move this bracelet and make it travel nearby." He pointed to the horsehair bracelet on Naomi's wrist. "May I?"

Naomi covered the bracelet with her hand. She whispered, "I've never taken it off, since that day."

"What day, Naomi?" Abigail felt strange about prying, but her curiosity took a good hold.

"The day my husband died. He gave it to me the night before. It makes me feel like he is with me all the time."

"Oh my gosh. Naomi, I am so sorry."

Nobody said a word. Desperate to help, Sergius looked around and then took off his shoe. "Would this do?"

Naomi then closed her eyes, put up her hand, and nodded to herself. "No wait. I think I'm ready for this. Here."

The three of them watch in amazement as she reluctantly pulled it off and handed it to Daniel's eager palm. "Thank you, Naomi. I am humbled by your offering. Now, I am going to create a location equation based on this bracelet. Then I will change it to the equation which will place it on Sergius' wrist. Once I've done that, I tap it three times and have the new equation clearly in my mind," Sergius looked down and saw Naomi's bracelet now on him. It was a bit tight and he just looked up and grinned.

"Wow. That *was* really cool." Abigail's eyes got bigger and she focused on the hologram in front of her. The equation was long, yet Daniel explained how to break it down in smaller chunks. He then had them recite it back to each other with a fun game. "I am going to toss a ball to you. Once you catch it, begin reciting the equation. Stop at any point in the equation and toss the ball to the next person. Once they catch it, they will need to continue where you left off. Got it?"

They all nodded and played toss for about forty five minutes. It was slightly stressful, yet they finally had it down.

Daniel was very pleased with his students. "Wonderful work everyone! Now I will show you how to change the equation ever so slightly."

This went on for another couple of hours until they mastered how to make the equations change to different times and places. Sergius finally felt his brain completely full and requested they pick up again the next evening. "I am pretty sure I will dream about this all night. I think I know how to bend this equation as well as I can groom a horse!"

Abigail and Naomi laughed, as Daniel nodded slowly. He turned very serious and said, "I understand. We will meet again tomorrow at the same time. Until then, dream well and begin to speculate how you might locate your inner helices. Even if you have no clue, just allow your mind to get quiet and ask your body to show you, before going to sleep."

They all agreed and shook Daniel's hand. He sent them to their respective homes. They arrived without a hitch. Sergius was especially grateful there were no mishaps this time.

Abigail's dreams were dark. Horses were stampeding over her small frame. Fires were all around. She felt trapped. Voices were shouting with an intense vibration. These voices were in an indistinguishable language and grew louder until she finally woke up with terror. Abigail started hyperventilating, freaking herself out even more. She felt betrayed. She thought her nightmares were a thing of the past since she had met Levidia. *I guess this confirms that the Murmori are still out there.* It took a few minutes before she could focus on her alarm clock. The red glaring numbers read 1:43 am. She sighed and closed her eyes again. She still trembled from the horrible feelings. *Levidia! Where are you? I need to speak with you. Please show yourself.*

Levidia floated through the wall and right next to Abigail's bed. "I know what you would like to ask. I am so sorry that I couldn't be there for you in your dreams. I can't be everywhere at once. That's the real trick of it all. For now, please know that you can wake up and create a more lucid dream."

"Lucid dream? What's that again? I remember Naomi mentioned it before."

"You will feel very relaxed, on the brink of sleep, and then you can just decide where you would like to go. Why don't you try being with Rafi?" Levidia kissed her on the forehead and disappeared.

Images of the buckskin stallion formed in her mind. Her breathing slowed and her energy quieted. He was very glad to see her and they rode around Naomi's facility for over an hour. She finally drifted back to sleep and almost slept through her alarm.

Waking for school was a challenge. She had less and less desire to be there anymore. With the time traveling evening classes, she was putting two days in one. It was taking a toll on her. Her mother noticed, as she could hardly keep her eyes open for her breakfast.

"Abigail, are you going to be all right? I wonder if that concussion has caused you to feel lethargic. Do we need to get you some multivitamins?" Evelyn was growing more concerned about her daughter.

"I'll be fine, Mom. I'm sure I will snap out of it soon."

Evelyn gave Abigail a big hug and whispered, "I can take you after school to visit the horses today, if you like." Abigail smiled widely and nodded. "Oh, that would be wonderful. Thanks Mom!"

It was excruciatingly difficult to focus on what her teachers were saying. She kept daydreaming. She would drift back to the ravine and find Sergius back on the Paint horse. She was surprised by how many times she thought of him now. She was grateful that he smelled better. Especially since Naomi taught him about the magical world of showers.

Then she began to wonder why she was even in school. It felt like a holding place for children to stay while their parents got some reprieve from their constant demands. She felt as if these classes had nothing to do with what life was all about. She wanted to learn more about physics, time travel, horseback riding, and how to impress a certain young Roman. Suddenly she was being called on in geometry class to go to the board and figure out a formula. It looked familiar, with a right angle triangle, but she was unsure and wondered if she would remember what to do.

Then it happened. She had a flash of genius. *Why don't I jump back in time to where my geometry book is wide open in front of me?*

Then the equation immediately started flowing in her mind. *Wait. I can totally do this. It will be a great way to experiment.* From the time it took her to walk to the board and put a piece of chalk in her hand, she went back to last Thursday night, saw her book on her lap, and memorized quickly what the Pythagorean Theorem entailed.

Although Mr. Mattina was most impressed with Abigail's work, he whispered to her at the chalkboard, "Abigail, I could have sworn you disappeared for a second on the way up here."

Abigail retorted as if she was in class with Daniel, "Well, I wasn't sure I remembered how to solve this, so I might have slipped out for a second."

He stared at her dumbfounded but didn't say anything. Abigail suddenly realized she was looking at a human teacher and not her angel guide. She quickly slumped back into her seat and thought, *Whoosh. That was a close one!*

When the bell rang, Mr. Mattina asked Abigail to stay after class. His C student was suddenly doing A+ work. He was convinced she had cheated somehow. "Abigail, listen, I don't think anyone else noticed but me. All the kids seemed to be texting secretly under their desks. I am trying to make sense of what is happening here. Are you sure there isn't something you want to tell me?"

Abigail shifted her weight back and forth and hugged her books closer to her body. She looked down and softly said, "I'm not sure what to tell you. I could try and explain, but I don't think you will believe me. Maybe one day." As soon as she said that, she knew she mistakenly amplified his interest even more.

"Abigail, tell me the truth. How did you do so well on the board? Did you happen to look at someone's work on your way up there?"

Oh, that's what he meant. She took a moment to come up with a story. "So, um, I've actually been working with a tutor. He's been really helpful."

He stared at her for a few moments. She attempted to look innocent. Being a seasoned teacher, he was quite adept at knowing when his students were lying. He wasn't convinced, but dismissed her anyhow.

When Abigail got home, her parents were waiting for her at the kitchen table. Her father started the conversation, "Hi honey. Listen, we need to talk. We got a rather unusual phone call from one of your teachers today. He asked if you were working with a tutor. Why would you lie? Is there something you want to tell us?"

Evelyn couldn't hold back, "I thought we agreed on no more secrets. We've never had a teacher call about you before. Abigail, honey, please tell us what's going on."

Abigail sat down and dropped her book bag on the floor. She let her head rest on the table for a moment, as her parents exchanged concerned looks. Nervously, she replied, "I don't know if I can tell you what's going on. Even if I did, I don't think you'll believe me."

"Is it drugs, boys, stealing, anything like that? Am I getting warm?" Evelyn was grasping at straws.

"No, no, it's nothing like that at all. It's just that, well. I have been chosen to do something, um, well, very special. That's all I think I can say right now. Please don't ask me to explain anymore. Just know that it is all good, really."

"Chosen? Abigail, who chose you? You aren't being lured into a cult are you? Do you even know what a cult is?" Albert was getting very distressed.

"Seriously, Dad? No way! I'm fine, really. Don't you guys trust me? I'm still your daughter who loves horses, reading, and wandering in the woods. I'm just not prepared to explain the latest events of my life. Can't a girl have some privacy?"

Evelyn jumped up from the table. "Sure, privacy is one thing. But seriously, Abigail. I'm really worried."

Albert took a moment to observe his daughter. He noticed she wasn't behaving like a typical rebellious teenager. She had a certain sadness that he couldn't put his finger on. He wasn't sure how far he could push her, before she never spoke to him about anything. He decided on a compromise, "Since this was the first time this has happened, we're going to let this slide."

Evelyn glared at her husband. "Albert, she needs to understand this is not acceptable."

He didn't waiver. "When you're ready to tell us, please know we are here to support you."

Evelyn stomped off to her study and closed the door a little louder than she intended.

Abigail and Albert stared at each other in silence for a few minutes. Tears began to stream. Albert hugged his daughter and finally said, "Honey, we really are here for you. Let me know if we can help in any way."

Abigail nodded, wiped her tears, and scooped up her backpack. She headed for her bedroom and decided to quiet say under her breath, "Dad, I found the answers you've been looking for. It's all possible."

He spun around and turned his head sideways. He hadn't heard what she said, and didn't want to upset her further, so he just responded with, "I love you." Abigail waved softly to him and shut her door.

Once in her bedroom, Abigail sighed, sat down, and thought, *Well, maybe doing time travel while in school wasn't such a good idea.*

Briggs appeared as soon as Abigail had that thought. "Abigail. What were you thinking?"

"I am so sorry, Briggs. I really thought it would be a useful tool, you know, to practice."

"I am quite sure Daniel would be disappointed to hear about this. Didn't he make it clear that there are real dangers to dabbling in time travel without having your equations perfected?"

Briggs paced Abigail's tiny room. Her head was brushing the ceiling, as she racked her mind to think of something to say. This youngster was crucial to the mission, but she couldn't fathom the gravity of her mistakes. It scared Briggs. This was her last chance for assisting Earth. She finally said, "Abigail. Please know that this mission is of greater importance than you can even imagine. Please don't experiment anymore. Will you promise?"

Abigail was crying at this point. She felt terrible. The pressure was getting too much. She whispered, "Yes, I promise."

Briggs gave her an enormous hug and then floated up and out through the window.

CHAPTER TWENTY SIX

The First

Abigail had trouble focusing. Her fingernails had the intoxicating smell of horses on them. She was grateful that her mother still drove her to the barn, even after the phone call from school. She took another whiff of her hands and then looked over at Daniel, "How do we find these spirals? This hologram is moving too quickly for me."

Daniel walked over to where she was sitting and put his hand on her head. "Close your eyes and breathe three deep breaths. Once you have calmed your mind, imagine tiny spirals inside your body. Once you focus on that image, get them spinning fast, then slow, then move them all around. If you can do that, you have successfully located your inner helices. I know it sounds simple, but this is how it all works. The simple answers are usually the most overlooked."

Naomi was taking notes this evening, making sure she would be able to review throughout the day, in between riding. She didn't want to miss any part of this lesson. She struggled with memorizing all the minute details. She was very jealous of how Sergius was picking it up so quickly.

Sergius did the exercise Daniel described and seemed to be exuding more confidence than ever. A few moments went by and he jumped up impatiently from his chair. "I am most certainly at the ready for another adventure!"

Daniel smirked and shook his head. "Sergius, I really need you to focus on these equations first. If you don't have this down perfectly some very detrimental things can happen. Do I need to remind you that even I made a mistake the first time we traveled? We certainly can't afford to lose you." Sergius looked a bit defeated.

"But I feel like we have been drilling for too long. I can't sit still much longer, Daniel. Let's commence already."

Daniel sighed. He decided that the three of them needed to decompress. "How about a change of subject? Would you like to hear more about my story?"

They all perked up and nodded at the same time.

Daniel continued, "My original form took shape before men began recording history properly, although I'm fairly certain my likeness is painted on some caves in Europe. I was enthralled with all the animals around me. I could have long conversations with the fish in the stream, the birds in the trees, and the weary dogs who would wander near my feet. One day, I saw a herd of horses and was completely spellbound. I had never seen this type of creature before. They were much smaller than today's horses. They were very much like the Fjords you see in modern times. I had the mind to follow them and wonder what it felt to move like them. The more I observed, the more I followed and became obsessed with the idea of moving with them.

They let me get close enough to touch them one day. It was while I was fishing. A mare and her foal were coming up for a drink and I could feel her hot breath on my shoulder. She seemed just as curious about me, as I her. For a few moments, I simply took in this feeling of connection. Then I slowly turned around and placed my hand softly on her neck. I began scratching the crest of her neck and she moved into this feeling to get a better scratch, as if showing me where she needed my hand. It was the most amazing feeling. Man and horse, together in that moment, for no other reason than to simply enjoy each others' company."

Abigail and Naomi had tears in their eyes. Sergius, with a knowing smile, put his hand on Daniel's shoulder. He felt Daniel back in that moment. He softly said, "It is a precious thing, to feel this trust with a horse." Sergius now understood why Daniel was their mentor.

Daniel felt the love from his students and shook his head, regaining his composure. "It was many months of this type of interaction before I even attempted the idea of riding these magnificent beasts. It happened quite by necessity, as we were all running from a predator. The mare and I were having a similar moment while I was on a huge rock. I was scratching her back when we heard something coming from the woods. The herd and I turned and saw a huge mountain lion on the prowl. Without thinking much of it, I slid onto the mare's back, put my arms around her neck and we all took off at a full gallop. We ended up quite a few miles away in the safety of another forest. I slid off of her, still in shock from the fact that I was able to ride her, stay on, and begin to enjoy the feeling of that movement. Then I looked down to see the chaffing on my legs and how my hands were shaking. There was nothing like that first ride. I am sure all of you understand that feeling; although this was I'm sure, a bit more primal than your experiences. At least all of you had the luxury of tack between you and your horses."

Abigail wanted to know more, "What did the mare think about all that? Did she allow you to ride her again?"

Daniel sighed. "No, my dear Abigail. That was indeed my only ride in that lifetime. A little later that month, that predator finally caught up to me. I decided to stay in spirit form for quite some time. When I came back to human form, I jumped forward into time when horses and riders were much more accustomed to each other. I helped a great many horses and riders get more comfortable with their jobs in life, yet always remembered that first ride in the most visceral way."

Naomi stood up, "Daniel, are you really saying that you can remember you past lives?" He nodded.

"Wow. It really is an honor to know you. Thank you so much for being here and teaching us. Like Sergius, I am ready for another adventure, although I do realize all of this information must be processed carefully. I'm finding it difficult, to say the least, to continue with my every day chores."

Daniel spun around and clapped. "Sorry, I get so excited when I think about you three going out on your own. It will happen so much sooner than you realize. I think you're all pretty close to memorizing this equation, correct?"

They all nodded. Sergius decided to stand up and walk around the room and recite the entire equation. Abigail and Naomi stared at him in awe. He was a remarkable human with the most dedicated mannerisms. They both longed for this type of sensibility. It seemed lost in their time period.

Daniel beamed with pride, "Well done, Sergius. You are proving yourself ready! My dear ones, it is time. Tomorrow you will begin. Tonight, I want you to simply dream of your favorite horse. Ask to see them right before you drift off to sleep. This will prepare you."

They left and Levidia arrived to get the update from Daniel. She looked at him expectantly.

He got right down to it. "Hello dear Levidia. They are certainly moving forward well. However, Abigail is still very unstable. She could use a boost of confidence. Naomi has glimmers of joy, but her sadness prevails. Sergius is certainly the most audacious, yet he needs to be more focused. Perhaps a reminder that he is part of a team. Can you bring that out in their dream time tonight?"

"Daniel, you realize keeping the Murmori away from them is exhausting by itself, don't you?"

"Of course. Of course. But I can't do all of this alone. They can only listen to my words so many times. They must feel it in their essence."

"I will see what I can do." She pondered for some time. Her hands trembled and she shook her head.

Daniel put his hands on hers. "Levidia, I have faith in you."

"Oh Daniel. I never imagined that an angel could be so scared."

"Yes, but we are blessed to feel all emotions, even in this dimension. Go on now. Believe you can create what is needed."

She sighed. Then smiled as the ideas came streaming in.

Levidia rushed off to find Rafi, Dotune, and Keeper. She asked for their assistance. Their friends were beginning to find their power, but they needed to expand the possibilities of all that they knew before. She instructed them each to find their designated human and jump into their dreams.

Abigail dreamed that Rafi took her to mountain tops where they encountered more horses. This herd was attempting to relax into the idea of interacting with humans. Abigail telepathically told them they were safe and to trust certain younger humans who were learning how to ride them without pain. They would even experience how to build muscles to become stronger and more secure in their bodies to carry their humans with ease. These techniques were ways to help them create a sense of peace on the planet like never before. She wasn't really sure why she was relaying all of this to them, yet this message came loud and clear to her. Abigail felt she was becoming a new type of horsewoman, destined to show others how to be kinder to these magnificent creatures. She was exuding confidence and joy, finally a much needed shift from the woes of daily school life.

Naomi was completely enamored with creating scenarios for helping others with her darling steed. She could feel Keeper do canter pirouettes under her without her touching his reins. It was a magical feeling indeed. After a few of these movements, small children began to flock and ask her incessantly how she did that. She began to explain her movements in detail. She then stopped herself, as she realized it had nothing to do with technique at all. Naomi laughed out loud and simply told the children she wished it and it happened. She explained further, "If you have joy in your heart, clarity in your mind, and a very relaxed body, all that you dream up will appear. It seems simple, yet you will need to practice. It's just like how you play all day with your imaginations. Never forget that, little ones. It's truly why we're here in this world. People will tell you to stop dreaming, yet they are just jealous. They have sadly forgotten how to create their world. You know this to be true, don't you?" The children all nodded, took hands and created a beautiful circle around the horse and rider. They began walking, then skipping, hand in hand, then broke away from the circle, one by one, as they formed a moving spiral. Naomi laughed again once she realized what they were doing. It was the best dream she had ever experienced. She could finally feel joy in its purest sense. She felt a huge shift happen and she cried in her sleep with happiness.

Sergius and Dotune were leading a herd of horses across galaxies. Sergius couldn't stop feeling the spirals within him and around him even if he wanted to. They were spinning faster and faster. He could feel the adrenaline rush all over him and loved every second of it. They rode through stars and more swirling galaxies, as if they both had huge wings and no regard to the fact that oxygen wasn't available in space. Dream time was handy that way. Sergius was then pulled into Abigail's dream and watched her on the mountains. He then jumped into Naomi's dream and saw the children laughing and skipping. He wondered if they could see him too. He noticed that they felt his presence, yet were too involved with the happenings of their dreams to acknowledge him. He didn't mind. He enjoyed being the watcher, the caretaker, the presence to help his fellow horse lovers.

It was then he had a flash of taking Daniel's job when he decided to 'retire'. He woke with a start and his hands were still in the position of holding Dotune's mane. He stretched out and noticed the sunbeams beginning to drip into the living room. It was a little chilly in the room and he was grateful for the extra blanket at the end of his cot. He pulled it up over his body and simply enjoyed the images from his dream to float up and away into those sunbeams.

CHAPTER TWENTY SEVEN

Shifting

Abigail felt like she was floating along. She knew the time was so close to go on her mission that she could practically taste it. She smiled more and shrugged off any strange looks from her classmates. She even felt herself having compassion for Thomas, the boy who put gum in her hair last semester. He was struggling with reading aloud his book report. He obviously didn't understand the themes.

Although so many of the concepts seemed selfish and abrasive, she did remember how the author emphasized the grandiose notion of never compromising oneself. Thomas was stumbling out his words and basic thoughts about the book. She felt her classmates were worlds away from what she was experiencing. Instead of her old instincts to feel annoyed or bored, she noticed how her heart got bigger and she sent out love to each of them going through their own struggles. *So this must be what it is like. Making the decision to have compassion and connect, no matter what your situation. I wish all teenagers could learn this.*

Abigail smiled widely at Thomas as he went to sit down. He stared at her in disbelief and she felt a sense of pride with how far she had come in her new way of thinking about *everything*.

Naomi's lessons that day were in the same vein. Her adult student was struggling with finding the right timing with her upward transition to canter. Her sitting trot was lovely, her positioning was correct, yet Naomi knew that something internally was holding her back. After the fourth attempt, Darby began to get a little silly and tossed his head, making the student a bit nervous. Naomi motioned for them to meet her in the middle of the arena, "Melissa, take a deep breath and close your eyes for a moment, while I hold Darby. Listen to his breath. Start breathing in sync with him. Now, start to notice what your heart is telling you right now."

Melissa opened her eyes with a quizzical look. Naomi continued, "Really, this will help, I promise. I do believe there is something inside of you that isn't ready for the canter transition on your own. You were fine on the lunge line earlier while I encouraged Darby to step up. Now that you have complete leadership, I wonder if you are nervous about your own power."

Her student began to take deeper breaths, while tears started streaming down her face. "You always know what to say, Naomi. Thank you for that. I think I'm ready now. I must own my power and go for it."

Naomi smiled and waved her off with an enthusiastic fist in the air. Melissa and Darby promptly trotted around, took a deep breath together, and had the most gorgeous, springy canter transition Naomi had seen in quite some time. They cantered around a few times and then enjoyed a lovely cool down walk. Naomi turned around to see Sergius sitting on a rocking chair on the observation deck. They smiled at each other and he bowed his head to Naomi.

Sergius had just finished cleaning out the barn and decided to watch Naomi's lesson. He was so impressed with the subtleties that Naomi possessed as a teacher. With each student presented to her, she carefully shaped the horse and rider combination like moving pieces of clay. It truly was an art form that he felt honored to observe. It felt very much like the dream from last night and he was eager to continue his journey with this amazing horsewoman.

He thought, *Incredible, she really knows how to relate to both horses and humans beautifully.*

Naomi turned around, stared at him and thought, *Did I just hear his thoughts?*

"Sergius?" He looked up in amazement as he realized what had just happened. His mouth flew open and he swallowed a fly.

He started choking and she ran over to him. "Sergius, are you okay? Do you need some water?"

He coughed a few times, threw his hands up, and said, "I am quite well, Naomi." She patted him on the back.

"So did that just happen?"

"You mean, did I hear you? Um, yes. You said I related to horses and humans beautifully."

Sergius was shocked. "That's exactly what I said."

"Whoa. This is unbelievable."

They sat down in silence. Naomi decided to test it on her end.

Thank you Sergius! I love my job.

You're welcome. They stared at each other in disbelief. Then smiled widely, as they realized their telepathic connection had been created.

We have to tell Daniel! Naomi was giddy. She jumped up and grabbed Sergius, practically dragging him along. "Let's go now." Naomi's mind was spinning so fast, she forgot her equation to get to Daniel's. Sergius got there before her, realized she wasn't with him, then went right back. He raised one eyebrow, about to taunt her for being so slow. He noticed she was staring at the ground and must have felt sheepish, so he decided to restrain himself. *Sergius, I totally blanked on the equation.*

Ah, I see. Well, I will recite it again.

Naomi nodded and they arrived at the large door simultaneously. They charged through and Daniel stood up with eyes wide, "What happened? Everything okay? You a tad early."

"We did it!" Naomi started running around like a horse. Sergius laughed uncontrollably at this burst of childlike behavior. Then he just had to join in. They galloped around like crazy and Daniel started to chuckle.

Abigail appeared just in time to see the wild party happening without her. "What's up?"

Naomi cantered right up to her student. *Abigail! Sergius and I figured out how to speak like this.*

Abigail stared at Naomi. She waited for her to say something.

"Well?"

"Oh, you mean you couldn't hear me?"

"No, sorry. Did you say something?"

Naomi's wind was taken out. "Oh, Abigail, I'm sorry. I thought for sure you could understand. Sergius and I...we did it. We telepathically connected. It's working!"

"Oh, that's great." Abigail sat down and looked around the room. She wasn't sure what to say next. Abigail looked longingly at them. She felt completely left out, but didn't want to squash their excitement. She looked up at the ceiling and attempted to hide her tears.

Daniel tapped her on the shoulder and handed her a tissue. She mumbled quietly as she dabbed her eyes, "Thanks." He nodded slowly and turned to the others, "Okay, let's start with the two of you. Practice this communication for a bit. Hopefully, Abigail, you will catch on."

Who was the first horse you ever rode, Sergius?

His name was Cesar.

Really? That seems so, well, obvious.

What do you mean?

Never mind.

And who was the first steed to grace you with a ride?

Her name was Brigadoon. She was a gorgeous chestnut with a flaxen mane and tail. I was eight years old and completely smitten with her.

Sergius smiled and opened his eyes. He then took in the sadness emanating from Abigail. He walked over to her quietly and said, "I know you can do this too. Why not think of us as horses? You are so adept at speaking with them. It would seem this is all the same, would it not?"

Abigail looked at Sergius, now with tears streaming down. "You make it sound so easy. But horses seem to have a clearer connection. When I try and hear either of you, I just get static, like a bad phone line."

Sergius shook his head. He had no idea what she meant. Naomi wasn't about to give up. "Listen, I have an idea. Why don't you start chatting with Rafi right now? Get that connection really strong. Once you do, then focus your heart into mine. I will think of a story for you."

Abigail was intrigued, but didn't want to sound too hopeful. "Well, it's worth a shot." She took a deep breath and connected with Rafi.

Daniel looked around at all three of them. He was relieved to see them finally working as a team. He then brought his attention to Sergius, who kept shifting in his chair. Sergius was clearly nervous and seemed like he wanted to leave the room. Daniel felt his anxiety, walked over and whispered, "What is it Sergius? Can I help you with something?"

He shook his head quickly and looked away. He wasn't sure how to express his fear that Abigail might learn what he was thinking. His cheeks began to burn.

Daniel focused in on Abigail again. "Well, anything yet?"

She opened her eyes. "Not really. I said hello to Rafi. I felt him encouraging me and a little nudge from his muzzle. Then, as I tried connecting with Naomi, I felt a twinge of sadness. Then I saw a hay barn filled to the brim with alfalfa. I figured that was just Rafi giving me a clue he was hungry."

Naomi gasped, "Actually, Abigail, that was my thought. I was sad because I've always wanted to fill my hay barn completely with top quality hay. That's one of my goals for my herd. So far, I can only afford coastal hay."

"Oh, so it worked?" Abigail was confused. She didn't hear any words or know that she even got a message from Naomi.

Daniel put his hand on Abigail's shoulder. "It's a start." He then stifled a sigh. Everyone was hoping they would have moved along faster than this.

Sergius felt the others' confusion. He remembered his dream about being the caretaker and protector. He felt it was time to step up. He stood and said loudly, "Abigail, why don't you try this connection with me. I'm obviously not going to think like a horsewoman. I have many battles to tell and surely, you will hear something quite spectacular."

Abigail smiled shyly. "Spectacular, huh? If you say so."

"That's the idea." He sat down and closed his eyes. Abigail shrugged and did the same. Her heart raced at the idea of connecting with Sergius' heart. She had to calm down. *What am I going to do? I have no idea what to say to him. What if he figures out that I've been thinking about him a lot?*

Sergius scrolled through his most daring adventures in his life. He wanted to find the most impressive one but kept seeing Abigail's face pop in, each time he thought of a different story. He finally thought, *Oh my, she's just so pretty.*

She opened her eyes and blushed. "You really think so?"

He whirled around. "Uh, uh." He knew it worked.

"What did he say?" Naomi was now very impressed that they connected so quickly. "No wait, try and tell me with your thoughts."

He said I am very pretty. Abigail's heart raced again.

"Well, well, well. Sergius! I had no idea you felt that way." Naomi suddenly turned into a big sister teasing a younger brother.

"I didn't really mean for those words to be conveyed." Sergius then looked away. He was very embarrassed. Abigail's heart dropped.

"Oh, so you don't think she's pretty?" Naomi enjoyed making him squirm a bit.

"I didn't say that."

Abigail then sent a clear message to Naomi. *Stop already. This is embarrassing everyone!*

Naomi smirked. "Our emotions are clearly creating a successful connection. Oh my! This is getting exciting. I mean, we can hear each other. Daniel! It's working!"

Daniel applauded. "Congratulations. It is time to move forward." He then had them all hold hands and in unison, to recite their basic equation. The power of them saying this out loud was palpable, so much so that Daniel felt the need to take in quietly how they were feeling. He walked around the three, pausing at each of their heads, noting how their energy was emanating, growing stronger, and rapidly shifting from calm to ecstatic. Sergius was exuding a sense of relief, mixed with pride in how he handled his decision to connect with Abigail. His connection worked out well. Actually a little too well. Daniel hoped these tiny sparks wouldn't distract them from their mission. Naomi was indeed finding a more joyous way about her. He smiled again as he thought of her running around like a wild pony earlier. He then took a deep breath, as he honed in on Abigail's essence. She had gained tremendous confidence with this new telepathic connection. He had even more faith in her than she had in herself. He was also sure that the unexpected compliment helped boost her ego as well.

"Excellent. Now, I realize this might be a challenge, but you will need to bring your energy back to a very calm and focused state. If you get too excited, the equation might become fuzzy in your minds. Since you are charging yourselves with the equation, it must be absolutely clear. You have memorized your equation for coming back here. That is by far the most important. If you forget it, you might get lost. However, the security is in having all three of you travel together. You have each other to help remember how to come back. And trust you will be able to communicate. Try it now, please."

They all gave each other nervous glances, as if suddenly realizing the daunting nature of their situation. Abigail gulped, then squeezed Naomi and Sergius hands a bit tighter. *We've got this. I know we can do this.* Naomi smiled and Sergius nodded. They both heard Abigail. The telepathic connection between the three had commenced. They were now ready for Daniel's instructions.

CHAPTER TWENTY EIGHT

The Mission Begins

Daniel sat down and began to lay out the scene. "This first task will be quite uncomfortable at first. It is unlike anything we have attempted before, yet I have so much faith in all of you."

He tapped the round table until a hologram of a massive sea ship appeared. Daniel whispered as the image zoomed in and they could see who the passengers were. "The year you will be traveling to is 1510. This is at the height of the slave trade off the coast of West Africa. This ship is owned by the Portuguese and is sailing from an island called Arguin toward Senegambia. They bring horses, saddles, copper, tools, wine, and cloth to trade for slaves. The Portuguese then get gold for the slaves, up and down the coast. I know you are already wondering why you are being sent there. This is indeed a dark time for this area and you are to show a select few that there is hope, joy, and love to be found amidst the darkness. Your mission will be completely covert. You will be sent in as slaves who take care of the horses in West Africa. You will know how to speak the language and you will look just like the other slaves in their bodies. This will take some adjustment, of course. The plan is for you to meet with three other slaves and teach them your ways of communicating with horses. Show them how horses can help them find a sense of peace. Invite them to join you. This might take a week or two. Remember, while you are gone that long, it will only be minutes in your time here. Your parents won't realize you are missing, dear Abigail. Naomi, Joe will most certainly continue to watch over your horses. Do any of you have any questions?"

The three of them stared at Daniel, as if all taking a nice sabbatical with Briggs. He sighed, realizing that he had lost, and then looked into each of their eyes for a few moments, sending a feeling of love and hope. Sergius broke the silence, "How are we supposed to know who to talk with and what to say?"

Daniel nodded and looked at Abigail, hoping she would be able to answer this. Abigail's eyes widened, "Who me? Really? Well, let me think."

She closed her eyes, took a few deep breaths and focused in on her heart space, much like Levidia had asked her to do for her very first task which seemed ages ago now. All of a sudden, the answers began flooding in.

There will be an internal glow from each of your new friends. You will be able to feel it in your heart and know that they are ready for a new beginning, a new way of thinking, and a longing for leaving their situation. They haven't lost hope in life. You will see it in their eyes. Simply connect with them exactly the way you connect with your horses; heart to heart. Remember how you learned to speak telepathically. For spirit is spirit. It doesn't matter if it is horse or human form. It is all the same.

Abigail relayed this information to the others. Naomi put her hand on Abigail's shoulder, "I know we can do this. You had confidence before we even knew what the mission was, right? We have come so far. Now we get to really be put to the test and spread our knowledge far and wide. To infinity and beyond!"

This made Abigail laugh, as she did remember watching *A Toy Story* as a child. Sergius just raised an eyebrow. He had no clue as to what they were referring. He was just glad it put Abigail more at ease. The three of them took hands again and listened to the next set of instructions carefully.

Daniel stood up and pulled a piece of paper from his pocket and read aloud a message from Levidia.

"Thank you, dear travelers. You are truly pioneers in this universe. We wish you so much love and light on your journey. Listen very closely to what you need to do: As soon as you find yourselves in your new bodies, take some deep breaths and connect to your heart. Remind yourself who you are and why you have arrived. Then look around and raise your hands above your heads. That way you will be able to identify each other and know how to stick together. Once you have settled into your form, immediately get to work on volunteering to be closer to the horses. Each horse has three attendants. One who provides the food, one the drink, and the last cleans the muck, maintaining the stable area. After making contact with your new prospects, remind yourselves to keep connecting with your hearts and whisper the home equation to yourselves each night. Never forget this. When you feel you have made sufficient contact, you may return back here with them. In that moment, once they agree to come with you, the strings of the Universal Web in that specific area will have a greater possibility of being Re-Connected. Then you will receive your next mission. May you continue to spread light and joy wherever you go! Good luck."

"Wait. What happens if it doesn't work?" Abigail couldn't hold back her doubts.

Daniel didn't want to hear about any more concerns. He was ready for them to get moving, "Oh how I wish you could just be bold and dive in, Abigail. But I understand your need for truth. To be honest, this whole plan might not work at all."

This was met with complete silence. He looked at their faces and watched the color run out. He pressed on, "If this plan doesn't work, I'm honestly at a loss for your answer. It frightens me too much to think of it not working. But my dear travelers, we must all move through our fear."

Sergius knew exactly what to say next. *I will promise to protect you both. Fear not, fair maidens.*

Naomi and Abigail smiled at this sweet sentiment and then were surprised to actually be comforted.

Daniel then said, "Oh and here is the most important thing to remember. You will all need to hold hands for your return. That way you can ensure everyone makes it back. So remember, hold hands, recite the equations, and good luck!" Daniel threw his fists up, over his head with authority.

It was finally happening and they took deep breaths as the new equation was presented in front of them. They started imagining their DNA, their helices within, spinning faster and faster. They studied the equation and allowed it to trickle in through their minds and into their bodies. A spiral in front of them appeared, they stepped in and they were swooped away.

Daniel sat down and let out a huge sigh of relief. He tilted his head back and whispered, "They're on their way, Levidia. Please keep watch over our young travelers." Daniel saw the faintest glow of white wings rush past him through the window. He knew she would be there, just in case.

Abigail, Naomi, and Sergius felt their bodies tumbling and spinning so fast that they weren't sure what they were seeing or what was going to happen. They wanted to scream, yet knew it would best to remain quiet and relaxed. As soon as they did, the darkness they were in began to part. They were thrust into their new bodies quite abruptly and found themselves in a dimly lit room, packed with other slaves. Some were singing softly, others crying, and some just stared blankly at the sliver of light shining in, examining the sea as it rolled on and on.

As instructed, each of them stretched their arms over their heads. They were divided by two other slaves sitting in between them. They all nodded to each other in acknowledgment, without trying to seem strange. None of the slaves seemed to even notice them, so they felt relieved, then wondered for a moment where these bodies actually came from. Abigail shuddered as she got the feeling that hers was beaten so badly that it had passed away a moment before she popped in. She guessed that would explain why her body ached terribly. She spoke telepathically with the others.

Are you all right? Do your bodies feel as awful as mine?

Naomi's eyes were wide as she responded, *Abigail, I think we just grabbed the dead guys' bodies. I am freaking out.* She started breathing rapidly and rocked herself back and forth, causing the others on the bench to rock and become annoyed.

Sergius went into protector mode. *Naomi, hear me. Try to relax. Breathe. Focus on my words.*

Sergius closed his eyes and began to focus on his heart. *I've been in some terrible situations before, yet this is by far the worst. You will get through this. Imagine you are on an unruly horse. You must remain calm and centered so you don't get bucked off. We will get through this together. It is clear to me now, why we were sent here. This is most certainly a low point in human existence. It would be most impressive if we could shine any bit of hope here.*

Sergius' words soothed Naomi enough to stop her from rocking the bench. Internally, she was still freaking out.

The stench was almost unbearable and the three of them remained in silence, observing, with hands over their noses. The rest of the voyage consisted of conversations between Abigail and Sergius, as they desperately tried to come up with ideas to keep Naomi sane. The ship finally docked a few hours later. Then they heard a noise that made their hearts leap. The sound of hooves were moving above them. Horses were being led out of the ship. The three nearly stood up in excitement, yet caught themselves, remembering they needed to be covert.

All of the slaves were pushed and pulled quickly off the massive ship. Rain clouds began to form above them and the sunlight disappeared. Whispers of fear and confusion circulated among them. Apparently rain storms were very rare.

Abigail suspected it had to do with their jumping into this time and space. She focused on her breathing. She tried to ignore the bruises and stinging pain all over her scantily clad body. She was barefoot, sore, and trembling. *Oh crap. I think we are going to be auctioned off.* Abigail had a minor panic attack that was similar to Naomi's, when they first arrived on the ship. She noted where Sergius and Naomi were in the line, just in front of her. There was more shuffling and pushing as they approached a huge entryway by the port. There were hundreds of slaves, merchants, and animals bustling under the archway of Senegambia. The three travelers sent love to one another, attempting to soothe their nervousness. And then they realized what was about to transpire.

Sergius was the first to be chosen for attending a prince's horses. He nodded toward Abigail and Naomi, whispering in the most respectful way possible that they knew about horses as well. He gathered that he must have caught the merchant in a very good mood as he laughed, shrugged and pulled the two out of the line. They all sighed and gave silent, grateful glances toward each other. Suddenly, another merchant caused havoc, claiming to have already paid for Naomi. The original merchant barked back and they began fighting. Fists flew. All the slaves were pushed and pulled again. The three had no idea where they would end up.

Abigail fell and was trampled upon by the fighting merchants. She yelped and was assisted to her feet by the slave behind her. *Sergius, please, try to calm them. Can you help us somehow?*

Sergius had an idea. He moved quickly to the horses and walked them over to Naomi and Abigail. *Get on, quickly. Show them you know how to ride.*

They did as instructed. The merchants were shocked into silence. They stared at the three slaves and then began bartering for the three together. The original merchant had deeper pockets and won with his bid.

They were required to each lead two horses at a time, following his four pack camels.

They walked for hours on end. There were six others chosen to be part of the caravan. The first three attended to the camels, while the other slaves walked behind each horse, all with their heads down, staring at their feet. They mumbled to themselves. Naomi noticed how the one closest to her was reciting a form of poetry. She was amazed that she could understand the language and feel all the emotions from this sad soul. He looked up at Naomi when she asked his name. He seemed confused, as if they had already known each other for quite some time. "I am called Ibris. Mai, are you all right? Have you forgotten your friends already?" Naomi just shrugged. She brought her attention back to steadying herself between the two skittish steeds.

Ibris continued his quiet soliloquy. *The thoughts in my mind are all mine. The love in my heart will never die. This body I inhabit will fade away. I must continue to pray for better days.*

The trek seemed endless, they stopped only to give the horses some water and fodder that was carried on either side of the camels. The slaves were parched and sucked up the water when they were permitted to drink; after the horses quenched their thirst. The main merchant shouted at them, "These animals must be treated like royalty. If anyone forgets that, you will be killed."

Abigail was trembling by now. She was having trouble communicating to her charges, as she was still acclimating to her own strange body. They seemed to settle down by the third hour, by pure exhaustion she gathered. It was in the fourth hour of walking that she began to hear whispers of them chatting to one another. The bay Barb spoke first: *We will never know the beauty of our rolling greens again. This land is so dry and barren. Do you think we will survive long?*

The gray with the red halter arched his neck and snorted. *No my friend. This is a sad lot. I've heard we have maybe two years at most. There is a deadly fly that bites us and we will never be the same in our bodies.*

Abigail started to cry as she heard them. They both looked at her and wondered what their handler was thinking. She then decided to reach out to them. *I am not as I appear. My dear horses, I was sent from another time to connect with you and your caretakers. I have two other friends here, just like me. We want to give you a sense of hope, love, and freedom if you choose. My name is Abigail Freedman.*

As they heard her, they both raised their heads in unison. The bay continued his conversation with the gray. *Could this really be true? I've never spoken with a two legged before. He seems really beaten up. Perhaps he is simply hallucinating and found a way into our conversation?*

The gray looked deeply into the body that carried Abigail and responded. *I think this one is for real. I have a funny feeling. I am glad we are here together. Although this fate might be a bad one, at least we can be heard.*

Abigail nodded and scratched them both on the necks. They seemed surprised to get such an affectionate feeling and decided to continue the walk in a more relaxed manner.

Abigail looked behind her to see the older man following them. He stared at her with an emotionless face. She wasn't quite ready to begin chatting with him.

Sergius, ever the thrill seeker, decided to connect with all of the other slaves in his vicinity. The one behind him wasn't interested in having anything to do with Sergius, so the camel attendants were Sergius' main focus. They all began to sing an entrancing song about spirits flying around. Sergius thought about how they truly jumped into a most peculiar, yet fitting predicament.

The song started out very quiet and ended in a big crescendo. The merchant didn't seem to mind, since it reminded him of his childhood. He hummed along and hoped nobody would notice.

They arrived at the fringe of the humble palace, with large huts all bunched together. Sergius stood quietly, waiting for instructions, while Abigail began to do a little dance, realizing she had to go to the bathroom and wasn't sure how that was going to work while she held onto the horses. Naomi kept looking from front to back; feeling like having the visual of both Abigail and Sergius would comfort her more during these eerie events.

The merchant began barking orders for three slaves at a time to go to a hut with gigantic buckets in front. One was for water, one for fodder, and the other for manure. "You will bring the horses inside and attend to their every need. Water can be found at the stream we passed an hour ago. Fodder is along the banks of the stream to collect. The manure will be dumped outside the palace garden. You will sleep in the doorways so if they try to escape, they will wake you by stomping on your bodies. That will be the least of your concerns if that happens."

Abigail, Naomi, and Sergius stared at each other, eyes wide, nodding in such a way to reassure each other. This was such a foreign way of life and it truly unsettled all of them to their core.

Abigail was relieved to finally be in the shade with her two new horse friends. Once she felt the other two slaves were settled in, she stepped outside to relieve herself. She was amazed at the ease of peeing while standing. It made her want to giggle, despite all the sadness around her. She thought, *Being in another body was definitely not something I expected for our secret mission.*

Abigail then telepathically chatted with Naomi and Sergius. They all agreed that they should get some rest and begin getting to know the others tomorrow. Once night fall hit, they slept without dreams.

CHAPTER TWENTY NINE

Searching for Hope

Sergius woke up early, before the other slaves. He diligently began brushing the horses with just his hands and softly hummed to them. The other two slaves woke up to this sound and stared at him curiously. After a few moments, they fired questions at Sergius, as if he was a foreigner. "Who are you really? We saw you die on the boat. How did you come to be here with us? We've never seen creatures like this before. How do you know what to do?"

He was at first very annoyed at this inquisition, yet remembered his job was to connect with the others, so it was best not to be on the defensive. Sergius stopped grooming and sat down on the hut floor. It felt cool and dusty. Hearing the horses crunch on their fodder comforted him, as he sensed the slaves' nervousness about him. He wanted to alleviate their fear. Sitting felt to be the most appropriate way to begin explaining himself. He remembered how Naomi did that to help ease Topsana. He took a deep breath and began to speak in their language. "Gentlemen, please excuse my strange behavior. It is true. I did die on that ship. I am a new soul in this body. One that is here to explore different ways of life and to help you understand that there is hope in this world, no matter how bleak our days might be. I have been sent here to help you learn about these horses, for they have magic of their own. If you choose to believe all of this, you can also travel in the way that I did to get here with you both. You can travel, leave this life, and begin anew, if you so choose. You have that power."

The two slaves locked eyes and shook their heads. The next thing Sergius knew, he was on the ground about to be choked out. "What nonsense is this? Did the heat go to your mind, Nkiruka?"

Sergius struggled out of their hold, but was extremely dizzy from loss of oxygen. "Apologies. Really, I am not feeling myself."

"What do you take us for? Do you think we are stupid?"

Sergius realized he came on too strong, "I just created this story to keep myself from being so sad. Please forgive me."

They shook their heads and waited for him to explain himself further.

"And as for these beasts, I feel a strong connection to them. They seem so noble. I wanted to get to know them better."

They weren't convinced. "You have gone completely crazy."

"This might be true, but I beg of you to believe me. I will try and prove it to you." Sergius then jumped up on the horse he was grooming and started asking for a turn on the haunches to get them spinning in place. The other slaves were speechless and now even more terrified.

"Never speak to us again."

Sergius heart froze. He decided to go back to grooming the horses, to help bring him back a small piece of comfort. Neither of the horses seemed to want to chat with him either. He felt completely defeated. He fought back the tears for these strange men, the horses, and himself. He quietly sent a telepathic image to Naomi and Abigail. They both felt his feelings of failure. They were devastated as well. Naomi sent him an image of hugging him. She didn't know what else to do. Sergius responded. *Be sure you don't overwhelm them. I certainly did. That is where I failed. I rushed into this far too brashly. Take your time with your explanations.*

Naomi took his advice and had a bit more luck with her two fellow slaves. The horses suddenly became restless in the hut. The three of them struggled to settle them. As they calmed, Naomi asked Ibris if he would be open to talking to her about where they came from. Ibris looked at her in a quizzical way, "Mai, you really have lost your mind. Of course, I will remind you. Perhaps then you will come back to us."

Ibris recounted how they used to play as children, being quite

154

mischievous by stealing the girls' toys in their village and hiding them on the rooftops. Once the girls discovered the location and climbed to the tops, he and Ibris quickly moved the ladders away. The girls were trapped until they promised to give them relief from their evening chores. It was a wild game that they loved to play often. That is, until the girls smartened up and decided to find long sticks. Once the boys hid the toys on the roofs, the girls climbed on each others' shoulders and reached up with big sticks to knock their toys down. Then they chased the boys with their sticks. That ended the game. Naomi, in Mai's body, let out a huge belly laugh. "Well, those girls were quite clever. What did we expect?"

Ibris simply nodded and continued to stare at Naomi. He noticed how his friend felt so comfortable around the big beasts and wondered where that came from. He then had a flash of an image that Naomi was attempting to send to him. He stood up and backed into the corner. He whimpered, "What are you, really? Is Mai even still alive?"

Naomi walked over confidently and put both hands on Ibris' head to calm him. "Ibris, please don't panic. I come from another time and space. This is Mai's body, but my name is Naomi. I hope you can understand that I mean you no harm. I am here for a very specific purpose. If you like, I can explain more. If this frightens you too much, I will be quiet from now on."

The other slave, Folami, glared at the two of them with his mouth wide open. He had never met either of them and really thought they were both crazy. He wondered if they put on this show to avoid the reality that they were trapped in this harsh life.

Naomi attempted to make eye contact with Folami. He quickly looked away and shook his head. She turned away and realized that Ibris was her best bet for connecting the dots in this strange world.

Abigail was getting to know her two horses. They seemed very receptive to her and it gave her an idea. *Naomi, Sergius, I think I will try and convince these horses to come back with us, along with the humans. That way, we can be sure to have a larger source of positive energy, since Sergius was unsuccessful.*

She decided to share with the horses all about Daniel, Gavrantura, and the other horses she had met so far. She was lost in a telepathic conversation, when suddenly the other slaves grabbed her on either side and started to hit her on the arms. She was so taken aback by this shocking onslaught that she shrieked. They were yelling at her, "Who are you? What is going on here? Why are you acting like this? Why are you treating us like you don't know us at all? We are your brothers. We are always in this together. Your mother would be ashamed that you're ignoring us. Snap out of this trance and talk to us already!"

They threw down her already incredibly sore body and she gasped for air. She whimpered and looked up at them with tears in her eyes. "Forgive me. I am not myself. Seriously. I am not who you think I am. I am going to give you all the truth I know. Once you hear what I have to say, perhaps then you will understand how I came to be here."

Kayode and Kwame put up their hands as a sign of resignation. They waited for Abigail, in the beaten and tired body, to begin her story. She told them all she knew, beginning with how she met Rafi, Levidia, Joe, Naomi, Sergius, Daniel and now them. It took her quite awhile to explain all of these stories, yet time was all they had, in between the long walks to fetch water, fodder, and dumping manure. As they listened, they grew quieter. They finally left her alone and told her to go back to talking to the horses.

While Sergius continued his quiet ways, the other slaves in his hut continued to ignore him. Sergius decided that not all battles could be won, especially with trying to convince them about his wild adventures.

One evening, Sergius had trouble falling asleep. When he finally did, he was in for a shock. He dreamed of riding Dotune through a battle field.

What is this pure energy? The Murmori had found him. They began fighting over who could drain his energy first.

Sergius was leading an army to glory and about to finish his last conquest, when he caught a glimpse of his enemy charging him. He gasped when he realized it was Abigail. She had a fierceness he had never seen.

Where did he come from? We've never felt such strong, clear, ample energy before. We must know how to get more.

A blood curdling scream came from the crazed young woman, as she swung her sword towards his neck. His head flew off and he could see the ground bouncing in front of him. Then hooves came toward him to stomp on his bleeding head. He could feel pain and then he was floating around, looking at all the other bodies Abigail was angling for next. He wanted to throw up, but couldn't.

Drinking from his essence is intoxicating. We will remain here all night.

The two slaves in Sergius' hut began shaking him. He was moaning so loudly, the horses were getting antsy. The slaves didn't want to get beaten for causing a stir in the middle of the night.

Sergius gasped as he came out of his nightmare. He couldn't get the images and feelings out of his head. There was no way he could go back to sleep. That morning, he was exhausted and shaken. He had to connect to Abigail. *That was the worst night of my life. The dreams were so vivid and brutal. I couldn't escape.*

Abigail was gathering fodder for the horses as she heard this message from Sergius. She cried immediately, feeling how lost he was. *I think the Murmori found you. I am so sorry. Those nightmares are the worst.*

Abigail, I understand now what you have been dealing with.

I guess they are getting more powerful and figured out how to find you, now that you're in their time and space.

Please know that I am even more committed to defeating this evil. I will do whatever it takes to assist on this mission. I'm at a loss for words now. I am unsure of the path to take us to victory.

I wish I had an answer for you, but I am hopeful that Kayode might be willing to come back with us. Also, Naomi mentioned last night that Ibris was open to listening to her. Have faith.

Abigail would randomly relay a story to the other slaves as they did their chores. There were moments when they even laughed, as they attempted to take in all of these fantasies that their once brother, now supposed strange girl spirit, was relaying. Kayode was the first to speak one evening, about a week into hearing all about her stories. "So, Miss Abigail Freedman. What is it that you are here to do, exactly?"

Abigail was shocked to hear her name come from this man. *I think they are really beginning to believe. Oh boy. Now I need to figure out what to say next.* She sighed and looked deeply in Kayode's eyes. He smiled. He had once told her that his name meant, "he brought joy" and she thought this was quite fitting given the circumstances. Although she was fluent in his language, she still struggled with how she wanted to convey her message. She started, then stopped, then started again. "Well, Kayode. Thank you for hearing me. I would like to know if you care to join me on this journey? My friends and I are going to help humans and horses in all different parts of the world, from different time periods, to search out joy, peace and find their inner strength. Does this interest you?"

He looked at her again, studied his brother's body, and reminded himself that it wasn't his brother any longer. He closed his eyes and said. "If there is a way out of this mess we call a life right now, I would love to believe you. But I simply don't. I have only been listening to you this whole time to stay distracted. You are wonderful entertainment, but you can stop pestering me now."

His brother, Kwame, was not interested in hearing more either. He frowned, clearly still missing his brother and walked outside to leave the two of them alone with the horses.

Abigail yelped out. "What? Oh no. Oh no." She really thought she had him convinced. *How could I have been so stupid. He's been playing me this whole time.*

After two weeks of trickling in her stories, she thought she had felt sparks of excitement coming from Ibris. One day his eyes glazed over from hearing yet another tall tale. She had just finished telling him how she learned to speak to the horses through her young student. "Mai, it is time you stop this foolishness. If you continue telling me you are this Naomi woman, you might as well stop speaking. My brother is dead to me."

Naomi was crushed. Her hope was washed away in one statement. *Oh Abigail, Sergius, I have failed.*

Sergius covered his face with his hands. He sent back this idea, *Ladies, I believe we have worn out our welcome in this land. Let's meet in Naomi's hut tonight. It is centrally located and we can discuss our next steps. There must be another way.*

They agreed to meet. They had to find a new course of action.

They each tried to sneak out and before they knew it, all three were quickly tied up and brought outside. One of the slaves had alerted the soldiers about this meeting. They were not about to allow an uprising.

Bound by their feet and hands, whips and shouts echoed in their stinging ears. They screamed and begged for the pain to stop. Abigail's horses broke loose from their bounds in the huts and jumped in front of the whip holders. They too were beaten as they desperately tried to protect their new friend. Abigail was able to send one last message to her horse friends before she lost consciousness. She sent them a visual of how to connect with Rafi. Her last thought focused on the hope that they understood. She couldn't bear the thought of leaving them behind.

The beatings lasted an hour before they finally came to a halt. Tears, blood, and groans were the only things left in the others' consciousness. Abigail had passed out completely.

They woke the next morning, barely able to move. Once untied, they were expected to carry on with their chores. If any of them were to digress, a repeat of the nightmare from the previous night was guaranteed. They decided it was hopeless. They just needed to get out. Sergius sent an idea to Abigail that they should all use their equations separately to bring them back to safety at Daniel's castle.

We should really make haste. I believe the sooner we escape, the better our chances are of continuing these missions. Otherwise, we may forget why we came here in the first place.

Abigail was numb. *I can't believe this is happening. I sure hope the horses figured out how to connect with Rafi. My only hope is that they can help move along this mission somehow. I don't really remember what I even said to them.* Although she was still shaking, she asked what Naomi thought they should do. Naomi couldn't fathom how this was feasible. *Don't you remember that Daniel told us we had to hold hands first? I do agree that we have to get out of here! But we must get together somehow.*

Abigail panicked. *Naomi, there's no way we can find each other now. We just have to go it alone. We can do this. We've come so far already.*

Naomi was still nervous, *We really don't have a choice, do we? Let's go.*

Abigail took a deep breath and recited the equation. In that same moment, Naomi did the exact same. Sergius followed suit and hoped it would work.

Naomi made it back to Daniel's without a hitch. She looked around. The other two weren't there. She looked up at Daniel in a panic. "Where are they?"

Daniel shook his head and motioned for her to sit down. "Naomi, I can't talk right now. I need to get in contact with Briggs and Levidia. Please, just rest here for a bit."

Naomi wasn't keen on sitting around. "No. Daniel, what the hell is going on? How could all of you let this happen? I am done playing around here. Do you realize we were almost killed back there? We were beaten senseless."

Daniel closed his eyes and scrunched up his face as he heard the anger pouring out of Naomi. He whispered, "I am sorry. I don't know what else to say. This mission is more perilous than any of us could have imagined."

Naomi shook her head. "I'm going back home. I need to be back with my horses." *I don't know what I would do without them now. They're my only true friends. They deserve better than this. Maybe I can find a way to help them once I'm home.*

Daniel lowered his head, "Of course."

Naomi wanted to punch the walls. Instead, she took a deep breath and headed back to Willow Tree.

CHAPTER THIRTY

Caught in Limbo

Abigail and Sergius felt the familiar spinning from the spiral. They expected to be back with Naomi and Daniel but found themselves in darkness. They could hear the Murmori reverberating in their minds. They both started to shake. *We have found the travelers. We can keep them as our trophies. I wonder how many others we can find next. These two are incredibly strong. But not for long. Soon we will have their entire essence within us.*

Abigail spun around and couldn't see anything. She could only hear their words. *Sergius, can you hear me? Where are you?* She heard nothing for a few minutes. The Murmori were keen on listening to her speak. Then they responded. *Ah, you have learned how to communicate in the same way we do. Well done, young one. You will soon become one of us. The drinking is nearly complete.*

She couldn't let this happen. After all they had been through. *Sergius please. Say something.*

I am here. Sergius appeared in flashes, three times around Abigail. One right in front and two on either side. The flashing got faster and it was as if he had been cloned. *Which one are you?*

Sergius didn't respond. All three reached out for her. Abigail's neck hairs stood up. She wanted to curl up and pull covers over her like a child. Only she wasn't in her bed. She was in the dark, swirling around a strange dimension. *How can I trust any of this?*

Levidia's first test suddenly popped into her consciousness. Abigail took a deep breath and focused on her center, where she discovered that original golden globe of power. Once she concentrated, the other two Sergius clones drifted away slowly. She reached out to the strongest image of Sergius and grabbed his hand tightly. *Breathe into your center. Recite the equation again.*

The Murmori shouted now. *NO. WE ARE LOSING THEM. GET BACK HERE!*

Sergius and Abigail found themselves breathless, lying across the round table next to Daniel. They had returned to safety.

Daniel hurried over to them and wrapped them both in blankets. "Thank goodness. You made it."

CHAPTER THIRTY ONE

Fast Moving Guide

Angels could lower their frequency for only short bursts, in order to observe the events on the Earthly plane. The manifestation of an angel was easier, when closer to their original human time line. The farther back in time an angel went, the more energy it took. Levidia had witnessed just a small portion of the African mission. She met up with Briggs after Sergius' encounter with the Murmori. She knew it wasn't looking good.

Briggs was distressed. "Levidia, I don't think you saw what happened after you left the travelers."

"Oh no. What is it?"

"They were separated before they could travel back and were beaten endlessly. Their spirits have truly been trampled upon. We almost lost Abigail completely."

Levidia wasn't prepared for this additional setback. She put her hand on Briggs' shoulder to steady herself. "Please tell me that they are all right now and back at Daniel's."

"They are indeed."

"What about the strings? Is there still hope for that area to be Re-Connected?"

"No. That mission has failed miserably."

"Will any of this be possible?" Levidia's voice shook. She couldn't bear another failure when they had already come so close with these new Re-Connectors.

"I don't know, Levidia. What other choice to we have?"

Levidia nodded and thanked Briggs for her support. She then flew off on Prometheus and fought back the tears in her eyes.

CHAPTER THIRTY TWO

Back to Safety

Abigail took one look at Daniel and Sergius, then collapsed on the floor. Daniel whispered, "You are safe now."

Abigail had an overwhelming sense of betrayal. She couldn't keep it to herself any longer. Although exhausted, she had to speak, "Daniel, why were we left to be beaten? Why couldn't you or Levidia or Briggs swoop in to help us?"

Daniel sat down to collect his thoughts. "I am sorry Levidia could only be there for a short time watching you. We can't be everywhere, all the time. Otherwise we wouldn't have called upon all of your assistance in the first place."

"A great help we were. We totally failed."

Sergius looked at Daniel sternly, "And we were caught in limbo. Did you know this? Why did you not assist there?"

Daniel turned his back to them and hid his tears. "I knew that you were just caught in limbo. We were certainly blind sighted with that as well. You know Briggs couldn't help there. Otherwise she would have been discovered. I am incredibly impressed that you got out, before we found a solution. You see, you are gaining more power."

Abigail wasn't interested in praise. "We've come so far only to be pushed into despair. I just don't get it. Why should we continue any more of this?"

"You are showing more bravery than any of us could have ever imagined. What you have been through has been no easy task. Sometimes, it is necessary to experience extreme depravity to appreciate ecstasy. This first task was the hardest on you physically. You deserve some time to just relax. We will need to regroup to figure out what in the world to do next."

Sergius gave Daniel a concerned look. Abigail couldn't stop crying and yelped, "Seriously? Don't any of you really know what's going on? If we're going to do any more of these so called missions, I want a guarantee we will be safe."

Daniel quickly ran over to Abigail and put his hands on her knees. She kept looking down as he repeated these words. "My brave young traveler. Please forgive me. Please forgive all of us."

She looked into his desperate eyes. She searched for any hint of forgiveness within her. She wasn't sure if she could muster any.

"This is an experimental mission. There are many lives at stake here. If you don't continue, the Murmori will conquer all of humanity. Please hang in there and forgive our mishaps."

Abigail sniffled as Sergius came over to comfort her. He put his hands on her shoulders. She let out a whimper and then said to Daniel, "There is nothing in the world I want more than to stop those nightmares and keep the Murmori at bay. I just wish I knew we were better protected."

Daniel stood up and silently nodded. "I am deeply sorry for your anguish. Please accept my apologies and know that I will do whatever I can to keep you all out of harm's way. But these are dangerous missions, to say the least. Don't lose heart. Please. You've already proven you could survive the worst."

Abigail found herself back in her bedroom. It felt extremely strange and yet overwhelmingly comforting all at once. She flew open her door and rushed out to see who was home. She had no idea what time it was and just wanted to see her parents again. She gave them the biggest hugs she could muster, while they exchanged curious glances with eyebrows raised. Her Mom whispered, "Abigail are you okay?" She just held on tighter and whispered back, "Yes, I am now."

Sergius was positioned outside of Willow Tree Farms' gate. He ran to the house. Joe was sitting on a rocking chair reading the latest

166

Practical Horseman. A teapot began to sing. Joe looked up to see a distressed Sergius. He put a cup in front of him and patted him on the back. "No need to be saying a word. Just rest there, son."

Sergius only had a few sips of tea when he decided to commune with Dotune.

Naomi was outside, regaining comfort from her herd. Keeper was the first to greet her. He nickered loudly and she gave him the biggest hug around his neck. He brought his massive head around her and hugged her back.

Dotune has just relayed some good news, Naomi. Abigail and Sergius did make it back safely. In fact, Sergius is already in your home.

Oh Keeper. Thank you so much for telling me. She cried into his mane as she hugged him tighter. She then turned around and jumped for joy. She saw Sergius making his way to the pasture. *You were right, here he comes!*

Sergius gave Naomi a big bear hug. They didn't need words in that moment. They were just grateful to be where they were. Dotune then trotted up to his friend and gave him a nudge on the arm. Sergius simply stared up at his dear friend, with silent tears in his eyes and whispered, "It is so good to see you." Dotune nudged him again and playfully nipped him on the hip. He spun around and galloped off, sending Sergius the message. *Sergius we have been on this journey for a long time. Prepare yourself for more. Rest well.* Sergius nodded slowly and followed a relieved Naomi back into the house.

They found sleep easily and awoke grateful that the nightmares did not come. Joe dutifully fed all the animals and prepared a brunch of omelets, muffins, and a fruit platter. They ate slowly and enjoyed hearing the horses outside.

"Naomi, do you think we will be able to continue?" Sergius was thinking about Abigail more now, especially with her outbursts upon returning. "I mean, I have the strength, but Abigail is really shaken and angry. How are you?"

Naomi didn't know how she was. "Sergius. This whole adventure has totally messed with my mind. I can't tell what is true or real anymore. I am glad to be back home and with my horses, but, I am not sure how much more of this I can take."

Sergius nodded. "I understand. Really. I'm hesitant to tell you what happened on our way back. But I think you should know. Abigail is the one who saved me from the Murmori. I believe she is the key to succeeding in this mission. We will need to find a way to convince her to keep going. Even if you decide to be done with it all, perhaps you can at least help her?"

Naomi studied Sergius' pleading facial expression. She realized he had found deeper emotions on this journey. She admired his perseverance. It inspired her. She sighed and quietly responded, "Yes. I will continue to assist. You and Abigail are so dear to me now. My thoughts last night when you weren't with me turned to such despair. I couldn't bear it if I lost you both."

Sergius hugged Naomi, feeling like he had just found the older sister he had always wished for. There was a undeniable mutual respect and admiration between them.

Sergius whispered, "We are enduring a multitude of painful experiences."

Naomi nodded and thought about the physical pain. She cringed as she realized it was nothing compared to the heartache of missing her late husband. Pain was so normal to her at this point. However, she was very adept at hiding it. She thought that Sergius had probably seen his fair share of loss in his life of duty and stewardship in Rome.

Naomi suddenly looked at her watch. She realized she was going to miss her first lesson. She was about to jump up to grab her phone when Joe put his hand on her arm. "Little lady, don't you worry about a thing. I put a notice up that lessons were postponed for this whole week. I wrote something about you having to go away for an unexpected family emergency. It's time you learn how to do some real relaxing. I've got this covered."

Naomi nodded, yet had trouble wrapping her mind around how she was going to pay for the next feed bill coming up in a few days. As if reading her mind, Joe walked over to her phone, and told her to open up her banking app. She plugged in the password and looked at him in shock as she saw her account had three times as much as it did when she left. "How did this happen?"

Joe shrugged. "Beats me how it's done. 'Suppose when you're working on these higher frequencies, your basic needs are automatically accounted for. Special type of manifesting, I reckon."

Sergius smiled at her. He was beginning to realize how much modern people were seemingly troubled by so many things he couldn't begin to comprehend. He was relieved to know that Naomi could be comforted as she continued on this journey with them.

"I can't imagine how I might assist you any further. But please, Naomi. Let me know how I can help here. This must be the most challenging part of all. Keeping your wits about you in this world, when you've now experienced such different ones."

"Thank you, Sergius. I think you have a better idea than you know. Although I'm beginning to think I shouldn't have looked through that looking glass."

He looked at her quizzically.

"It's a reference to a book. I think it's on my shelf. Although, I wouldn't recommend it right now. We've got enough on our minds."

He simply nodded and went outside to clean stalls. With every pile he threw in the wheelbarrow, it allowed him to filter out his negative thoughts and find a sense of peace.

CHAPTER THIRTY THREE

The Confession

Levidia and Daniel shared a bottle of wine at the round table. Levidia let out a nervous laugh. "This mission is certainly tricky, to say the least. I'm afraid I let the travelers down. I am at my wits end to try and make it up to them."

"Not only that, but Abigail and Sergius were caught in limbo with the Murmori. Did you know about this?"

Levidia covered her eyes with her hand. "Yes. Briggs told me."

"Isn't it a miracle that Abigail saved Sergius?"

She took a long sip of her wine. "Truly. Why do you think Abigail succeeded?"

"I've noticed a certain spark between the two."

"Maybe that's what we're missing, Daniel. A deeper bond. They need to feel more physically connected. The horses know about this, but the humans, well, they haven't felt it yet."

"Levidia, I think you're on to something. Whether it could be more, I'm not sure."

"How shall we fuel that fire?"

Daniel poured Levidia the last of the bottle. He looked up for a moment, hiccuped, and his eyes twinkled. "Let me make a suggestion. What about a party in their honor? That might help them form a deeper connection."

Levidia placed her hands on the table and stared into Daniel's eyes. "Brilliant. I will send the invitation right away. Let's hope that is the answer. Thank you, Daniel."

"You're most welcome. In the meantime, I will scan the planet for other possible strings. I have some ideas, but I would like to chat with

Briggs first for confirmation. There will be many pieces at play."

"Thank you. I sure hope you come up with something. I am drawing a blank and I fear Briggs will not be here much longer. The Murmori are so powerful now, they might discover her string."

"I know. Levidia, I will do my best. These three are certainly the best Re-Connectors I have ever met, but they need to raise their spirits back up if they are to succeed. This party idea might be the ticket. Joy is one of the main ingredients for this recipe."

"I will make the arrangement now."

Daniel watched as she gathered up her silvery shawl and walked back over to Prometheus. They were off in a lightning flash.

The alarm blared for awhile before Abigail could even understand who she was, where she was, and what that crazy sound was coming from above her head. She opened her eyes to see her father standing over her. "Abigail, Abigail? Are you all right? Your Mom and I are very concerned. This alarm has been going off for ten minutes. You're going to be late for school. Are you sure you can go? Do you need to stay home today?"

Abigail wiped her eyes after hitting her alarm clock harder than she was expecting. She sat up and mumbled, "Dad, oh, my, yes, um. Could I please stay home? I am having, actually, some really weird feelings today. I think it might be a girl thing. Do you mind? Where's Mom?"

"She's in the kitchen. Abigail, what's happening? You look like a wreck. Last night got us worried with the way you ran out and hugged us so tightly. It seemed like you are in some sort of trouble. We can't go anywhere until you tell us what's going on."

He grabbed her by the arm and sat her down at the kitchen table. Evelyn looked at Albert with concern, then stared at her daughter, and waited for an explanation. She had insisted that her husband help get to the bottom of her mysterious behavior.

Abigail's heart raced as she tried to decide if she should really tell them everything. *I could have been lost forever last night. I think I better tell them in case I never come back. I can't hold back anymore. They are my parents after all. What's the worst that could happen if I tell them?*

Albert looked concerned as he watched the turmoil in his daughter's eyes. "Come on, Abigail. Please tell us now. We know something is up and we need to know exactly what it is. No more secrets."

She took a deep breath and just let it all spill out. "Well, I have no idea if you're going to believe me or not, but here's the short version. I've been selected to be an adventurous time traveler, who communicates with horses on Earth and from another planet. I have two dear friends who have joined me on this journey. I've been traveling a lot and that's why I was so tired this morning. Please don't freak out. I'm sure you guys must think I'm nuts by now, but I promise you, it's really happening. It all began just a little bit before I started riding at Willow Tree Farms."

"Who are these friends?" Evelyn wanted to know who was filling her daughter's head with such nonsense.

"Sergius. He's um, an exchange student. And, well, Naomi. My riding instructor."

"What? Albert, get me her number. We need to call her right now and read her the riot act. I thought we could trust her. Why would she lead Abigail down such a rabbit hole?"

Albert stood in shock. He didn't know what to say but started walking toward the telephone.

"Wait! You guys. Seriously. Please don't call her. Please don't."

They stopped for a moment and stared at her. Evelyn shook her head, "Why shouldn't we call her? Are you lying about all this? What are we supposed to believe?"

"Mom, Dad, let me prove it to you. Please. At least give me the chance to show you that I'm not crazy. Just give me a few minutes in my room. I promise you will understand after this."

Albert and Evelyn shrugged. They had never seen Abigail so determined. "Fine honey, go ahead." Albert gave Evelyn a sideways glance and wondered if she was going to agree as well.

"You have five minutes. And then we are calling Ms. Naomi Drake."

"Mom, I will be back here in three. Promise." Abigail scurried off to her room.

Evelyn and Albert sat down and waited in silence. They weren't quite sure what to say. Evelyn was nervous that her daughter was having a mental breakdown and wondered if it had anything to do with her recent concussion. Albert was equally concerned, but thought very deeply about their recent conversations. He then had a flash of her inquiry several weeks back. *Could it be?* He was ever so hopeful that time travel existed, but then wondered if all of his stories over the years had imprinted on her. Perhaps she conjured up these grandiose notions as a form of escapism. *What if all of this was my fault?* He was nauseous.

Abigail closed her bedroom door. *What am I going to do? Think, Abigail. Think.* She jumped on her bed and covered her face with a pillow. In the darkness, she focused on her breathing. An idea began to trickle in. *Observe them when they first met. Find that club they always talked about. Figure out exactly what they said to each other. Yes. That's it.* She immediately went to work on an equation where she could spy on her parents.

She was whisked away to New York City, where her father played the guitar in a band for the summer. It was 1995 and the club was called CBGBs. She then saw her parents flirting with each other. *Whoa. Dad looks so weird in that flannel shirt and long hair.* She heard every word.

"Can I buy you a drink?" Albert leaned closer to Evelyn.

"I'll have a Cosmo." Evelyn looked past Albert, trying to keep her cool.

Wow. I've never seen Mom wear her hair like that. She looks gorgeous.

"So what are you doing the rest of your life?"

Seriously Dad? What kind of cheesy line is that?

Evelyn chuckled. "Well, I was planning on being the top groupie for Bon Jovi, but I'm keeping my options open."

Albert tried to keep a straight face. "Why not be my groupie?" As soon as he asked her this, his trembling hand dropped his drink all over Evelyn's top.

Smooth move, Dad!

"I'm so sorry. Here, let me help." He grabbed the first napkin he could find. Unfortunately it was full of salsa. Now her breasts were soaked and ready for some tortilla chips.

Oh crap. Dad. That is so embarrassing. Look what you did!

Evelyn's face turned red and she pushed away Albert's hand. "I've got it. Don't worry. I'll be right back." Evelyn jumped up and ran to the bathroom. As Abigail rushed past her Dad to follow her Mom, she overheard him say something interesting.

"That is the woman I am going to marry. Just you wait and see." His drummer pat him on the back. "Go get her, tiger. That is if she'll still have you after being such a top notch dork."

Abigail pushed open the bathroom door. It smelled putrid. Her eyes watered and she slipped into a stall before her Mom even noticed her. She overheard her talking to another woman as she rinsed her shirt. "I can't believe I met the man of my dreams in this dive. I just wish he had shorter hair. That grunge look just isn't my thing." The other woman hiccuped and leaned over the sink. "Honey, anything's possible with enough imagination."

Evelyn pushed the door, left and Abigail came out to pretend to wash her hands. The woman was still standing at the sink and looked her over. "Aren't you a little young to be here? And where did you get those shoes? Wow. They are so cool." Abigail looked down and realized she was wearing a pair of barefoot running shoes. "Um, right. I'm just passing through. Oh, these shoes are specially made for me. Maybe you can order them in the future." The woman raised her eyebrows. "The future huh? Have you been watching reruns of Quantum Leap?"

Abigail had no clue what she was saying. "Sure, that's it." *I need to get out of here.* She had enough evidence to make her parents understand this was for real and recited her equation as she ran back into the stall.

She bolted out of the bedroom after two minutes and forty five seconds. She blurted out, "Remember CBGBs?"

"Of course. We've told you about that club many times." Evelyn wasn't impressed.

"Well, Mom, you ordered a Cosmo. I had no idea you drank those."

"Lucky guess."

"Sure, but then you guys never told me that Dad spilled a drink on you. Let alone the salsa."

Albert's eyes got bigger. "You promised to keep that a secret, Evelyn. When did you tell her?"

"Albert, I would never embarrass you. I still haven't told anyone. Only your drummer knew and he died before Abigail was born."

They both turned back to Abigail. "Hey, I've got more for you."

"Mom, then you ran to the bathroom and you had a chat with a lady in there. You said you couldn't believe you had met the man of your dreams in a dive like that. And..."

"Okay, that's enough. I get it. Don't say another word."

Albert cocked his head. "What?"

Evelyn then realized she needed to hear if Abigail truly knew what came next. "Well, I guess you can go on." She nervously put her fist to her mouth.

Abigail then realized that her Mom never told him that secret wish. "So, I was going to say that you hoped he looked a bit more refined. Right?" She winked at her relieved mother.

"Oh and then the lady by the sink said anything was possible with enough imagination. The restroom in that club was really gross by the way.'"

Evelyn stood up and paced the kitchen.

"And Dad, you were so cute. You told your drummer you were going to marry Mom. He then said, "Go get her tiger." Albert and

175

Abigail said it in unison. His mouth fell open. "And then he called you a top notch dork."

"Wait, what? Albert, you never told me that."

"It's true. All of it."

Her parents were stunned. They looked at each other with tears in their eyes.

Abigail took the lead, "So, are you guys freaking out? Are you able to go to work? Talk to me. Will you be okay?"

Evelyn stood up and quietly gathered her belongings, too afraid to look at her daughter. "Abigail, I'm going to need some time."

Albert hugged Abigail. As he leaned over, he whispered, "This is really something. I need some time to digest the ramifications of all this. We will have to talk more about it later."

He floated out the door. *My daughter just time traveled. She just saw my younger self. What if things change forever now? How will anything be the same again? My daughter is a time traveler. My daughter just time traveled. Oh my god.*

Abigail knew this was quite the ripple in her family dynamic. She was the most grounded in the moment. "Be careful today. I am sorry to scare you, but you needed to know. I love you guys."

As Albert walked out the door he calmly stated, "Get some good rest. I will call you later to check on you."

Abigail watched him leave and then put her head on the table. *Whoa. That was a close call.*

CHAPTER THIRTY FOUR

The Invitation

She went back to bed and slept for another four hours. Her home phone rang several times before she stumbled out of bed. She expected to hear her father's worried voice on the line. Instead she heard this. "Ms. Abigail Freedman is respectfully invited to attend the Festival of the Hawk and Crow Feathers this evening. Will she be attending with an escort?"

"Excuse me, who is this? What?"

The caller cleared his voice. "Beg your pardon, madam. Please see the formal invitation on your kitchen table with all the details. I am simply the messenger." The dial tone was all Abigail heard after that. She turned around with the phone still in her hand to see a shiny black and brown envelope sitting haphazardly next to the pile of mail. She picked it up and saw it was indeed addressed to her. As she opened it, she caught a glimpse of something flying right in front of the kitchen window. She looked up to see ten hawks and twenty crows all dispersed amongst her backyard. Abigail decided to sit down to read the invitation. She thought, *Wasn't this supposed to be my resting time?*

The invitation read:

Ms. Freedman, you are cordially invited to the
Festival of the Hawk and Crow Feathers.
Please dress in your most formal (yet comfortable) Earthly attire.
You may bring one guest with you.
Meeting point: Your hammock
Time: After you have gone to bed this evening,
get up and go outside at precisely 3:14 A.M.

Abigail sighed. She was still half asleep. She closed her eyes and tried to imagine what this festival party thing was all about. Then her thoughts drifted to Sergius and her stomach flipped. She hoped he would go with her, but wasn't sure how to ask him.

Sergius and Naomi were still in their pajamas, lounging in the living room, when Abigail called. Naomi jumped up, startled at hearing the phone ring, and smiled brightly when she saw the caller id. "Abigail! How are you feeling? Did you just wake up?"

"Hi Naomi. Whoa. Seriously. I've never felt this tired in my life. Yes, I woke up just a few minutes ago. Naomi, um, I actually had a strange invitation. Um...I was invited to a party. There were very specific instructions. Well, it said I could invite just one person. I'm not sure what to do..." Naomi nodded a few times and then smirked.

"Hey! Abigail has something to ask you!" She quickly handed over the phone.

He looked at Naomi quizzically and took the phone to his ear. "Hello Abigail. How are you?"

"Hi...Sergius, oh. Um...Listen, I have something to ask you. I just received a mysterious invitation to a festival. It said I could take an escort." She hesitated, then continued. "Would you like to join me?"

Sergius' heart began to race as he considered what this would mean. He nodded and then realized Abigail couldn't see him. He was, after all, still getting acquainted with modern technology. "I would be delighted. How shall we proceed?"

He could hear Abigail sigh and she explained the strange time and place they needed to meet. He agreed to dial in his equation to meet her at 3:14 AM and not a minute earlier or later. They both hung up the phone and felt their cheeks burn.

Naomi watched the young man float back down to the couch and put his feet up. She suddenly had a rush of memories come in of her late husband and longed for him deeply in that moment. Naomi shook her head as if to help her snap out of this feeling and told Sergius she was heading out for a quick ride on Keeper. Before she walked out, she turned and said, "You know, I think I have some old suits left in that back closet. They were more of my husbands' clothes. I think they will fit you well for your date."

He looked up with eyes wide and asked, "What's a date?"

Naomi stopped dead in her tracks. She turned around and sat down on the couch next to the young man. "Well, it means that two people who like each other, decide to do something together. You know, so they can see how much they enjoy each others' company."

"Oh, I see. And that will lead to a marriage ceremony?"

Naomi laughed and then promptly stopped when she saw the seriousness in Sergius' eyes. "Not exactly, Sergius. You see, in these times, most people can date for weeks, months, and years. Some don't even choose to get married. It's all about what feels right for each couple."

"How peculiar. Then how do you know if you own your woman?"

"You never own a person, Sergius! At least not in this time and space!"

She shook her head and reminded herself how different he really was. She tried to calm down and explain it rationally, without getting too emotional. "Listen, our world is all about people being equal, making their own decisions about their lives. This includes women, Sergius. We don't have to be sold or forced into marriages anymore. At least not in mine and Abigail's culture. With that in mind, please remember she is very young. Younger in her mind than I am sure most of the women are, where you come from. Take it slow and don't expect too much. Do you understand?"

Sergius nodded slowly. "This really is a strange time. Thank you for your advice, Naomi. Enjoy your ride. I think I will take a respite."

Naomi patted him on the shoulder and quietly slipped out toward the barn.

Even though her body was moving at a snail pace, Abigail could hardly contain her inner excitement. Just moments after she hung up the phone from confirming Sergius, her father called to check on her.

She sounded flustered, which didn't help him think she was doing any better.

"Abigail, do you need me to bring home anything? Your mother mentioned as we were leaving, that there are some leftovers in the fridge. Please eat and rest some more."

"Thanks Dad. How are you doing at work?"

"Trying to keep my cool. Abigail, this is some pretty wild stuff to take in."

"I know Dad, believe me. See you later. Love you."

Abigail hung up and went into her room to ransack her closet for clothing. She really had no clue what to wear. She wasn't ever one of those fashionable girls at school. She was always content to wear jeans and a simple shirt or sweater.

She stared at the possibilities and decided on a long black layered skirt with a turquoise button down top. She remembered getting a pretty belt for her birthday last year that she hadn't even tried on. It ended up going quite nicely with the two pieces she picked out. *Maybe I won't look so bad after all.*

Abigail struggled with the realization that something had to be done with her hair. Leaving her frizzy curls down felt too cumbersome and her now go-to ponytail felt childlike. She went into her mother's bathroom and found a scarf she had admired for quite some time. She took it and wrapped it a few times. She created a beautiful headband to show off her face. It allowed her hair to be halfway pulled back. This felt like the best compromise.

At dinner, her Mom wasn't sure what to say to her. Her Dad had called earlier to say he was going to be late, since he couldn't wait to discuss time travel with his physics buddies. Abigail decided to create a distraction. "Mom, you know that scarf hanging in your bathroom? Do you think I can borrow it?"

Evelyn seemed happy that Abigail was taking an interest in changing her look, knowing this was inevitable with a teenage daughter. She nodded and smiled at her.

"So how was work today, Mom? Were you able to focus? I know

this all must seem like such a shock."

"Actually, honey, I was trying not to think too much at all."

"Sorry Mom. Listen, I won't talk about it anymore. I realize you are pretty freaked out. Just know that I love you."

She stood up and hugged her, then headed back to her bedroom to leave her alone. Evelyn half smiled and walked slowly, as if in a trance, to her study.

Abigail laid out her clothes for the evening festival next to her bed. She could hardly wait to go to sleep. Carefully, she set her alarm to radio mode on the quietest setting to wake her up at 2:50 am. She didn't think it would take all that long to get ready. She dreamed about showing Rafi where the gray and bay were located.

Abigail almost slept through her alarm, as it was quietly crooning Cyndi Lauper's "Time After Time," an older pop song she had heard only a few times, when her parents had command of the radio. As she sat up in bed, she smiled and realized how fitting that song was. She flipped on her desk lamp and got dressed. After setting up her hair, she slipped into the bathroom to brush her teeth and put on some lip gloss. She looked at the time and it was 3:11. Her heart skipped a beat and she sneaked out the back door.

Sergius appeared right next to her hammock at 3:14. They awkwardly fist bumped each other, then leaned over, not sure if they should hug. Sergius lost his footing as he swooped down and grasped at Abigail's arm. He caused them both to fall into the hammock. They grinned shyly and held onto the netting, unsure of the next step. As it began to swing, they were pulled into a vortex. It was a bit dizzying at first, yet they felt comforted knowing they were together. The hammock disappeared and they were in front of a dark building with feathers adorning the doorway. They heard music playing inside.

Sergius grinned widely and looked Abigail over. She looked incredibly beautiful and he wasn't sure how to express it. He simply grabbed her hand, squeezed it a bit tighter and leaned down to kiss her on the cheek. She looked away and smiled all at once.

Sergius motioned toward the door, held it open for Abigail and said, "Shall we?"

Abigail blushed and then stared into his dark eyes. She felt her stomach do a few flips. He looked dashing in his suit. She walked through the threshold and only then realized they were holding hands. She smiled up at him and looked around to see the most peculiar people and creatures dancing all around. There were hundreds of tables set up, with food and wine and every kind of bird feather imaginable. The crows and hawks that Abigail had seen outside her window were now flying above her, shooting back and forth from decorated tree branches, to awnings, and trapeze swings. It looked like a bird's paradise. Sergius, still holding Abigail's hand, turned to her and asked, "Ready to dance?"

"Um, sure. I've never done this before."

"Neither have I. But I'm willing to take a chance. Are you?"

"Oh, well, okay..." She swayed to the music, but didn't know what else to do.

He looked around at the other dancers. He imitated the way they moved and started in on the steps. He whispered. "Abigail, let me take the lead." They moved in a disjointed way at first. "Relax, Abigail. I've got you."

As soon as he said that, she took a deep breath and they began moving effortlessly around the dance floor. They paused occasionally to dodge flapping wings.

Sergius leaned over and whispered in Abigail's ear, "What kind of festival is this again?"

Abigail raised her eyebrows and shrugged. As if they all heard him, the music stopped. A hawk landed on Sergius' shoulder. "Welcome Ms. Abigail and Mr. Sergius! Tonight, you will celebrate with your feathered friends. Sergius, you were the first to travel into the future for this journey and we are deeply humbled by this gracious act of courage and thoughtfulness for the beings in this universe. Abigail, you were the first to escape the Murmori's hold and were even able to save your Sergius. We were astounded by your efforts. So, without further ado, we would like to dedicate this evening to you both.

Please, dance with us some more and try and fly if you dare."

The music began playing again. They twirled and laughed for a good hour. Finally, after pure exhaustion, they were guided to watch a short demonstration of how to fly. Abigail remembered her training with Levidia and decided to have a go. She closed her eyes, imagined herself floating upward, and engaged her inner core power. She opened her eyes to see Sergius still holding her hand on the ground. She felt like a helium balloon floating above him. "Come on, Sergius. Go for it!"

He laughed and as the joy filled his body, he was amazed that he began floating up with her. He looked around, felt a moment of disbelief, panicked and promptly fell on his behind. Abigail rushed down to his side. Sergius grabbed Abigail's arms and brought his face close to hers. They kissed while the birds flew every which way above them. Feathers flew down and began to cover the lip locked couple. Sergius couldn't believe where he was. It felt like a dream that he never wanted to wake from. Abigail forgot all of her sadness, nervousness and worry. Time stood still and she was in heaven in that moment.

CHAPTER THIRTY FIVE

Naomi's Fate

Sergius could still taste Abigail's lip gloss when he woke up on the cot in Naomi's house. He licked his lips, rolled over, and felt a warm, tingling sensation. He had never been in love before. He thought of Abigail and himself in the distant future and wondered what was in store for them. He took a deep breath and noticed a faint sound of galloping. Sergius jumped up and looked out the window. He was still fully dressed and although a bit crinkled, his clothes still looked just as dapper as the middle of the night. *Sergius. Get out here.* Keeper beckoned him outside. Sergius saw all the horses running back and forth along the fence line. Something seemed wrong. His heart dropped. Naomi was lying on the ground, not moving.

As Sergius ran toward Naomi, Keeper explained what he thought had happened. *I am so sorry. I spooked when I heard two new horses running around in the far pasture. Naomi flew off before I could steady myself underneath her. I am so so sorry.*

"Sergius, oh my goodness. That happened so fast. When did you wake up? Did you see what happened?" Naomi spoke quickly but still hadn't moved.

Sergius shushed her and assessed the situation. "Naomi, can you feel your toes?"

Naomi immediately began to panic. She couldn't. She felt numb everywhere. She took a deep breath so she wouldn't pass out and then the tears began streaming. Sergius wasn't sure if he should try to move her. "How do we get assistance?"

"Oh. Okay. Here's what you need to do. Pick up the phone inside and press the buttons 9-1-1. Then explain you need an ambulance at

Willow Tree Farm. The address is 114 Manor Road, Greenville." Naomi struggled to get the words out. She was getting freaked out more than she expected. This was scarier than being in the strange body in Africa. Now she was in her own body, but she couldn't feel much of it.

The ambulance came ten minutes later. Sergius sent a telepathic message to Abigail, who then grabbed her parents to drop her off at the barn. It was a Saturday, although all the days felt like they were folding into themselves. Abigail arrived just minutes after they took Naomi to the hospital. Naomi insisted that Sergius stay behind and help Joe with the horses. She would call later when they knew what was wrong with her.

While Abigail's heart fluttered at seeing Sergius that morning, she was too panicked about Naomi to let that distract her. She looked at Sergius and asked, "Do you think she will be able to walk again?"

Sergius couldn't hide his worry. He stared at Abigail and let his tears well up. His silence was extremely profound and Abigail threw herself into his arms and they hugged for a long time. She finally whispered, "Naomi will be okay. She is strong. She's been through so much. Besides, no matter what, she's learned how to time travel and jump into other worlds. Perhaps she can go back and erase this completely?"

As soon as these words came out, Levidia came circling down from the sky. "Abigail. Sergius. Come with me. It is time to meet with Daniel again right now. He will show you how to help Naomi."

Abigail shouted. "How could this happen to Naomi? I thought I made it clear that we were to supposed to be watched over. No more danger!"

Abigail was about to throw a fit, but Sergius put his hand on her shoulder. This calmed her enough to allow Levidia to scoop her up.

They gulped as Prometheus began moving. He was so big it seemed like there was room for at least three more people on his back. His wings flapped diligently and they spiraled up to the clouds. Abigail was wedged between Levidia and Sergius and couldn't stop her mind from racing. *I still don't know why this happened with Naomi. Don't we have enough to deal with already?*

Levidia heard these thoughts and hushed her. "Abigail, please listen. This had to happen, just like your fall from Jasper. There is an experience Naomi has to have. This was our idea. Really. Trust that we have thought this through. We believe this is the key for success, so please don't be cross with Daniel or myself."

Abigail got very quiet and let her tears stream. She leaned back against Sergius and he held her waist tighter.

They finally jumped into a cloud and found themselves just in front of Daniel's building. As Sergius and Abigail slid off the magnificent beast, Levidia told them to be brave. She also knew what Abigail was thinking. "I need to go find Briggs now." And off she flew.

Naomi lost consciousness on the ambulance ride. She drifted into a dark place. She found herself in a room with a young girl, pacing around, trying to figure a way out. Just as Naomi was about to speak and ask why the little one was so nervous, she froze. In the corner was the most intense beast. It looked at first like a horse, but it had enormous ram horns. Its eyes were round like marbles, practically popping out of its head. The eyes were the darkest black she had ever encountered. Her stomach turned as she realized it was about to charge them both.

Instinctively, she jumped in front of the child, in hopes to protect her. As soon as the beast was about to make contact with Naomi's body, it reared up, started pawing the air and flipped over. It then became more crazed as it struggled to its feet. Naomi and the young girl now cowered in the corner together. They had no idea how to get out. There were no doors. Just four white walls and the three of them trapped inside. Naomi was surprised to find that she wasn't bleeding or bruised, just shaken. Then she realized the beast was just as afraid. She took a deep breath and started talking to him, just the way she had learned from Abigail.

You are safe. We are not here to hurt you. We will figure a way out of this.

The beast started running in circles, and then charged each wall, attempting to break through. It kept looking back at Naomi. While its eyes made her repel, she could feel a softening develop in its body. She hoped she had gotten through to it. The little girl was grabbing a hold of Naomi so tightly that she lost feeling in her right arm. She finally looked down to examine her face closely. It was tear-streamed, yet clearly looked like her younger self. Naomi gasped and blacked out again.

Daniel had Sergius and Abigail sit down and reassured them that they needed to proceed with assisting Naomi. He taught them a breathing technique to alleviate their worry and connect with her.

"Take a deep breath through your nose for a count of seven, filling your belly. Pause for three seconds, then exhale through your mouth for a count of ten. Pause for two seconds and repeat six more times. While doing this, allow everything around you to get quiet. You can even close your eyes and appreciate the entire universe as you breathe. Now, as you do, imagine Naomi in perfect health. Send her this image and your love."

Naomi jolted back to wakefulness as she felt this energy coming at her in the form of an energetic hug.

She looked around the hospital room and felt very foggy. The doctors stood over her and asked her many questions. She finally blinked a few times and began to form words. "Yes, I can feel that. No I can't feel that. Wait. No, I do feel a tingling." She closed her eyes again and trying not to panic, focused on sending love back to Sergius and Abigail. She fell back into a deep sleep.

CHAPTER THIRTY SIX

Home Planets

Abigail and Sergius felt a rush of love from Naomi and they instantly knew she would come back to them. They looked into each others' eyes and got completely lost for a short moment. Daniel cleared his throat. The smitten ones quickly looked away and shyly smiled. Daniel began speaking before any more awkward moments could transpire.

"My dear friends! I realize this has been a harrowing experience, to say the least. However, we have concluded that we must press on. A new mission has been developed. We are anxious to hear if you would even consider partaking on this next quest. And if so, would you like to wait and see if your Naomi will be joining us?"

Abigail's eyes narrowed, "We *must* wait. I have faith she will be back. Really, I don't see why we should go on without her?"

"Yes, Abigail. I agree. However, it is most important that we continue on as quickly as possible. As you know, the Murmori have discovered Sergius. I can only speculate that they have figured out that they might be challenged. They are accelerating at an alarming pace. The amount of nightmares Levidia has reported is dismal, to say the least."

Abigail shuddered. Images from all of her night terrors began popping in her mind. She grabbed Sergius by the hand and attempted to focus on his strength. It surprised her how fast that worked. She felt his love pouring into her hand and it washed away any fear she ever had. As she held his hand tighter, she felt a pulse that reminded her of a drum beat from her favorite song. She got lost in the moment as she hummed along in her mind. Then she stuttered, "Serg, Sergius.

Whoa. All I had to do was hold your hand. The scary images dissolved instantly. Daniel, there's got to be something to this."

Daniel nodded, "Ah. Now you're on the right track."

"Maybe that has been the key to this mission all along. The physical sensation of love."

Sergius kissed her on the cheek and whispered, "I've just thought the same." Abigail felt goosebumps down her neck.

Daniel chimed in again, "My dear travelers, please listen carefully. The Murmori are counting on humans to forget what it is like to fill themselves up with love. They came in during times of war, slavery, and despair. They figured out how to dismantle the strings of the Universal Web. All they had to do was foster the fear and chaos during those times. They've created a subconscious notion in humans that they are designed to suffer and feel pain. Their nightmares reinforce this notion. Every time they create a strong terror, their force field around Earth gets larger. If you can somehow inspire others to feel love within themselves, a revolution can truly be had."

"Abigail. You were able to save me from the Murmori. I know you can do the same for others." Sergius squeezed her hand tightly, then kissed it softly.

She blushed and then stood up. "Daniel, I've been too afraid to ask this until now. But, where did the Murmori come from?"

"Ah, that my dear, is the very scary part. They are from everywhere. Any being that has passed on can choose to become an angel, like Levidia, Joe, and myself or...like the Murmori. They come from every planet. Earth, however, has the most. These dark spirits thrive in numbers. Unfortunately, they are very good at recruiting new spirits. Their power is intoxicating. I've brushed by them on occasion, in between lives. I can't honestly say that I hadn't considered joining them. But do you know what stopped me every time?"

"What?" Sergius was intrigued to hear this. He was shocked to think that Daniel could have switched over to the other side.

"My connection with horses. This is why you were all chosen."

189

Abigail was equally shocked. "Whoa. So our love of horses are the true weapons against the Murmori?"

"Precisely."

"But how are we supposed to use that to our advantage?"

Daniel stood up and met her eyes, "Isn't it obvious by now? Talk to your horses. They will teach you. Learn from them and then, perhaps, you will have more confidence to continue. We are putting our faith and trust in you three. Go back to your horses, now. Once you find out their unique message, we are hoping you will be able to continue on the next mission. Good luck."

Sergius and Abigail went back to Willow Tree Farm and meandered around the paddocks. Joe greeted them and wanted to cheer them up. "Hey, how was the festival? Did you two love birds have a fanciful time?"

They looked at each other, then back at Joe. They both blushed and nodded. Abigail spoke first, "It was a wonderful time."

"Yes, it really was." Sergius grinned like a young school boy.

Joe then quietly walked alongside them. Abigail started thinking more about everything that had just happened. Last night's festival reminded her of a dream she once had. She felt compelled to tell Sergius in that moment.

"I was ten years old, and had fallen asleep quickly that night. My dreams were stranger than I had ever felt them, but in a good way. They were crystal clear, familiar, and comforting. I often had the worst night terrors with freaky voices waking me up. But this dream was so beautiful that I even woke with tears in my eyes from happiness."

Sergius was eager to hear more and motioned for her to continue. She whispered, "I was told that I was going to visit my family; my real family, on another planet. I wasn't even scared or surprised in my dream. I was taken back in a wormhole-like tunnel, with misty starlight all around, just swirling. When I landed, I was inside a circle. Creating the circle were six huge beings, over seven feet tall, all cloaked in robes that looked like crow feathers. They welcomed me with such love and gratitude. I never told anyone about this dream until now. I think it's all beginning to make sense."

Sergius' eyes welled up with tears, as he suddenly remembered a similar dream when he was about the same age. He looked around and quietly began, "Well, this just brought back a rush of memories for me as well. It was very similar, only the beings around me were short, about five feet tall and they were cloaked in hawk feathers."

Abigail closed her eyes and leaned again the fence. They all stood in silence for a few minutes. Joe broke the silence, barely being able to contain his excitement. "Did y'all know you're talking about home planets?"

They stared at him blankly.

"Now think about that festival you attended. Quite profound, wouldn't you agree?"

"What do you mean?" Sergius wasn't connecting the dots.

"Abigail, Sergius, listen closely. Those dreams were little memos from your past lives. I'm speculating they arrived on your tenth birthdays, to let y'all know they was still watching over ya. That's just about the ripe age for learning about such things."

He proceeded to explain how Earth was the original meeting point for many beings in the universe. Often travelers would get lost or confused, yet were always allowed to go back to their home planets when their missions were complete on Earth.

"But with the strings dismantled from the Universal Web, that just isn't possible anymore. Without those there strings, other beings just can't travel to Earth. Y'all have been summoned to work as a team, to Re-Connect all the strings. That way you can become ambassadors for your home planets."

Abigail's eyes began to get heavy.

Sergius quietly asked, "Are you all right? Please don't fall asleep right now."

"Oh, Sergius. I can't just can't seem to keep my eyes open."

Sergius tried to open her eyelids. She giggled. "No really, it's fine. I just need a little nap."

"But there are too many questions left unanswered. What about Naomi and the mission? Do you think she will be able to join us?"

Abigail yawned, then mumbled, "Sergius, I think I am about to find out." She passed out in Sergius' arms. He brought her into the house and let her body rest on the couch. She fell into dream time quickly. Briggs was waiting for her.

Abigail Freedman, I must get you to the next door quickly. I am glad you honored the message of taking a nap.

Abigail felt Briggs' large hand assertively take her arm and whisked her away to a long corridor. She looked up at Briggs and smirked. *I really didn't have much of a choice. It was as if someone pulled the plug to my energy source and I simply had to sleep.*

Briggs didn't respond. She was clearly on a mission. She found the door and ushered Abigail in. *Now go through and don't you worry about a thing. Remember, you are powerful beyond measure. Never forget this. I will see you soon, I am sure.*

Abigail pushed through a large wooden door, with tons of moss growing around it. She stepped out onto a huge, plush green meadow. Beyond the meadow was a forest. Abigail continued walking toward it. There were hundreds of beds hanging from tree limbs, all covered in shimmering lace. She was drawn to a willow tree and there was Naomi, lying peacefully in that specific bed. Before she got closer, Abigail noticed how many bodies were in all of these beds. They were not all humans and noticed a few cats, dogs, birds, and even iguanas. Abigail tried not to get distracted by the strangeness of all this and instead focused on her beloved friend and trainer. *Naomi. I am here. Briggs brought me here. What can I do to help you?*

Naomi didn't move. Instead, the lace surrounding her body began to shiver and puffs of smoke encircled Naomi's body. Abigail got a little nervous as it was getting harder to see Naomi's face. She worried that she might not be alive anymore. *Naomi, please! Let me know you are here with me.* The smoke drifted up and Naomi's hands moved a little and that was all Abigail needed for reassurance.

As Abigail watched the smoke, an idea washed over her. She sent this message to Naomi.

Naomi, do this. Imagine your body in perfect health, hovering above you. Study it, thank it, and then allow it to merge back into your body. This is called your perfect, healthy blueprint that was assigned to you at birth. You can simply call it in and remind it to bring you back to wellness.

She then took her hand and thought of all the riding lessons this dear woman had offered her. Abigail filled up all of her memories and love into her hand. She hoped that would be enough to bring her fully back.

Naomi got the clear message. *My perfect blueprint? What in the world?* She decided to take a deep breath and listen again. *Interesting. This is something I never would have thought of. I wonder how many people know about this. Wait, I need to focus. What did she say again?*

Naomi tried to remember. The thoughts trickled back in. *Imagine my body in perfect health above me. Got it.* Her blueprint began to crystallize over her and it shined like the brightest stars in the night sky. Overwhelmed with joy, Naomi realized just how divine her body really was. She then wished everyone on Earth could experience this knowledge. She took some more deep breaths and sent immense gratitude to this image floating above her. She then invited it to merge back into her. It settled in like a nice down comforter on a frigid morning. She felt her entire body tingle and she promptly fell asleep again.

After what seemed like an hour, Naomi coughed and sat up slowly. She seemed shocked to see Abigail.

"What are you doing here? Where am I? Do you know what's going on Abigail?"

As she squeezed Naomi's hand again, Abigail sighed and then whispered, "Well, I thought this was my dream and you just happened to be here. Maybe we are in the same dream together?"

"Abigail, I think the force is strong with us. " They both laughed at the *Star Wars* reference. But that is really what it felt like to both of them. Naomi whispered to Abigail, "You know, up until I met you, I thought I would be content to just teach riding and if I died, it didn't really matter. Now I see that I can make a bigger impact in the world, and even other planets. My goodness! This really is a wild ride."

Abigail turned to Naomi. "Can you feel all of your body parts? Please, Naomi. Please come back with me."

Naomi stared out in the distance. "Yes, of course. Why would I want to get off the horse now?"

Abigail began to stir on the couch. Naomi found herself in the hospital room, luxuriating in the feeling of all her fingers, toes, kneecaps, ankles and oh, hairy legs under her robe. She thought, *I really wish I shaved more often. One of those doctors was really handsome.*

The doctors scurried around her and performed more tests. Then they seemed shocked. The first doctor leaned over and spoke softly, "Naomi, you had a bump to your spine. We thought you might be paralyzed. However you are recovering at rapid speed. It will only be temporary. You are very, very lucky. We will check on you this afternoon."

CHAPTER THIRTY SEVEN

A Slight Delay

Rafi called all the horses over for a conference. He had just finished guiding the two new horses to Gavrantura first, and then back to Willow Tree. It was time to get everyone involved in the final mission.

Dotune, Keeper, Rafi, Brouteen, and Shantoo stood in a circle together. Brouteen's dark mane flipped up with the wind. *Friends. Fear not. I received a message from the elders while Rafi was guiding the two new horses. Our humans are still getting organized, but we are set to go. We will assist the humans on a journey. If we are successful, then more of our benign friends from other planets can join us in these adventures.*

Rafi touched noses with the other three horses while Brouteen relayed her message. He then paused for a moment, taking in this conference with gratitude. *Thank you all for being so willing to do this with me. It is amazing to think how far we have come and what we are about to embark on. Dotune, you were the first. Do you have any words of wisdom before we leave?*

Dotune thanked Rafi for his acknowledgment. *I am quite honored that you asked this. We must convince our human friends that they are magnificent beings. If they can believe in their own power, they can learn to speak with all the other horses in the world. With this connection, those horses can then help humans stay focused on love and light. This will elevate the Earth's vibration and allow for the strings to be Re-Connected.*

Shantoo swished her tail. *Do you really believe they can do this?*
Dotune nodded. *We must try. Are you all with me?*
The other four snorted in the air, with their heads held high. They

were ready for anything.

Abigail wiped her eyes and found Sergius sitting on the couch next to her, rubbing her back. He smiled as she opened her eyes. She leaned over on his chest and sighed. "She's going to be all right."

Joe nodded as he heard this and offered Abigail a small piece of chocolate. Her eyes lit up. "How did you know? Chocolate always makes me feel better."

Joe tipped his hat, "Well, now, you know I've been reading a lot of magazines. Sergius, look here, this is how you keep your little lady happy."

Sergius smirked and then nodded.

Abigail giggled and munched the delightfully sweet morsel. She then stood up with a quiet determination.

Joe smiled. "I reckon you two are eager to visit Miss Naomi. She's at St Daniel's hospital just twenty miles from here. She called about an hour ago, saying she was feeling much better. I'll stay here and keep watch over things."

Abigail laughed and said, "St. Daniel's? Ha! Good one, Joe." She waved to him, mouthed thank you, grabbed Sergius and motioned for him to jump in the driver's side of Naomi's dually. She was eager for him to catch up to her modern ways. This involved pushing him past his comfort zones and learning more about modern equipment.

He stared at her dumbfounded. "Abigail, I don't know how to work this beast of steel. Remember, I'm not of your time."

"Really? Sergius, where's your sense of adventure? I will explain as we go. You are older than me and I only have my permit. If we get pulled over, we can say you just lost your wallet. Easy peasy. Stick with me, mister."

Sergius grumbled to himself and then opened up the passenger side door, helping to launch Abigail's tiny frame into the large truck. He then slipped into the driver's side where the keys were already sitting between them. He stared at the wheel and then back at Abigail. He decided to grab the wheel and shout, "Onward!"

Abigail burst out laughing and dangled the keys in front of him, "Ahem. Sergius, you need to insert this little metal device just next to the wheel thing that didn't listen to you."

He grabbed the keys and tried to figure out where to click it in. Abigail stretched across and got the truck started. "Now, push your foot down on the left pedal and move this stick to the reverse position."

Sergius placed his heavy foot on the gas and revved the engine, causing them both to jump and nearly hit their heads on the top of the truck. "The other pedal!" Abigail screamed and laughed all at once.

Sergius sighed and did as instructed. They began to back up and nearly hit one of the pasture fences. Abigail quickly grabbed the wheel and spun it to the right to position them toward the street. "All right, now push that left pedal down again, move the stick here to drive and then switch pedals."

They bucked forward and started doing sixty miles per hour out the gate. Sergius was frozen in fear and Abigail shrieked, "Slow down, take your foot off the pedal quickly! Please!"

The truck was coasting now and Abigail decided it might be less risk for her to get caught behind the wheel, than for him to continue driving so perilously. She got him to put the truck in park while his hands were still shaking. "I would have conquered this steel beast." He was secretly grateful to be back in the passenger side.

"Oh, I'm sure you would have. Sergius, you are quite the rider."

Abigail had to hold back her laughter from Sergius' nervousness about driving a vehicle. After all they had been through; it was amusing to see this tough young man fumbling so much. They pulled up slowly to the hospital and found a spot large enough to park.

Once they found Naomi's room, the doctors kept insisting that they wanted to keep her for several more days for observation. Abigail suspected they just wanted to increase her hospital bill, since it was apparent that Naomi felt way better and was even walking on her own to the rest room. Surprisingly, Naomi didn't seem keen on leaving all that quickly either. Abigail couldn't figure her out. In their shared dream, she seemed eager to get going again. Finally, Sergius asked her bluntly, "Naomi, is there something here that is holding you back?"

Naomi blushed and actually put her finger to her lips. She motioned for them to sit down and decided to chat with them telepathically.

This is a little bit embarrassing. While I am truly happy to see you both and eager to continue this journey, I've actually been chatting with a young doctor here on and off all afternoon. He even brought me my Earl Grey tea, when clearly he's super busy.

Sergius stood up and squeezed Naomi's hand. "All right then, dear Naomi. Why don't you wait here another night, get to know this doctor friend and just meet us tomorrow? Would that be, um, easy peasy?"

Naomi nodded and giggled as she realized Sergius was learning more of their modern ways of speaking. She motioned for them both to give her a hug. "Gently please. I am still really sore from all this."

They waved goodbye and left holding hands. Naomi smiled to herself, happy to know those two were really a couple now. She was especially excited to see where her flirtations might end up in the next few hours with Dr. Erdene. Naomi leaned her head back on the pillow and sighed. She had not felt like this in a very long time.

CHAPTER THIRTY EIGHT

Riding Lessons

When Sergius and Abigail pulled up to the stables, they were surprised to see Joe had saddled up Dotune and Rafi. He had heard from Daniel that the horses needed to impart wisdom. A ride was in order. He wasn't surprised that Naomi wasn't with them. He already knew where her heart was, after the earlier phone call.

"Daniel has instructed y'all to learn from *your valiant steeds*, I believe he said." He excused himself and went back inside.

They mounted up and began walking around the arena. "What do you think we should do?" Abigail was excited to ride with Sergius.

"Well, I think we just need to get quiet for a bit and simply ask." Sergius closed his eyes and allowed his hips to follow the motion of Dotune's large stride.

Abigail nervously closed her eyes as well and grabbed a chunk of Rafi's mane. She waited for him to begin speaking as she tried to relax in the saddle. Her stirrups were a bit too long and she decided to just drop them as they meandered around.

Abigail. It is wonderful to have you here with me, yet again. Take a few deep breaths and start to really appreciate this moment. How often do you let yourself just relax? Especially now with these wild happenings and thoughts swirling?

Her tears started streaming rapidly. He continued.

Good, good. I can feel your heart opening. It is interesting that the first question you asked when you arrived on my back was, What should we do? What I would rather you think about is What should you be? You need to be confident, powerful, and feeling love from every particle of your body. Sergius has helped you with that, am I correct?

Abigail blushed and rubbed his neck softly. *Yes, yes he has.*

Perfect. Now, keep that feeling tone of love and spread that everywhere in the world. Go on. Start with sending it to me, then Sergius, then Dotune. When you feel it spread, allow it to trickle out to all the horses in the world. Both here and in other time periods.

Her thoughts went back to the horses from West Africa. She sent them love, hope, and appreciation.

Abigail, I am so proud of you. You are doing exceptionally well with this concept. You are a joy spreader and one of the true Re-Connectors now. Breathe that in, my sweet friend. Keep that love exuding from you and anytime you feel anxious, remind yourself to come back to this feeling yet again. In other words, never get off the horse.

Abigail opened her eyes and looked over at Sergius. "Would you like to know what Dotune told me?"

"Of course."

"Horses are filled with pure joy. They are immune to the Murmori. If humans can connect with horses and that joy, they can protect themselves from the Murmori. Abigail, your connection with that joy and these horses is what allowed you to save me from the Murmori."

"That makes total sense. No wonder Rafi was just explaining to me how to find my joy."

"Are you ready to engage in joy at the gallop? These thoughts from Dotune have brought me much exhilaration."

They laughed and raced around together. The horses were just as thrilled as their humans to feel the thunder of their hooves in unison. Dotune was particularly impressed.

Sergius. I am truly enjoying the feeling of showing you what it is like to move like me. This body is a wonderful vessel for spreading love and joy. I understand now, completely, why Briggs chose horses for this mission.

Sergius beamed. *Dotune, you are a very wise being. I am ready to charge forward. Although the Murmori are extremely powerful, I believe if anything can break their hold on Earth, it has to be this connection.*

I think so too. Let's keep this bond strong.

After this first ride, they went to spend some time with Joe in the house. He had prepared a feast of fried chicken, mashed potatoes, and green beans. They ate their lunch quickly and started chatting about their introduction to horses. Sergius began, "Abigail, what were your first thoughts during your initial ride?"

"Hmm...let me think. Something like, oh my goodness, please make my butt stop bouncing!"

They all roared in laughter.

"What about you, Sergius?"

"Well, let me think."

"You mean you don't remember?"

"That's not it at all. I was just a wee lad. My father would hold me while exercising the horses in his charge. I don't remember ever not riding."

"Oh wow. No wonder you are so connected to them."

As they were helping to clean up the plates, a crow began cawing loudly. Abigail ran outside to see it fly over her head and then drop a piece of paper perfectly into her outstretched hand. She ran inside and began reading the Lauren's message.

Congratulations on finding your telepathic connection with humans and horses. Your final mission will involve much riding. It would be wise for Joe to team up with Shantoo. Of course, the others know their steeds, Sergius with Dotune, Abigail with Rafi, and Naomi with Keeper. The eight of you will be assisting a unique herd of wild horses. They are called the Tahki, also known as 'spirit' in the land of Mongolia. The year you will be traveling to is 1925. It is a year where the numbers of these horses are dwindling. They are important to the hearts of the Mongolians, for they are known as the heartbeat of that proud nation that honors horses immensely. In your time, these horses are nearly extinct. Briggs has recently discovered that this area is where the Murmori learned to dismantle the strings. You must find a way to prevent this. Levidia will explain more later. Please have Naomi read this when she returns.

Abigail was breathless as she read and stumbled on some of the words. She wasn't completely recovered from her last mission and this new mission sounded quite daunting. Sergius sensed her hesitation, "Abigail. Remember what you just learned from Rafi. We can do this. The horses will be our guides this time."

This gave her more comfort, but she still couldn't help feeling the butterflies in her stomach.

Joe rocked quietly in his favorite chair. He pondered why he was chosen to go. He knew better than to question the Laurens at this point, but he figured it was getting pretty dire if he had to be included. He wondered if his energy could handle this journey.

Sergius grabbed Joe. "Why don't you come and ride Shantoo now? I think we can all ride around together finally."

"Now you wait just a moment there. I need some more time to finish up with this here surprise."

Sergius lifted his eyebrows, as he took in that Joe was putting together some sort of baked treat. He wondered where Joe got all of his skills to put together such fine tasting food.

"Sustenance is rightly important for all of us, Sergius. You'll find that comfort food can bring us back to a vibration we all need to be in. Especially when that food is done up just right."

Sergius laughed and said he would see him out there. As soon as the door shut, Joe finished mixing up the ingredients and leaned over to look at the recipe he had been hiding on a chair, under the table. It was for an upside down cake. He wasn't sure what that really meant or tasted like, but the photo in the magazine sure was pretty.

This activity helped soothe his troubled thoughts. *I've certainly mastered how to stay in this here time and space for longer than I could have imagined. But going back in time? I don't know how long I will last. Sure hope Briggs has some sort of special magic for me.*

Later on, with the arena lights blaring, the three of them rode around like a drill team. Abigail suggested they do a loop around the property on a short trail ride. They stopped in front of the gray and bay. All the horses whinnied at them as soon as they passed. Abigail took a moment to realize who they were and then smiled widely. Rafi sent her the image of how they arrived safely. She stroked his neck and whispered, "Thank you so much. You are truly a remarkable being." Rafi beamed at the feeling of appreciation coming from his favorite human.

CHAPTER THIRTY NINE

Flirting

Naomi opened her eyes to see Dr. Erdene smiling over her, checking her chart by her feet. She blushed, then quickly said, "Well, if you hadn't noticed, nothing has changed on that chart since the last five times you looked at it today. Well, nothing except maybe one thing."

The doctor's eyes fixed on Naomi's and then he coyly smiled. "What's that?"

Naomi decided to take the plunge. *After all, what is scarier? Flirting or jumping through time and space?* "My heart. It seems to be skipping beats here and there."

They both laughed and he sat down at the foot of the bed.

He paused and then took a deep breath. "Would you please do me the honor of going to dinner with me next Saturday?"

Naomi was speechless. She thought *Well that was direct. What should I say? I have no idea if I will even be in this century next week.*

"Dr. Erdene, I would really love to..." She hesitated.

"I think I hear a but coming on. Perhaps I should get you a bed pan?"

Naomi's mouth opened wide and then she got the joke. "Oh my, that was a good one. No, seriously, I am flattered. I'm just not sure where I'm going to be next week. Would you please give me a few days to get my body back in order and I can get back to you?" As soon as she said those words, her cheeks turned red, realizing it sounded a little funny. She looked away and laughed.

Dr. Erdene then said, "Please, call me Alex. Of course. You need to rest and get your life back on track. Let's do this. No phone calls. You can meet me here at the hospital next Saturday night at 7:30 pm. There is an amazing restaurant around the corner that I would love to take you to. The food is incredible. Much like your smile."

Naomi laughed again, "All right, you sweet talker, get out of here already. I will meet you here that evening at 7:30 pm. Not a minute later. That is, if I am in town."

He smiled widely and kissed her hand. "I will sign your release papers then, now that you have sort of agreed to go out with me. You can leave in the morning. That *was* a yes, right?"

They both laughed again, pretending as if he was holding her hostage. Naomi nodded and then said, "What a relief. Thank you."

Dr. Alex Erdene swiftly walked out of her room and spun around with joy, once he closed the door behind him. He nearly bumped right into a nurse with his excited movement. The nurse looked back at him and just shrugged, not really knowing how to handle the usually very serious doctor's sudden burst of joy. She had worked with him for almost three years and neither she, nor anybody in the hospital for that matter, knew much about his private life. He was always very quiet, respectful, and focused. He was an amazing doctor who seemed married to his occupation. This wasn't uncommon amongst the overworked neurosurgeons.

The next morning, Naomi took a cab home. Just before pulling up to the gate, Naomi noticed a strange sight. Two men were riding together who weren't her students. She thought, *Who are they?* Then it all clicked in. *Oh I see.* As the cab dropped her off at the entrance, she tipped the driver well, and walked as briskly as she could toward the arena. Then she took in the sight and was shocked. Sergius and Joe were riding together in the most beautiful way. As soon as she approached, they halted and waved at her. Sergius then trotted over and smiled.

Naomi spoke first. "You've been busy, I see."

"Yes. This is part of the final mission. I'm so glad you're all right. Did you want to call Abigail over so we can get going soon?"

"I think I want to relax in my house for a little while, if you don't mind, Sergius." She smiled to herself at his eagerness to see Abigail again.

"Of course, I am sorry. I will help throw hay with Joe."

"Thank you, Sergius. I am going to hug Mr. Keeper than rest a bit. I will see you later."

Naomi walked to Keeper's paddock. He immediately nickered at the sight of her. *Welcome home Naomi. I am ever so relieved to see you. I am so incredibly sorry about spooking with you.*

Naomi wrapped her arms around his neck. *Don't worry at all. You are perfect. I love you.*

He mouthed her back a little, pretending to mutually groom her, but in the softest way possible. He felt happiest around his human.

CHAPTER FORTY

Compromised

Daniel worked tirelessly to create the travel equations. Levidia popped in to give him support. "Daniel, this mission is our last hope. Please quadruple check your deciphering."

"Of course. You think I don't know this?"

Her tears welled up, "I'm sorry. I'm just so nervous."

He said sharply, "I am too. Believe me."

There was something about his tone that made Levidia question him, "What are you not telling me?"

"It's nothing. Just know that once I give you the program with the equations, I'll need to make myself scarce."

"What? Why?"

He took a deep breath, " Levidia, I understand intimately how dangerous this mission will be. You see, I was in Mongolia during that time. The Murmori are very powerful. I was almost recruited. That's where I was faced with the decision to stay in the dark or to become an angel. Obviously you know what my choice was. If I don't step out of the way, I'm not sure what the consequences might be."

"Are you out of your mind? How could we even fathom this? Why would you agree to this? We need to come up with a different plan. Quick!" Levidia was rattled.

"No. Levidia, this is the place. I have a very powerful sense they need to be there. After all, Mongolia is where the humans and horses had the strongest connection. It must be where the Murmori learned how to dismantle the strings."

Levidia sat in silence for a few minutes. She couldn't think of any other place where the Murmori's hold was so strong. She finally looked up, "Stop right now. Let's start a new equation immediately. There hast to be another place they can go."

Before Daniel could respond, they both felt a tingling sensation and froze. Briggs materialized in front of them. "Stop fighting, both of you. Time is running out. You really need to get a move on. My string is beginning to fade and I can hear the Murmori on the other side. They are getting closer to discovering me. We have no choice, we have to stick to this plan."

Levidia cried out, "This can't be happening! I thought we had a little more time."

Briggs shook her head, "Please, Levidia. Please send them on their mission immediately. Please convince them they are the true Re-Connectors. I must go. I have one last place I can hide."

She then turned to Daniel, "My friend, you know what to do. Please stay safe."

Daniel and Levidia watched Briggs walk through the door. Daniel noticed something peculiar. A few spots of rainbow light were pulsing on the door, as if the String had started to dismantle already.

Daniel suddenly jumped up and ran towards it, to get a better look and gasped, "Do you hear that?"

"No, what?"

"Now I can hear the Murmori too."

"Are you kidding me? Daniel, this is no time to be joking around."

"I am dead serious. Briggs was right. They really must have found her string. Give me a moment. I can almost make out what they are saying. I think I can hear three different voices."

Oh Yes. Now that we've had a taste of that pure essence, we must find it again...

It shall be done. Their equations have a residue. We also know who is helping them...

It is curious they intend on heading to our original headquarters. It seems they are on a quest to defeat us. They will never succeed.

"Oh no. Levidia, they know about Mongolia. This is terrible."

"What? There is no time to lose. Can you create a more protected equation?"

"I will do my best. Go and grab the travelers and bring them here right away. I will have their equations ready by the time you arrive back."

Levidia hopped on Prometheus and headed to Willow Tree Farms.

CHAPTER FORTY ONE

Time Blips

The eight of them created a circle in the far pasture. Each horse had their chosen human aboard. Levidia showed up in the middle of the pasture. "I have more information. You will need to know this for your final mission."

She initiated a hologram of the Tahki horses in Mongolia. They were quite short, stocky, and had manes that stood up. They were running along plains, with mountains in the background.

Even though this hologram was only about two feet tall, the travelers felt like they were right in the thick of the galloping hooves. It was breathtaking.

"Listen closely. You are about to travel to Mongolia. The Murmori found it to be a perfect area to grow their numbers. They could remain covert in that vast land. In the simplest of terms, it was their base of operations. They learned there how the connection between humans and horses held the strings intact. That's where they began dismantling the strings. They started to figure out ways to sever the connection between horses and humans. This is why it is imperative that you go there now. We had hoped that we wouldn't have had to send you there. It is the most dangerous area, since there are so many Murmori. That's also why Briggs decided to send Joe with you. Joe, remember how you first found Abigail?"

"Yes ma'am."

"The amount of power in that connection will serve you well for this jump back in time. Can you remember how to do that?"

"I can." Joe gulped. For the first time, he felt real fear.

"Good. Now, Briggs is counting on all of you. You are to meet up with the Mongolian nomads. Remember, the Murmori have infiltrated every area. Be on your guard. They may find clever ways to manipulate you."

Abigail looked at her friends' distressed faces. The love she felt for all of them washed over her. For the first time in her life, she finally felt like she had true kinship. She felt the urge to boost their morale somehow. "Come on, everyone. We can do this. We've come so far already. Besides, we are the most bad ass time traveling, telepathic equestrians I know!"

They tension lifted and they all laughed quietly except for Sergius. "Yes, although I have no idea what a bad ass is, Abigail. I hope you aren't referring to a donkey?" He looked especially handsome to Abigail when he was confused with her modern speak.

"Ha! No, not at all. I was just trying to make a point that we are amazing, Sergius. Don't worry. Come on, we've got this!"

Levidia continued in a more hushed tone, "I need you to understand the gravity of this. These horses were some of the first puzzle pieces on Earth. Without them, the rest of the pieces won't shine as brightly. The new ones are nearly extinct. You, my dear ones, will need to go there and make sure they this does not happen. You see, every piece is important, whether they are in bodies or in spirit. They find ways to inspire, connect, and create as they enjoy their magnificent participation, being a part of the universe. For the future horses in the world will inspire many other beings and raise Earth's vibration. It is difficult to explain the magnitude of this mission in words. You must now go to Daniel's castle where he can give you the proper equations." She then disappeared.

They dialed in their equations for their home base, Daniel's castle. They arrived just outside where it should have been. There was no sign of the castle, nor Daniel.

"What is going on?" Naomi spun around with Keeper. He felt her anxiety and started pawing.

"I have no idea." Abigail dismounted from Rafi and started shouting, "Daniel! Daniel! Where are you?"

Sergius panicked as well and joined in on the shouting, "Briggs, Levidia, Daniel! Where are you?"

Joe remained calm. He closed his eyes for a moment and saw Levidia flying right back to them, "Hush now. Levidia is on her way here. Quit your fussin'. She heard us all right."

Levidia and Prometheus swooped in. She was shocked to see the castle was gone. "Oh no. It has already begun."

"What are you talking about?" Naomi shrieked.

"There is another major factor at play here. I can't keep it from you anymore now. Daniel is actually going to be one of the Mongols you encounter. I don't know which one he is, but he will be there. This was the time where he made his decision to become an angel. You must find him and make sure he stays on that path. If you don't, everything will have changed. You might not even have a home to come back to."

Abigail leaned against Rafi. *Holy crap.* She looked over at the others. They were speechless. Naomi was pale. Sergius had his hand over his eyes. Joe stared at Levidia and spoke up, "Levidia. Why'd you have to go and say something like that? You know they were just getting all revved up."

"Joe, I'm sorry, but they deserve to know what they're up against. Also, it gets worse. The final string is faltering. The Murmori were able to hear our plans. They have already gone back to Mongolia and I am quite sure now, since the castle is missing, that they have increased their hold on Daniel. I have no doubt they have sent reinforcements back in time, much the same way as we are sending you."

Abigail cried out, "This is so messed up."

Levidia couldn't hide her tears any longer. "It truly is. All of our destinies are hanging on your next moves. And there's nothing I can say to reassure you at this point. Good luck."

Levidia knew the equations were lost. It was up to her to get them to their destination. She had them all link arms while on top of their mounts. She ushered them to Mongolia and then quickly disappeared. Besides, that place had such low frequency, it was nearly impossible for an angel to remain there for more than a few minutes. She needed to conserve her energy. She thanked her lucky stars that Joe, at least, had more residue from his human life than Levidia. It brought her great comfort that he would be able to be there for them in this perilous time.

CHAPTER FORTY TWO

Mongolia

The travelers were gently placed behind a huge hillside. The horses' breath was visible in the crisp air.

The horses transformed into the Tahki, while their riders stayed in their same bodies, cloaked in vibrant colored clothing. It took a moment for the riders to adjust to their smaller mounts.

Abigail spoke quietly at first and then remembered herself, she quickly switched to telepathy. "Let's see if we can scope things out around this hill. Oh wait." *Sergius and Dotune, why don't you go first?*

The pair nodded in unison and moved in a careful, collected walk. As soon as they made it around the hill, Dotune froze. Sergius sent a message to the others. *That was fast. It seems we have already encountered the Mongolians. Go ahead and come around the hill, slowly. Let's not startle them.*

There were eight nomads in the distance; three men, two women and three children. The women drove the wagons pulled by camels, while the men and children were riding on top of square like saddles on scrappy looking horses. Their intense eyes and dirt filled faces stared out into the distance. The children trotted toward them. They were expert riders and couldn't have been more than four or five years of age. The leader of the nomads quickly followed suit, shouting at the small riders to stay back. "We don't know who they are. Don't be so reckless!" The children pulled back on their reins and their horses spun in place, ready to make a change from their exhausting trek.

As soon as Naomi came around the bend with Keeper, she gasped. The nomads were now thirty yards away. She could see shadows and dark figures circling around all of them. *Oh no. I think I am actually seeing the Murmori. They have these people surrounded. Can you guys see this? I'm going to be sick.* The shock of seeing the entities made Naomi dizzy. She fell off Keeper in slow motion and wretched several times. Joe flew off of Brouteen, and rushed to her side. He stroked her back. She grabbed his arm and then slumped over. Joe whispered, "Y'all go on. I will stay right here with Miss Naomi until she's feeling herself again. I don't rightly know why she had such a strong reaction to seeing those there evil beings. I'm speculatin' it has to do with her time in the healing tree. Be careful."

Abigail's eyebrows raised. She wondered how Joe knew about the tree. Sensing this, Joe responded, "Briggs tells me nearly everything she rightly knows. Don't you go forgetting we are all connected." Abigail closed her eyes for a moment. She was satisfied with his answer and sent Naomi a message. *Don't worry, Naomi. We've got this.* Naomi whimpered and rested her head in Joe's lap. Abigail and Sergius nodded quietly and pressed on. They couldn't see what Naomi just witnessed. They had a sudden rush of knowledge pour in as they rode forward. They knew now how important each of their powers were to this mission.

Sergius looked over at Abigail. *Let me take the lead. I think I can convince them to let us ride alongside. You work on talking to the horses.* Abigail was relieved to hear that Sergius was interested in speaking with the humans. She had no idea what to say, anyhow. *Works for me, Sergius.*

The leader puffed up and spoke forcefully, "Who are you? How did you arrive? What do you desire?"

Sergius took a moment to respond. He was again surprised that he knew exactly what he was saying and how to use the right words to respond. He took a deep breath, "We mean no harm. May we join you on your journey for a short time?"

The nomad was suspicious. He introduced himself as the leader, Batbayar, and motioned for them to ride next to his three children. He then nodded to the other two men. Before they knew it, Abigail and Sergius found themselves lassoed. They were now prisoners.

Batbayar said smugly, "We are rounding up our herd of horses. When we sell them, we will see what kind of a price we can get for you as well." Abigail and Sergius struggled at first. Then Sergius relaxed. *Abigail, it is not necessary to resist. We can observe all the same like this. Let's search among these nomads for Daniel.*

Abigail was tense. *I know you're right. But I just can't bear the thought of being a slave again.*

I will never let that happen to you. Be strong like I know you are. Concentrate on sending a message to Joe and Naomi. Tell them we have been captured.

I will. Abigail then reluctantly allowed the men to tie her to Rafi's saddle. She knew Sergius was right, but couldn't help crying. She regained her composure a few minutes later and sent Naomi the cry for help.

We will follow behind and do our best to stay hidden. Naomi found her strength and mounted Keeper again. Joe was ready and they rode out slowly. They noticed a single nomad also following the same path, trailing behind the caravan. Joe sensed his energy was on his frequency. "Naomi, I do believe this is a person of interest. We should catch up to him."

"Really Joe? Are you sure?"

"We're fixing to find out, but I have a sneaking suspicion that there fellow is one of us."

They picked up a trot and focused on their target.

As they continued riding, other nomads trickled in, pushing small groups of horses ahead of them. There were now over thirty nomads in the group and at least two hundred horses. The herd were all short, stocky, and wild. They intimidated and awed Abigail all at once.

Abigail looked over at Sergius. They needed answers. He asked one of the guards keeping them captive. "Where are you taking these horses?"

"Our leader has decided to sell off the herd. All but a few. He said we didn't need this many horses to survive. He was confident there would be more traders willing to give us food and water with gold, rather than horses. He heard there was a place to sell horses and he desires to bring them all there. He is our leader, so naturally, we must do as he commands."

Sergius let out a large breath. "Oh, I see." He shot Abigail a sideways glance. She gulped. *This is a bad. I'll bet the Murmori are manipulating him to do this. I think I'm the one to help him escape their hold. I did it once. I am sure I can do it again. I will ask the horses for help.*

Sergius agreed. Abigail was getting stronger every day. He was so impressed with her determination. *Let's hope the horses will listen. They are immune to the Murmori, so their energy will be perfect if directed correctly.*

Abigail reached out to the wild horses. *Please hear me, Tahki. Your livelihood is at stake. The humans, your wonderful soul mates on this journey, are being held hostage in their hearts. They have decided to sell you to strangers. Please, do you have any idea what you can do to help?*

The horses didn't respond. They didn't have a heart connection with this human. They thought it was very odd that she was trying to speak to them. Rafi and Dotune sensed this challenge and spoke for their humans in unison. *You can trust these strangers. You will soon see that they are telling the truth.*

The Tahki were emotionally torn. They had a hard time believing that their humans were truly ready to sever their bond. On the other hand, they knew something felt wrong lately. The horses weren't able to feel into their humans' heart centers. There seemed to be a block. They responded to the new horses, *We are unsure. Time will tell.*

Naomi and Joe slowed their horses back to a walk when they reached ten yards away from the stray nomad. He had felt them coming. He turned around slowly and put up his hands. "Do not come any closer. I am protecting my people ahead of me."

"Please, we would like to assist. We know that your people are in trouble. We have come to help them escape the dark hold around them." Joe looked into the nomad's eyes and waited for him to truly see him.

"I see you. Yes, you are most welcome to assist. I desire to free my people from this dark hold you speak of and the creatures that have created it."

Naomi responded, "You can see them?"

"I am their Shaman. It is my job to see the spirits." He then turned to Naomi. "And where do you come from? You are most different from your friend here."

"Yes, I am. But I am learning his ways. Here, this will help you understand." She closed her eyes and sent him a telepathic message.

I am from another time and place. I can connect with horses, just as your people do. Please, we don't have much time. Can you hear me?

The Shaman was impressed. *Yes.*

Please, can you find a way to ensure the safety of our friends? They are being held captive by your people.

The Shaman's eyes lowered. "I don't know how to get through to them. They all walk with a dead look in their eyes now. They have forgotten how to connect with their horses. They have lost their joy. They are planning to get rid of their herd very soon."

Naomi and Joe looked at each other with fear in their eyes. "How is this going to work?" Naomi brought Keeper to a halt. "This seems hopeless."

The Shaman then turned around and continued forward on his path. Joe shook his head. He didn't have any comforting words.

Sergius looked around as they were pushed along the seemingly endless trek. The nomads looked lifeless. They hardly spoke. The silence was crippling. He could only hear their footsteps, an occasional snort from a horse, and the sound of the wheels on the wagons. *It is just too quiet. I feel like I am in a Murmori hold myself. I must find a way to break out of these desperate feelings.* While he was thinking of what else he could do, he noticed the herd of horses were getting very agitated. There was a commotion. He had to do something to calm them. He did what he had always known.

Sergius suddenly burst out with a beautiful melody. It was the song he used to calm his horses in Rome. Abigail whirled around. His song was so lovely, it gave her goosebumps. The horses took notice. They were intrigued by the sound vibrations coming out of this strange human. They hadn't heard anything like this in quite some time. Dotune pranced to his human's song. *That's it! Why didn't I think of this? Sergius, you are brilliant. That is exactly what comforted me when I first arrived on Earth. Keep going!*

The Shaman felt the reverberation of the horses. "It seems there is a spark of joy coming from the herd. Someone has found their voice again."

Naomi tuned in. It was Sergius. "Oh, that is my friend. Please. Can you hear him? His name is Sergius."

The Shaman tuned in. He heard the song, but then frowned. "While it is a nice vibration. It will not do. It is not a Mongolian song. Perhaps I can help him. I will teach him a song of my people." He sent the idea to Sergius. It was a childhood song that all of his people were familiar with.

Sergius was startled to hear a new telepathic voice. It was layered with Naomi's.

Sergius. We have just encountered a Shaman. He wants to teach you a new song. Please sing it now. This should help push away the Murmori. Do it now.

Sing this song and my people will hear you. Sing it loudly.

Sergius inhaled and began the sound vibrations that burst from his entire being. The nomads stopped the horses as soon as he started this new song.

The nomads began humming and could now hear Sergius and the

Shaman at the same time, singing a familiar song. The melody comforted them.

All of the nomads, except Batbayar and the two guards, joined in on the singing. The leader was furious. He was ready to move out and get the horses to the market. "Enough! We must keep traveling."

Sergius ignored the leader and continued singing. His joy was overwhelming. As he sang, the horses formed a tremendous spiral pattern. He looked over at Abigail, once he realized what they had created. She let her eyes settle on the spiral. *Whoa. Sergius. This is incredible. I am so proud of you.* He beamed back at her.

Naomi, Joe and the Shaman watched the scene from a nearby hilltop. They noticed as the nomads sang, the Murmori peeled off of some of them. They were unable to maintain their hold on those singing, as the nomads' joy intensified.

The trio on the hill then saw all the Murmori swirl around, then settle above the leader and his two guards. Batbayar's anger made him spit. He glared at Sergius, "I command you to stop singing. Guards, kill this outsider!"

The Shaman had arrived in that same moment, with Joe and Naomi close behind. The Shaman boomed, "No. Batbayar. If you want him dead, you must face him in single combat."

The nomads looked at the Shaman with reverence and lowered their heads. The Murmori continued to drain the essence of the two guards. They advanced on Sergius.

Abigail dashed toward all three of them, clucking to Rafi, "Hurry up, we can't let them do this." They slid to a stop just in front of the guards who were holding their swords to Sergius' neck. "Naomi, Joe, please! Send your love to the guards. Quickly!"

Joe spun and directed his most joyous memories toward the men. Naomi clenched her jaw, fighting back the anger at the way they held onto her friend. *Come on, I have to shift my emotions.*

Abigail felt Naomi's struggle. She turned to her again. *Please. Just close your eyes and imagine they are your favorite horses. Breathe in love and beam it right at their hearts. You can do this! We have to save Sergius.*

Blood began to trickle from Sergius' neck. He wanted to struggle, but their hold was too tight. He had to find a way to free them from the Murmori before it was too late. He could still hum. He continued the song from before. Their eyes got heavy. They held Sergius tighter around the arms. Sergius softly mouthed the words, "Please. What would your horses think right now. They love you and want you to do what is right."

The guards heard his words and hesitated. They then felt the love coming from the three others. They finally lowered their swords. Batbayar's eyes widened and he shouted, "What are you waiting for? Kill him!"

The guards refused to move a muscle. They looked stunned and felt as if they had just snapped out of a fever dream. The Murmori put all of their focus on the leader.

The Shaman rode up to Batbayar. "Now it is time you prove yourself worthy of leading us. Don't hide behind others."

Batbayar frowned and then looked up at the sky. He grudgingly dismounted from his horse. Sergius was released and untied. He moved forward toward the wild eyed leader, unafraid of his fate.

Batbayar edged closer and closer to Sergius, who then whispered, "Come, we don't need to do this." Batbayar's eyes flickered. His body went rigid as Sergius put his hand on his shoulder. They locked eyes and Sergius then felt a very familiar feeling. "Daniel?"

Batbayar stumbled backward, looking confused.

Sergius immediately sent the message to his friends. *Daniel is Batbayar. Now I understand why I must face him.*

The others heard him. Abigail gasped. *Please, Sergius. Be careful. Fear not, Abigail. I will find a way. I must.*

The Murmori continued to drape over Batbayar. He was consumed with darkness. He grabbed his sword and lunged toward Sergius. He yelled out in rage as he attacked. Sergius was a powerful human, conditioned by his many years of labor. He dodged the sword expertly and gave Batbayar a push so that he could get behind him.

Once he did, his days of wrestling with the other Strators kicked right back in. He swiftly disarmed him, grappled for both shoulders, and then his neck. Before Batbayar could struggle out, he was in a frightening choke hold. Sergius was being manipulated by the Murmori as well. They were egging him on to kill the leader. *Go on. Keep squeezing. He will be ours forever then. Your future will be dark. We will have all of you to feast from.*

Joe shouted, "Sergius, stop. Don't kill him. It's Daniel. Remember! We need him to live." Joe then motioned for Abigail to get closer, who squeezed Rafi into the herd of horses and to Dotune. She pleaded with him to help. *Dotune let's focus our love on both of them now.* Dotune heard her and sent his love to both Batbayar and Sergius. Abigail remembered her moments in limbo, and called in her most amazing memories of riding Rafi, the waterfall, flying around at the festival, and kissing Sergius. As she thought all of this, she sent these memories of love, light, and joy to Sergius. He blinked and looked up at her. He then changed his hold from around Batbayar's neck to through his arms and around his chest. He also used his legs to keep Batbayar from moving out of this new hold. Sergius felt the love from Abigail and it shocked him back into himself. He then thought of their beloved Daniel and sent love to him.

Batbayar's face contorted with turmoil, as light and darkness struggled within him.

While Naomi stared horrified at this struggle, she could see the Murmori, as well as Daniel and Batbayar's faces interchange. She then turned to the Shaman. "Please, tell your people to send all the love in their hearts to the leader they once knew."

As all the humans and horses focused their love and joy on Batbayar, the Murmori could no longer hold him. And suddenly he was free.

Batbayar collapsed. The sheer amount of alternating energies that moved through him, caused him to slip into a coma.

Sergius let go and stood up slowly. "He is still alive. Don't worry." He hugged Abigail tightly, as she softly repeated, "It worked. It worked."

Naomi stepped closer, she could still see the Murmori flying above all of them. *It's not over yet.* She pleaded. *There is one last thing that must be done. Friends, remember why we are here.*

Abigail grabbed Naomi's hand and added. *We are connected and bonded to horses.*

Sergius agreed. *Yes, we need to solidify our bond to push the Murmori out.*

Naomi thought for a moment about her first conversation with Keeper. Then she knew what to say, *Everyone, link up your hearts. Create a love connection and then beam it out all around us. Do it now!*

They heard her. The love began to shine outward, while the Murmori darted down to attack everyone. Joe's energy had drained completely and he fell off of Brouteen. He remained motionless under her protective legs.

Naomi, Abigail, and Sergius saw this happen at the same time. Sergius urged them forward. *Don't be distracted, we must keep this connection strong!*

The Shaman raised his arms up to the sky and asked his horse to spin slowly in place with just a shift of his weight. He began singing a new song, which excited all of his people. They joined in, while the three friends continued to beam love with the horses. Their location's vibration rose so high, the Murmori couldn't possibly be in the same frequency any longer. A huge dark cloud formed overhead. The Murmori evaporated with a resounding boom.

Once gone, a huge light enveloped the nomads and all the horses. The string had been Re-Connected. Rainbow light shone out from the edges. It looked like a huge tunnel from the ground shooting up toward the sky. Abigail, Naomi, and Sergius jumped up and down like little school children. "We did it!"

The Shaman stepped in and waved his hands over his leader. "You are most powerful humans, strangers."

He then moved toward Joe and hummed a quiet tune. "He will go back to where you are from. He will be safe." Naomi gave the Shaman a curious look, "How do you know?"

"You think you are the only one who understands this kind of traveling?" The Shaman smiled softly.

Naomi looked back at Sergius and Abigail. They raised their eyebrows and ran over to Joe's side. He whispered, "Y'all sure know how to raise a ruckus, now don't ya?" They all laughed as they realized he really was going to be fine.

The Shaman spoke again, "The evil entities have left for now, but they might come back." He pointed to Sergius, "You must take his place. My people are very fragile right now. They look to you as the leader, since you have defeated Batbayar."

Abigail spun around and stared at the Shaman. "What? Why? He needs to come with us. There is no way he can stay here and be your leader."

Sergius understood. He looked over at Joe and Naomi, then back at Abigail. "Friends, it is important that I remain here. I must ensure Daniel's spirit comes back as an angel and not a Murmori. I feel this is the only way. Please understand."

Abigail felt abandoned, even though she was still standing right next to him. "But what if you don't come back? I can't lose you."

"Abigail, I will do my best. You said it before. We are bad ass, right?"

She chuckled. "Oh, Sergius. You so get me."

He smiled and then kissed her deeply. They all looked away to give them a few moments.

The Shaman watched the three mount their horses. "The horses will be safe with us now. For that, we are all grateful."

They all hugged Sergius goodbye. He then said with his heart, *See you soon.*

Naomi, Joe, and Abigail recited their equation and traveled back.

CHAPTER FORTY THREE

New Beginnings

Abigail, Naomi, and Joe found themselves scooped up and placed gently on the softest couches they had ever felt. They opened their eyes to realize they were back in the floating building of their beloved guide, Daniel. They took a moment to rejoice in the fact that the castle was indeed back. Then their hearts dropped. Daniel was nowhere to be found. As she looked around the room, Abigail stood up and noticed something was amiss. The horses weren't there, nor were Briggs and Levidia. "Where are the others? What happened?"

Joe looked at the round table, "Look there." An envelope sat in the middle, addressed to the Re-Connectors.

Abigail tore it open and read:

The gratitude in my heart can't be quantified. You have Re-Connected the string in Mongolia and ensured the safety of mine. I am on my way to see Batbayar's soul in the Healing Tree, as you read this. Levidia is bringing him there. Fear not. Sergius will return soon. Please rest. Thank you so much.

All my love, Briggs

"Rest? But what about Sergius. I couldn't possibly rest, knowing he is out there, just waiting to make sure Daniel gets back."

Joe reassured her, "I understand. Although, sometimes taking a moment to relax all your worries is the best thing a human can do. Trust me, Miss Abigail. I know you fancy seeing your man again, so just believe it will happen and take a breather."

Abigail slumped down and looked to Naomi.

Joe gently placed his hands on Naomi's shoulders. "As for you. It's time to return to your life and take care of your horses, including the new charges. I was fixin' to tell you before this last mission that they are ready for just about anything. Maybe they can be lesson horses?"

Naomi smirked at this thought. *Horses from the past, who traveled to another planet, are now in my herd and might teach my students lessons? Oh boy.* She quickly looked at Abigail, as if expecting her to follow her back to the stables.

Joe turned back around. He cleared his throat, squinted his eyes, and squeezed out a speech he had memorized for this particular occasion, "Abigail, you are hereby invited to travel within the strings that have been Re-Connected, as Earth's ambassador. If you choose to continue to help restore the Web completely, you may keep this castle as your base of operations and learn more about traveling to other planets, including Gavrantura. But first, Abigail, you must go home and tend to some unfinished family matters."

"Whoa. That sounds intense. Well, let's just see what happens, huh Joe? Thank you so much for your help." She hugged him and he fought back proud tears. She then wrapped her arms around Naomi tightly. She whispered, "I sure hope Sergius makes it back soon and we can ride together." Naomi held on longer and thought, *Don't worry. We've got this.* Abigail laughed as she remembered those were the exact words she told Naomi for reassurance. She then took a long, deep breath and recited her home equation.

Abigail was back in her room. She jumped into her bed and pulled the covers over her tightly. Never in her life did she feel such comfort from her bedding. *I can't believe we did it.*

Her stomach rumbled. She couldn't remember the last time she ate something. As she stood up, she noticed her reflection in the mirror. She didn't even recognize herself. Flashes of horses, spirits and friends zoomed past her in the mirror. *What the? Oh.*

Whatever was in her heart, was reflected inside of herself. *Now, that's a much more interesting way to look at oneself. Especially when there is absolutely no more hair smoothing cream.* She laughed out loud. It was hard to believe how much that meant to her months ago. It seemed so trivial. She stumbled out of her room and into the kitchen.

Albert and Evelyn were eating brunch when Abigail appeared. Her frizzy hair was wild that morning and they couldn't help but giggle a little when she slumped into her chair at the kitchen table.

"Are you okay?" Albert was concerned.

"I think I finally slept without dreaming. At least I can't remember any. We rode a lot last night, on a very special mission." Before her parents could reply, the loudest cawing sound came from outside. There must have been about forty crows outside the kitchen window, going wild. Abigail jumped up and ran outside. She was still in her crumpled pajamas, barefoot, and sleepy-eyed. The breeze picked up and caused the huge wind chimes to play a song, along with the sound of all the black birds circling over her head. Abigail raised her arms and shouted, "Good morning beauties. What can I do for you?"

They quickly flew away and headed to the North. It was in the exact direction toward the waterfall where this whole adventure began. Abigail watched them fly away and suddenly had a tingling sensation all over her body. She remembered what it felt like to feel a horse's muzzle for the first time. She began to get very nostalgic about that first encounter, even if it was only about ten months ago.

She quietly turned around and went back inside. She smiled and sat down, as if still in a serious meeting with Briggs. Evelyn passed her a glass of orange juice. "Here honey, I think you should have some of this. It looks like you need a boost to come back to Earth."

Abigail put her head in her hand, took a big swig, and thanked her Mom. She then requested, "I know you both were hoping for a quiet day, but do you think you could take me somewhere special? I'd like to show you something."

They agreed and while her parents finished up their French toast, curious about this mystery, they were extremely pleased that Abigail wanted to include them in something.

Albert couldn't contain his excitement and jumped up and grabbed the keys, "I'll get the car started." Abigail looked down at her attire and smiled, "Dad, um, do you mind if I get dressed first?" They all laughed, realizing that none of them actually noticed she wasn't ready to walk out the door. Clearly they were all feeling a bit out of it with all the thoughts swirling in their minds.

The sedan slowly took the turn down Cuba Hill Road. Abigail rolled down her window and could already hear the faint sound of the waterfall. Her parents were surprised that she had negotiated them there so well. This was just a road off of the main one from school to home. Evelyn couldn't help but ask, "Abigail, how did you know about this place? We don't usually drive down this way, ever really."

"Oh, Mom, I love exploring, you know that. I just decided to go down this road when I wasn't ready to start my homework. I just followed my heart and my feet led the way."

Three car doors slammed and the crunching of feet on leaves were the only sound, besides the waterfall. As soon as they reached it, Evelyn gasped. "Abigail, this place, it's like from a dream. I swear I have been here before."

Abigail put her arm around her mother's shoulders. "I was told this was a place that all humans knew about, yet simply have forgotten."

Albert then looked up at the top of the waterfall and shouted, "What is that?"

Levidia and Prometheus burst out of the waterfall and shot out like a cannon toward their heads. All three of them scrambled backwards quickly. Abigail smiled and started to jump up and down.

"Good afternoon, dear Freedman family. I am so happy to see all of you here. It's about time we all had a chat."

Evelyn nearly fainted, yet Albert steadied his wife, by putting his arms around her waist. He smiled. It was the angel from his dreams. She was really here. *I am like a little school boy again. I can hardly contain my butterflies in my stomach!* Levidia motioned for them all to sit in a circle together. Prometheus was now grazing next to them, his wings the size of seven foot tall basketball players. Evelyn wasn't sure who to look at, since they were both such fantastic creatures. She pinched her cheeks, just as Abigail did during her first meeting with this guide.

Levidia got right into it, "Evelyn, Albert, Abigail, thank you so very much for meeting me here. I am guessing the Laurens gave you the idea, right Abigail?" She studied her parents' expressions. She could tell they were equally in awe and disbelief. "I assure you that I am real. I was the one who introduced your daughter to all of the incredible powers she has within. I believe she has proved that she can time travel, has she not?" Abigail's parents nodded. "Good, then the reason for this meeting is to tell you that she might be gone a bit longer than you expect for her next mission. If and when she returns, her life will have a much different purpose. Let's just say school work will no longer be a priority."

Evelyn began fidgeting and wanted to say something. Albert chimed in first, "Did you say IF she comes back? What is this? Are you saying we might not see our daughter again?"

Levidia closed her eyes for a moment and stretched her hands over her head as if reaching for the most perfect words to trickle in. "This is why I have brought you all here. I know it seems extremely difficult to swallow, but yes. She might decide to continue her adventures without coming back to her home base. But never fear. I shall show you the way to time travel, just as she did and you can create your own meetings together. How would that meet your fancy?"

The three of them all stared at Levidia for a few minutes without a word. Abigail's heart skipped a beat when she heard she might not come back. This was initially what she had always wanted, yet it felt extremely sad to hear it as a distinct possibility; knowing how she would miss her parents and they her. She then looked at her parents and said, "Well, I guess you can look at it as an extended study abroad program, right?" She was always trying to make them laugh in some sort of way. While this seemed funny to her, they weren't laughing.

Evelyn began to cry and Albert rushed over to comfort her. "Evie, darling. I think this is something beyond what we could have even imagined for our girl. She's never been too keen on following our paths anyhow. I think we should give this idea a wider perspective. This might seem crazy, although not too much now, but I've actually had dreams with Levidia in them. Way before Abigail was even born."

Evelyn shuddered a moment and then looked up at her husband. "This isn't as easy for me to take in. I will try."

Abigail hugged both her parents and then looked at Levidia with a gratefulness only a child who desperately wanted her parents to understand her completely, could. Abigail was instructed to head to Daniel's castle immediately. Briggs was waiting for her. She squeezed her parents' hands a little tighter. They felt they hardly knew their daughter now. She had grown so much, so fast. And then, in a flash, they were left sitting by the waterfall by themselves. Evelyn and Albert hugged each other tightly.

Levidia whispered, "I'll be back soon to teach you both how to travel." She waved to them as she climbed aboard the Pegasus and flew away.

Naomi found herself on her couch, stretched out and immediately thought, *I am going to need another working student. I wonder if I should change the ad somehow.* She laughed to herself and then rolled over to take a nap.

Her phone buzzed and she woke up with a start. It was her alarm telling her to get ready for her date in an hour. She looked at the calender on the phone. It was indeed Saturday night at six o'clock. She rolled onto the floor, stretched some more, and then crawled her way into the bathroom. She started talking to herself, *What am I doing. I hardly know this man. I should really focus on getting back into a routine here at the farm.*

Joe suddenly appeared from around the corner of her bathroom and chimed in, "Now listen here, Miss Naomi. You tend to your heart and I'll tend to your horses. You reckon that's a good deal?"

Naomi smiled widely and sighed. "Yes, Joe. Thank you, dear sir."

She then decided to shower and picked out a pretty sweater with a clean pair of jeans. Naomi felt surprised that she had clean laundry at this point.

As she drove up to the hospital parking lot, she was skeptical about how her date was going to go. She remained hopeful. She blushed as he kissed her hand at the entrance of the hospital. They made small talk about the weather as they walked around the block to the restaurant.

At the intimate dining table, Dr. Alex Erdene found himself so comfortable with Naomi, he revealed more about his background than he usually would on a first date. "My parents were Missionaries so I moved around quite a bit."

Naomi was curious. "Oh really? Where did you live?"

"Well, I was actually born in Mongolia where I learned to ride horses with the other young children, moved to West Africa as a teenager, and then ended up in the United States to pursue my medical career."

Naomi stared at him in disbelief. She wasn't sure if she should tell him where she had just been. Sensing it was time to pass the gauntlet, he leaned over and asked, "So, tell me about yourself."

Naomi thought for a moment, carefully deciding on how to reply. She laughed out loud and coyly said, "Hmm. Where do I begin?"

Before she could utter another word or flash him a coy smile, Abigail appeared at the table next to her. Naomi turned her head so fast, she nearly gave herself whiplash. She mouthed to her, *What are you doing here?*

Abigail jumped up, with tears in her eyes, and said, "Naomi, Sergius and Daniel are still missing. Neither Briggs nor Levidia can sense them anywhere or any when. Please help me find them."

Naomi stood up quickly and stuttered, "Uh, uh, Dr, this is my dear friend Abigail."

He had no clue what she was trying to convey, but Alex stood up and instinctively patted Abigail on the back. Naomi started shaking. She was ready for a rest. She knew she couldn't now. She politely thanked Alex for understanding that she would have to leave right away. "I would love to try this again, sometime. If you haven't already written me off as crazy."

Dr. Erdene looked Naomi in the eyes, took her by the hand, kissed it, and quietly said, "I would be honored. Please find me when you're ready. If you need me to go to Mongolia, I am sure I can arrange something. I still have friends there."

Naomi gave him a grateful smile. She then let his words sink in. *How did he know?* She shook her head and decided to focus on the task ahead of her. Naomi locked eyes with Abigail's red ones, "Let's go."

Made in the USA
San Bernardino, CA
08 April 2017